MEMORIES OF SANTORINI

JENNIFER SKULLY

Redwood
Valley
Publishing

MEMORIES OF SANTORINI
A ONCE AGAIN NOVEL

Book 6

There's magic on Santorini, beneath the beautiful bougainvillea, under the blue domes, and in the enticing Aegean Sea.

Angela Walker spent three glorious weeks on Santorini after she graduated from college. Three weeks that changed her life forever. Thirty years later, it's time to go back to that beautiful island and the warm blue sea, the only place where she was ever completely happy.

Thirty years ago, Xandros Daskalakis fell in love with a summer girl who came to his beloved island. When Ange had to return home, they agreed they'd meet in one year, a he believed he'd spend the rest of his life with her. But An never returned. Not for thirty years.

Now she's back. And she's brought her daughter wit Suddenly they all have questions that could cause an en massive enough to destroy their lives. Or bring them the happiness they lost so long ago.

Take a holiday to the gorgeous Greek Isles and feel the magic for yourself in this later in life, second chance romance.

Join our newsletter and receive free books, plus learn about new releases, contests, and other freebies: http://bit.ly/SkullyNews

ACKNOWLEDGMENTS

A special thanks to Bella Andre for this fabulous idea and to both Bella and Nancy Warren for all the brainstorming on our 10-mile walks. Thank you also to my special network of friends who support and encourage me: Shelley Adina, Jenny Andersen, Linda McGinnis, Jackie Yau, Kathy Coatney, and Laurel Jacobson. As always, a huge hug of appreciation for my husband who helps my writing career flourish. And thank you to Wrigley, who is once again crying at the door to come in, even though I only let her out a minute ago!

"You should tell her the truth." Her sister Teresa rolled the stem of her wineglass between her fingers, leaning in so the other restaurant patrons couldn't hear them.

"You know I can't tell her," Angela said, her teeth snapping on the words.

She'd had ample opportunity to tell Sienna the truth in the year since the divorce. But Angela's relationship with her daughter was already on tenterhooks. It had been since Sienna was eight years old.

"Angelina." Teresa, two years older, said her name the way their mother would, as if she'd done something wrong. "It's time Sienna knew what he's like."

Her ex-husband, Donald Walker, had been the driving force in Angela's life for the last thirty years, controlling everything, from the way she interacted with the children, to the charity endeavors she took part in, to the country club ladies she was supposed to make friends with. Even though they'd divorced a year ago, he was still controlling her through Sienna.

She breathed in, pursing her lips. "Sienna adores him. Telling her will only backfire. Donald will somehow use whatever I say to break any connection I'm building with her."

Teresa spread her hands, her voice soft and cajoling. "But things seem to be better between you and Sienna."

"That's why I'm not going to endanger anything right now."

The waiter chose that moment to ask if they wanted refills on their wine. Born of Italian parents, they'd been drinking wine since they were ten years old, though watered down at that time. Now that she was fifty-three—and no longer under Donald's thumb—Angela chose the best wines. Their father was a multimillion-dollar contractor, and their mother had been trying to make it to the top of the Silicon Valley elite for thirty years. The divorce had dashed her hopes.

The restaurant, an upmarket establishment in San Francisco, was relatively quiet for a mid-week lunch in early March. The conversations were muted, the ambience sophisticated, the patrons elegantly dressed even at lunchtime. Fresh hydrangea blooms decorated the tables, accompanied by crystal stemware and delicate porcelain.

After the waiter left, Angela went on. "That's why I want to take Sienna on this Santorini trip, to give us a chance to understand each other. Maybe down the road, when we have a better relationship, I can explain everything." She came from good Italian stock, and she used her hands to describe everything. "Right now, she doesn't want to hear anything negative about her father. She already thinks badly of me, the way he's always wanted her to, and I'm not giving him any ammunition before I'm ready."

"It's not giving him ammunition. Haven't you heard the old saying that the truth will set you free?"

Angela wished she'd never told Teresa the truth about her

marriage. And when she gave her sister a look, Teresa raised her hands. "All right, fine. I won't belabor the point." Thankfully, she changed the subject. "I really like the new haircut. I swear, you look five years younger." Teresa touched her hair, which today she wore in a chignon. "Maybe I should cut mine off too."

"William loves your long hair. But thank you. I'm glad you like the new cut." Angela hadn't considered it until her hairdresser suggested a shorter cut would be more attractive, the words *now that you're getting olde*r left unsaid. The March day had been cold and blustery, though sunny, and she patted the curls in place as if the wind had disturbed them.

Sienna blew in then, all eyes drawn to her lithe figure in neat business attire, pants, suit jacket, and low-heeled pumps. Her beautiful chestnut hair curled in ringlets past her shoulders. Both Angela and Teresa had black hair—at least before the gray crept in—but Sienna had dyed hers, as if she didn't want to be anything like her mother. And yet the likeness was unmistakable. Sienna had Angela's classic bone structure, the patrician nose, the full lips. But while Sienna, at five foot eight, had the statuesque figure of a Roman sculpture, Angela and Teresa were both more petite at five-four, buxom and curvy like their mother.

Over fifty now, Angela was a pale imitation of her thirty-year-old daughter. She no longer turned men's heads. Though turning a man's head was the furthest thing from her mind, she still wished for her youth, her beauty, and the alluring figure of a twenty-two-year-old.

The hug Sienna gave Teresa was effusive and heartfelt. "Aunt Teresa, I'm so glad you're here today."

When she turned to Angela, their hug was standoffish, as if Sienna couldn't bear more than her fingertips on her mother's shoulders and an air kiss that didn't connect.

The rift was Angela's fault. She'd allowed Donald to take

over. That was her mistake. She should have fought for her daughter's love every step of the way.

Sienna practically threw herself into the seat. "Thank you so much for ordering the wine." She smiled glowingly at Teresa as if her aunt was responsible for everything. "And thank you so much for the dinnerware."

Teresa had sent her a set of everyday plates because Sienna had complained about chips in the old stuff she'd bought when she got her first apartment six years ago.

"You're so welcome." Teresa leaned over to kiss her cheek.

"Happy birthday, sweetheart." Angela forced enthusiasm into her voice. "I'm so happy you could make it despite your birthday being last week." She held her hand out in a that-doesn't-matter gesture even though it mattered a lot. "But I've always said we should have a birth month, not just a birthday."

Teresa raised her glass. "Here's to turning thirty. And may the next ten years of your life be just as amazing as the last."

Sienna's face pinched, as if she thought the last ten years hadn't been all that great. But in the next moment, she painted a smile on her lips.

If only things between them could be different. Maybe on Santorini, they would be. That was Angela's hope.

"You look marvelous." Teresa fluffed one of Sienna's curls. "I thought you said you were going to cut your hair into a bob."

"I've got an appointment at the salon this evening."

Despite having her own new style, Angela didn't want Sienna to cut her hair. The length and the curls looked good on her. But Angela knew better than to say anything. It had been this way for years. Whatever Angela thought Sienna should do, her daughter would do the opposite.

Sienna touched her hair. "I have that interview, the one I told you about, and I want to go in with a fresh look."

"An interview? For what?" Angela regretted the question the moment she spoke. It was obvious Teresa knew things that Angela didn't. Sienna talked a lot more with her aunt than she did with her mother.

Sienna grabbed a bread stick, pulling off a tiny piece. She wasn't gluten free, but she complained about the empty calories of garlic bread and pasta. "I'm tired of working for a huge, soulless conglomerate. I want to be with a smaller firm, with fewer clients where they don't feel like I'm rushing them out of my office so I can bring in the next client."

Sienna was a financial advisor like her father, although Donald was head of his own company, managing billion-dollar hedge funds and dealing only with billion-dollar clients. He shunted the little guys off to his subordinates. Angela was dying to ask why Sienna didn't approach her father for a job. But working for Donald, where Sienna would be under his thumb, wasn't a good idea.

Teresa clapped her hands. "I wish you all the best of luck with the interview."

That's what Angela should have said in the beginning. Now she could only imitate her sister. "I know you'll get the job."

Sienna looked at her as if she didn't believe the good wishes. But she smiled. "Thank you."

"Tell us what you did for your birthday," Teresa said with an expansive gesture. "Every detail of the special day."

Sienna glanced Angela's way, a little wary along with something else. Sadness? Angela couldn't interpret the look.

"I took the day off, got a mani-pedi, pampered myself." She patted Teresa's hand. "Nonni and Poppa said they're coming out in July, and I thought we could have a family party. I really want to celebrate with them." She glanced at Angela again. "I didn't want to have a big party now and make them feel left out." She smiled at her aunt. "And of course I want you and Uncle William and all the cousins to come."

Teresa beamed. Angela was glad that Sienna's resentment of her didn't fall onto the family. Teresa had three girls, all a year apart and all college-age now. When Sienna was in high school, she'd been their babysitter and enjoyed every minute. Angela's parents had moved to Arizona when Dad retired a few months ago. Now their mother was busy building her kingdom in Scottsdale since she'd never been successful at empire building in Silicon Valley, as if the tech world didn't value a former construction worker, even if he'd built his business into a multimillion-dollar corporation.

Sienna went on with her description of the party. "I'm not inviting all my friends for this. I just want close family."

Teresa stole a glance at Angela, one perfectly plucked eyebrow raised. Angela knew why Sienna didn't want to invite her friends. She'd already had a big bash on her actual birthday last week. Of course, Donald called Angela to gloat. Sienna hadn't invited her because, Donald imparted with glee, their son Matthew wouldn't attend if his mother was there. If she and Sienna had a cool relationship, then she could safely say she had no relationship with her son, who was two years younger than his sister. He sent the obligatory birthday and Christmas gifts, but he rarely accepted her invitations to lunch. She had no idea how to repair their non-existent relationship. At least Sienna had given her openings she could step through, like the lunch today. But she'd obviously chosen her brother for her birthday bash.

Angela didn't call her on the slight fabrication. It would serve no purpose. "That would be wonderful. Nonni and Poppa will be so glad to see you this summer." Her mother didn't like the March rain in the San Francisco Bay Area, although this year they weren't getting much.

Sienna shut the door on any more questions and grabbed

her menu. "The waiter will be here to take our orders, and I haven't even looked."

He arrived shortly after Sienna had decided on the shrimp salad, dressing on the side.

Even though Angela knew all about weight gain at menopause—honestly, just a couple of pounds—she ordered the lobster salad with melted butter while Teresa went for the lasagna.

"This is a special day and calories don't count," Teresa said cheerily.

Sienna smiled, and in the half minute of silence, Angela decided there was no better time to make her offer. Sienna couldn't be buttered up. She'd either say yes or no.

"Sweetheart, I have a proposition for your birthday gift."

Sienna picked up her wine as if she needed fortification. "It's just a thirtieth birthday. You don't need to do anything special, Mother."

Angela hadn't been Mom or Mommy since Sienna was eight years old. She was always Mother. In the teenage years, Sienna had said it with capital letters and two exaggerated syllables.

"It's very special. And I want to do something to celebrate. Remember I went to Santorini right after I graduated from university?"

Sienna nodded, her gaze wary.

Angela pushed on. "I'd really like to go back, and I thought we could go together to celebrate your thirtieth birthday. I can show you all the places I visited. Since you went to work right out of college, you didn't have a chance to do anything fun. Maybe now is the right time."

Sienna jumped in immediately, as if she didn't even have to think up an excuse. "Mother, I'm trying to get another job. I can't go to a new company and suddenly take off for a trip to Santorini." A slight edge of disgust laced her voice.

Until today, Angela hadn't known about a new job, and Sienna's quick words squashed her hopes. She tried anyway. "Maybe we could do something between jobs. The trip will be on me. For your birthday."

Donald was worth millions, and Angela had wrangled a very good divorce settlement after thirty years of marriage. She could afford to take her daughter on a nice trip. Sienna had never asked her father for money. She had a modest apartment in San Francisco, and she paid for everything herself. Unlike Matthew, who had gone directly from university to work for Donald, Sienna had wanted to make it on her own. And she was doing so well. She'd even moved to something pricier than her studio apartment with the galley kitchen where she'd lived the first three years after graduating.

The problem was that making the trip between jobs meant they'd have to go fairly soon, but Angela had planned on June. "Or you can tell them you have a trip already in the works for this summer. That way, you get your feet wet and learn everything before you go."

Teresa was making an exaggerated eyebrow wiggle, as if she was trying to warn Angela that she was moving too fast and pushing too hard. But she wanted this so badly.

Sienna was adamant. "There's absolutely no way I can do that, Mother. If you'd ever been in the work world, you'd know that."

Angela felt the stick right up in her ribs, the pointy end jabbing her heart.

Sienna was nothing like her mother. They'd both gone to college, but where Angela had taken a month off for a European vacation, Sienna had gone straight to work. Where Angela had never used her teaching degree and instead married right after returning from that trip, Sienna had never had a long-term relationship. Through Teresa, Angela knew her daughter dated, but there'd never been a serious man. Sienna wanted to meet her career goals before she considered marriage and children. Angela wasn't sure Sienna even wanted children.

Sienna started, looked up. Angela could almost feel the kick Teresa had given her under the table.

"Why don't we do this..." At least Sienna didn't say MOTHER in capital letters. "Let me get through this interview, see where everything settles, then you and I can talk."

Angela answered with enthusiasm, as if her heart hadn't been trampled. "That'll be wonderful. We can talk about it later."

She smiled, though she was afraid that "later" would bring an even more explicit rejection.

2

Sienna felt a stab of guilt at the fall of her mom's features, though Mother tried to cover it up quickly. This wasn't how Sienna wanted the birthday lunch to go down, and she added, to take the harshness out of her words, "I'll really try, Mother. But this is a difficult time for me to get away. I'm sorry."

She hated herself for apologizing. Her mother had apologized to her all her life and yet still held Sienna back. As a child, Sienna wasn't allowed to go on a visit to the Exploratorium in San Francisco with her brother and father, or a fishing trip in the Sierras, or countless other outings because those excursions were for father-son bonding. When Sienna wanted her dad to come in for career day, her mom said he didn't have the kind of career that would interest the other students. They wanted firefighters and policemen, not stockbrokers and hedge fund managers. When she wanted to go to the senior prom with an older boy, her mother told her it wasn't appropriate, and he went with someone else. The worst, however, was that her mother always had her dad do the dirty work, making him say, "Your mother doesn't think

you should do that," as if she'd swallow it more easily from
Dad than from her mother.

But at thirty years old, she wouldn't be bitter anymore.
While she'd never felt close to her mother, she didn't want to
shut her down completely. She didn't want to be angry or
mean-spirited. It wasn't good for her.

So she turned on the charm, just the way her father could.
She'd learned that from him, watching his every move,
wanting to be just like him so that he'd love her. "This is so
sweet of you to take me out to lunch. That's all I need. It's
really special. Thank you."

Underneath, though, she wondered if it was Aunt Teresa's
doing. Her aunt had always been her confidant. She knew all
about the trials and tribulations of Sienna's relationship with
her mother, and she'd been sworn to secrecy. But then she
didn't put it past Aunt Teresa to be the angel on her mother's
shoulder, telling her how to fix things, which was probably
why her mother was offering the Santorini trip now. It was
Aunt Teresa's idea.

She went on brightly, changing the subject. "The party
with Nonni and Poppa will be fabulous."

"I can hardly wait," her mother said.

"I really should try to get out to see them." She gave a
very Roman shrug, just like Poppa would. "But work is so
busy right now. I'm hoping this new job will give me a little
free time." Instead of pushing more and more clients at her
to the point where she felt like she couldn't give any of them
her full attention. "But I'm so glad they'll be coming out."

She'd wanted to invite all her family to the party last
week, but Dad had said that Matthew refused to come if
their mother was there. Instead of having to make explana-
tions, she hadn't invited any of them and planned for a
summer party to make up for it.

She honestly didn't understand Matthew's antipathy. He

wasn't the one who'd always been told he couldn't do this or that. Dad let him do whatever he wanted. He was the golden boy, a carbon copy of their father in height and build, short brown hair and hazel eyes like Dad's. But when Matthew arrived that night, he'd acted like nothing was up. She'd have to get to the bottom of it eventually. During the party, however, wasn't the right time.

She steered the conversation to her cousins. "Tell me about the girls, Aunt Teresa."

They'd been much closer, treating her like an older sister, when Sienna had done all their babysitting. They'd talked about makeup and boys and that horrible teacher who was always embarrassing them. She had done her best to soothe their ragged edges.

"Sophia has decided she wants to go in for prelaw. And you know Charlotta, she absolutely loves that dance school. I think she can go all the way. At the end of the term, she'll be doing tryouts for the New York City Ballet."

"That's fabulous," Sienna's mother said as if she didn't know. Surely Aunt Teresa had told her.

"And Bianca landed the most amazing job at a CPA firm once she graduates in June."

Sienna's cousins were go-getters. Bianca wanted to be on the partner track for a huge firm. Whether it was accounting or law or consulting, she wanted in on the big action. "They all sound just as busy as me."

Then Aunt Teresa mentioned the elephant in the room. "And how are the plans for your father's wedding?" Aunt Teresa always liked everything on the table.

Sienna looked at her mother. Her face was pinched, her coffee-colored eyes suddenly darker. Sienna took after her mother in most ways, the same dark, curly hair, brown eyes, and olive complexion. The most she'd done to step out of her mother's beautiful shadow was to dye her hair chestnut.

And yet still she felt like an imitation of her mother and aunt.

Her parents had been divorced a year now. In Sienna's opinion, her dad had screwed over her mother. Yes, she got the Los Altos house and a decent alimony settlement, but Dad was worth beaucoup bucks. He could have been more generous, especially since he was the one who'd left Mother.

His fiancée Bron, short for Brianna, had sworn up and down they weren't having an affair before the divorce. She'd simply noticed how lonely he was, and she'd felt sorry for him. She was a highly paid executive assistant, and she wasn't stupid enough to ruin everything by having an affair with the boss. Once he'd divorced, however, all bets were off.

Sienna liked Bron. They had a lot in common.

And there was the baby, of course.

Sienna walked the tightrope, not wanting to hurt her mother's feelings, but not wanting to lie. And Mother knew about the baby. "It's going well. Bron wants to get everything out of the way now, before she's too far along." Bron was eighteen weeks, the baby due at the beginning of August. The wedding would be late September, and she was making all the decisions now before she got what she called foggy baby brain. "She invited me to the food tasting on Friday." Not wanting to hide anything, which would get way too complicated, she added, "She's asked me to be a bridesmaid."

Her mother's pinched face didn't change. Except for that blink. As if she was hoping it would conceal all the animosity in her eyes.

Aunt Teresa gasped loudly enough to turn heads. "You're really on board with this, Sienna? She's your age, twenty-five years younger than your father."

Her aunt said everything her mother wasn't. But Sienna didn't want to get in a war with her father's future wife, the mother of her half brother or sister. She wanted to be friends.

"Just think how that makes your mother feel."

Just as a twinge of guilt unfurled in Sienna's stomach, her mom jumped in. "I'm fine. I don't bear your father any ill well. He has the right to marry whomever he wishes and to start a new family." Uncharacteristically, she put her hand over Sienna's. "I'm glad you want to be friends with his new wife. Just because we're divorced doesn't mean you have to choose sides."

For some strange reason, her mother's words made her eyes prickle, and she said softly, "Thank you. I'd like my relationship with her to work. I want to be able to see the baby."

She'd always had a difficult relationship with her father, striving to earn his love even as nothing she did ever worked. That's why she hadn't gone to work for him the way Matthew had. She'd taken a job at some soulless corporation just so she did nothing that would disappoint him. Yet he'd been disappointed anyway.

In the last few months, though, things seemed to change. Maybe it was her friendship with Bron. Not that she'd become friends with Bron to get to her father. But she'd even asked him to put in a good word for her with the senior partner at Smithfield and Vine, the company she'd been interviewing with. The two men were good friends, and maybe it was nepotism, but she wanted this job. She wanted him to be proud of her. With his recommendation, she had an excellent chance.

So no, when Bron asked her to be a bridesmaid, she didn't turn her down.

Luckily, her mother changed the subject. "I'd love to hear more about this new job. Tell us everything."

Sienna did. Maybe, if she tried hard enough, she could leave behind all the resentment that had festered for as long as she could remember, making her question not only her mother's motives but everyone else's as well. It was even why she'd never let any man get too close.

But at thirty, she wanted to be a new person, one who no longer spent her downtime brooding about the past and possibly missing out on something good in her future.

✿

HAVING TAKEN ONLY A LONG LUNCH, SIENNA HAD RUSHED back to work once she'd demolished her sorbet.

"Don't get all mopey," Teresa told Angela. "She can change her mind."

"Not if she gets this job. Which I'm sure she will." Angela tucked her pain down deep. She had to believe that things would get better between her and Sienna. They'd come a long way. Five years ago, Sienna would never have met her for lunch, even if Teresa attended. And she hadn't been cruel in turning down the trip. She'd actually been polite. Didn't that mean there was hope?

"You can always go later, maybe in August or September, after she's acclimated to the new job."

Teresa always saw the bright side. But then she had three beautiful daughters who adored her and a husband who was as madly in love with her today as he had been when he married her. Angela, on the other hand, had two children who hated her and an ex-husband who couldn't get rid of her fast enough once he'd met a prettier, younger model. Had they been having an affair before the divorce? That pregnancy had come along fast. Not that she cared. She relished her freedom. The best thing Donald had ever done was divorce her.

Once he was married, and with a new baby, he wouldn't be so concerned with what Angela did. Maybe he could stop punishing her.

But that didn't change the trip she wanted with Sienna.

"If we wait, there'll be the baby and the wedding. We really need to go in June."

Teresa sipped her latte, licking the foam off her lip. "Wouldn't next year work just as well?"

She needed to go this year, exactly thirty years after she was supposed to return to Santorini. And didn't.

"It's not as if he's actually going to be there." Compassion softened Teresa's voice.

Angela knew he wouldn't be there. She wanted only to retrace her footsteps of that glorious graduation trip. It was a pilgrimage to her past. If by some miracle she saw him, she didn't have a clue what she'd say anyway. *Sorry I didn't make our date thirty years ago.* He would never understand.

She'd done what every young woman did on a fabulous holiday in a foreign country. She met a boy, falling head over heels for him. He'd wanted her to stay. She'd wanted him to follow her home. But they'd had two very different lives.

And she was engaged to Donald.

But they'd made a pact before she left Santorini. She would return home and end her engagement, giving her family time to get over the scandal. And time for them both to make sure their feelings were true. Then, exactly one year later, she would return to their favorite café on the Greek island, meeting him for their usual coffee and *bougatsa*, the sugary pastry she'd loved. And they would plan their future.

The memory of those long-ago mornings with him at the café made her eyes ache.

But she'd come home to face the wedding, her mother adamant she couldn't jilt her wealthy fiancé. The shame and scandal it would bring to the family was untenable, especially since her mother had worked so hard to make this relationship work. Donald's family was San Francisco elite, and Mama wanted into that circle so badly she could taste it. Maybe if Angela had been older, stronger, if she'd started working and had lived on her own a few years, she might have withstood the pressure. But she couldn't handle it, especially when her mother explained what her life would be like if she didn't go through with the wedding.

Angela could still hear her mother's angry voice, see the finger pointing in her face. "I told you to take your sister with you. None of this would have happened if you'd done what I said." But Teresa had already met William, her future husband, and she'd had no intention of taking off for Santorini.

Mama had berated her endlessly, telling her she was just a passing fancy to a Greek boy who was no better than a beach bum. It was idiotic to think he'd be waiting for her in a year.

There was no social media, and cell phones and email weren't the norm yet. Besides, the year apart was supposed to solidify their connection. They hadn't planned to get in touch. But he'd believed she would call off her wedding.

Instead, she'd finally accepted her mother's absolute certainty that he wouldn't show up for their reunion. And the only other person she'd ever told about the Greek boy she'd fallen in love with was her older sister Teresa.

"It's just a trip down memory lane," she told Teresa. "It was the happiest three weeks of my life. I want to visit all the same places. And if Sienna will come with me, maybe she and I can work things out."

"You can go anytime if all you want to do is relive memories. It doesn't have to be the middle of June."

But Angela needed to go to that café on the anniversary of the day she'd missed. She wanted to gaze at the bougainvillea climbing the white walls, the blue domes of the churches, and the turquoise Aegean.

She wanted to sit in the morning sun and imagine what her life would have been if she'd made a different choice.

But Teresa didn't believe in fanciful thinking. She was down to earth. With her beautiful, loving family, she could be.

All Angela had were dreams. And the hope that one day she and Sienna would find the closeness that mothers and daughters should share.

3

Sienna stomped through her apartment, tossed her phone on the bed, her whole world shattering as the receptionist's words repeated in her head.

Mr. Smithfield is canceling your interview today. He's already decided on another candidate. He sends his apologies and wishes you all the luck in finding the right opportunity.

She couldn't believe it. Her heart was racing, her hands were clammy, and she couldn't catch her breath. Was it a panic attack? Or was this how it felt when you saw your future crumbling?

She'd taken the day off for the interview, which was why she hadn't spent more time with her aunt and mom yesterday. She was dressed in her best blue suit, circumspect yet elegant, with a short jacket and a blouse that showed a hint of skin above the neckline. She hadn't wanted to be overtly sexy, but not androgynous either.

Tearing off the jacket, she threw it on the floor, ripped open the blouse, a couple of buttons flying, then yanked on the back zipper of her skirt, letting it fall to the floor where she kicked it aside. Her low-heeled pumps flew into the air as she kicked them off, one of them smashing into the vanity and sending her makeup crashing to the floor.

They'd decided on another candidate before she'd even had her third interview? It didn't make sense. Companies went through all their candidates, called you back for a second round if they liked you, then, if you really had the spark they wanted, they called you in for a third interview. Yet they'd made their choice without even talking to her again. It wasn't right.

She'd wanted this job with every fiber of her being. She would have shown her dad how good she was. Next to his firm, Smithfield and Vine was the top investment house in San Francisco. All his disappointment would become a thing of the past.

She clomped to the closet, pulled out her robe, sliding her arms into it and belting it tight. Thank God she hadn't quit her job, despite being sure she'd had this one in the bag. And thank goodness she'd canceled the hair appointment too. Why cut off her long curls for people who didn't even want her? Maybe the decision had been a premonition.

She probably needed to get out of town, try L.A., maybe Seattle. Or San Jose, the heart of Silicon Valley?

She made herself a cup of tea, then curled up on the sofa in her postage-stamp living room. At least her apartment *had* a living room with a separate bedroom and an actual tub in the bathroom instead of a shower stall. It wasn't a palace, but it was cozy.

Setting her teacup on the side table, she dialed her father. "Hi, Dad." She tried to sound upbeat even though her heart jammed her throat.

"Hello, Sienna."

He'd never had a pet name for her, not like he had for her brother, things like buddy or scout, terms of endearment. But never for Sienna.

"How did the interview go?" was his first question.

She shouldn't have asked him to put in a good word with the senior partner. Then she wouldn't have needed to tell him she'd failed.

Now she had to admit the truth. "They canceled me even before the interview, saying they'd already made their choice."

"I'm sorry, Sienna." His voice was soft, maybe with sympathy. At least he didn't say he was sorry she wasn't good enough for the job.

She couldn't help asking. "Did Mr. Smithfield give you any indication when you talked to him?" It sounded like begging, and she added, "When I go out to interview again, I don't want to make the same mistakes." She hated admitting that she must have blown the interview.

"I'm sure they just found someone more..." He paused, as if he'd been about to say something hurtful, and qualified the statement with, "Someone who's a better fit."

More. She'd always wanted to be more, but never was.

But this time, she'd believed she was a perfect fit. "Okay. I just thought maybe..." She trailed off.

"I would have told you, Sienna, if there was a problem. You can always come here." It sounded like a consolation prize, not something he truly wanted.

"Thanks, Dad." She absolutely couldn't go there. She'd constantly be proving herself. Even if her brother was two years younger, she'd never live up to him. "But I still want to try it on my own."

"I'll keep my eye out." A hint of annoyance crept into his clipped voice as he said, "Don't forget about the tasting at the caterers tomorrow."

She didn't feel up to it, and she'd have to leave an hour early, not that anyone would notice. She was just a tiny cog in a gigantic wheel. "I'll be there. No worries."

After hanging up, she called her brother. Matthew knew

all the scuttlebutt. "Hey," she said when he answered. "I was up for that job at Smithfield and Vine, but I didn't get it." She wasn't as leery of telling her brother now that her dad knew.

"Too bad. Good luck on the next one." He was terse, as if he was in the middle of something.

"Can you put your ear to the ground and find out what happened? I can't imagine why they canceled without giving me a chance."

"They actually canceled the interview?" His voice rose with incredulity.

"I didn't even get my third shot."

"That's shitty. They could've at least taken you out to lunch."

She wanted to cry, but she couldn't let Matthew hear.

"I'll put out some feelers," he said. "And I'll call you if I learn anything."

"Thanks."

"Sure." He hung up without saying goodbye.

With the day off, Sienna could have gone for a run or worked out at the gym, but afraid she might not hear Matthew's call, she binged *Squid Game* on Netflix. When her phone rang, she actually jumped.

"You won't believe this." Matthew's tone was harsh with disgust. "You're way better qualified than the asshole they gave the job to."

She basked in her brother's praise. "Who was it?"

"I went to university with him. Jeffrey Deck. We all called him Dick. He totally thought he was better than the rest of us, but he was an idiot."

Smithfield and Vine didn't hire idiots. And the guy was younger than she was, which meant he had less experience. She could only think he got the job because he was a man. Yet Smithfield and Vine were highly regarded for their hiring practices. They were colorblind and gender blind, even if your gender was fluid.

"What the hell?" she muttered.

"Just what I was thinking," Matthew said. "If I hear any more, I'll let you know." Then he added, in a near whisper as if somebody was listening, "You can always come here, Sienna. Dad's really not as bad as you think."

She didn't want to get back on the competition merry-go-round with her brother. She liked Matthew. Once she was out of the house, and even more so after he'd graduated too, they got along fairly well, even occasionally getting together for drinks.

That camaraderie was why she felt she could ask, "Why didn't you want Mother to come to my birthday party?"

She thought he'd stammer an answer, but he said, "What are you talking about?"

"You told Dad you wouldn't come to the party if Mother was there?" Her voice rose, ending it on a question.

"I didn't say a thing to him." She could almost see his shrug. "I didn't care if you invited Mom." Matthew didn't avoid their mother. He gave her birthday and Christmas presents, and yet he rarely saw her and didn't seem to have much use for her.

"She's really not as bad as you think," she told him. "I've had dinner with her a few times. She and Aunt Teresa took me out for a birthday lunch."

"I don't think she's a bad person." Matthew was silent a few moments. "But I didn't know you were ready to forgive her."

"I'm not forgiving her. I just decided I'm too old to hold grudges. It's not good for me."

He laughed harshly. "Are you saying I'm holding a grudge?"

"Look, I know we really don't talk much about how things

were when we were growing up. I'm just saying that people make mistakes."

"I know they do. And I'm not holding any grudges. It didn't bother me that you were her favorite."

"Her favorite? You've gotta be joking." He was rewriting history. "But you know how fragile Mother was. You and Dad were so close, she thought she couldn't compete."

Matthew laughed, not cruelly, just softly. "Maybe. Remember how she was when Dad was on a business trip?"

"I remember." Their mother always made their favorite meals when Dad wasn't around, tacos or fish and chips or lasagna, stuff their father didn't eat. He was strictly meat and potatoes. Then they'd play board games or watch movies. When their dad was away, Mother actually made the days fun. Maybe she actually had been trying to compete.

"Anyway," she said, "It's good for me to let go of all this animosity."

"Absolutely. And honestly, I don't have any animosity either." Maybe that was true, or maybe Matthew was in denial.

Once he'd hung up, the main point of the conversation hit her. Dad had said Matthew didn't want their mom at the birthday party. Yet Matthew hadn't said that at all. Her father was a lot of things, but she'd never thought he was a liar, and though she rarely confronted him, she needed to call him on it now. After all, it was pretty blatant.

Her father answered the way he always did, flatly. "Hello, Sienna."

He didn't ask why she'd called a second time in one day and waited her out. Which made it harder to confront him. She had to dig her fingernails into her palms to keep going. "I just talked to Matthew, and he says he never told you he wouldn't come to my birthday party if Mother was there."

Her father's long pause almost unnerved her, until he said,

"I'm sorry I wasn't quite truthful. It was Brianna—" He never called her Bron. "—who was uncomfortable about your mom being there. Since you and Brianna get along well, I didn't want the two of you to develop any bad feelings, so I told a fib. Don't mention this to Brianna, or she'll get upset that I treated her like a child who can't handle anything."

So Bron would be mad to hear he'd stepped in. Interesting. Her father usually never cared what anybody wanted. He just did what he wanted. Maybe Bron was softening him up a little. That was a good thing. But it was too bad Bron had to feel uncomfortable.

"I won't say anything. I want us to be friends, but please don't do stuff like that, Dad. Bron and I are big girls, and we can handle it."

"I never make the same mistake twice," he said, yet his voice didn't hold even a hint of remorse.

⚜ 4 ⚜

"**O**h my God," Sienna said, her eyes closed as she savored the lobster roll. "These are so good." She looked at Bron. "You have to get this. And the lobster bisque."

Bron nodded enthusiastically. "Absolutely."

The tasting would act as Sienna's dinner. After work on Friday, she'd driven down the Peninsula to meet Dad and Bron at the Burlingame caterer. They'd started with asparagus soup, followed by carrot soup, but the lobster bisque won hands down. "You should have those lobster-stuffed mushroom caps too. Make it a lobster feed."

Bron laughed. A blonde with blue eyes, and a model-thin figure—at least she had been model thin—she dropped her hand to her belly, caressing the eighteen-week baby bump. Bron's pretty features complemented Dad's good looks, his hair liberally littered with gray while his face remained relatively unlined. They were almost the same height, Bron only a half inch shorter than Dad's five-nine, which she compensated for by wearing flats.

The age difference was striking, Bron being thirty like

26

Sienna, while at fifty-five, her dad was a couple of years older even than Sienna's mom. He'd weathered the years well, but men always did without menopause sucking the life out of them, as her mother and Aunt Teresa often said when complaining about night sweats, crepey skin, and extra weight. Not that Aunt Teresa didn't look fabulous. And Sienna's mother was still beautiful, though she didn't laugh often enough.

Laughter was a skill Sienna needed to learn. She took after her mother in that way. But being around Bron made her feel good. When they went out for lunch or shopping on a Saturday afternoon, she swore she laughed more. It felt like an honor to be helping with the preparations. Bron's parents were in South Carolina and her brother and sister were back east. They wouldn't be coming out until a couple of weeks before the wedding. But Sienna didn't think of herself as second choice.

They tested additional hors d'oeuvres, delicate quiches, crispy bruschetta, lettuce cups filled with blackened fish.

Bron clapped her hands. "Now for the main course. They'll bring us filet mignon, lobster tail, pecan encrusted salmon, and coq au vin I'm told is to die for."

"Anything for vegetarians?" Sienna asked. It seemed the world was going vegetarian.

Bron put a hand on her arm. "They have an amazing lentil stew a friend said is delicious. We'll try that too."

"Count me out on that one," Sienna's father said. "And filet mignon and lobster tail are over the top."

Bron curled her fingers around his. "If this is going to be the event of the year with people talking about every detail, do you really want to scrimp on the cut of meat we serve?"

He gave her a look. Maybe it was indulgence, maybe it was weariness, or maybe it was love. "All right, you win."

Sienna wondered if that look stemmed from a need to

show everyone he deserved a young trophy wife, a Cinderella wedding, and a new baby. With the baby coming in August, they'd pushed the wedding out to the end of September. Neither of them seemed the least bit uncomfortable with having a newborn at their wedding. Maybe it was a badge of honor for her father, that he still had what it took. Honestly, she couldn't tell how he felt about becoming a father again at his age. He was unreadable to her.

As for her mother, she'd said she was fine about the wedding and the baby. But would she show Sienna anything different?

After choosing filet mignon, salmon, and coq au vin, plus lentil stew for the vegetarians, they moved on to the bridal cake. Bron dropped her voice so the caterers wouldn't hear. "I found a princess cake at a Danish bakery. It's filled with whipped cream and raspberry jam and covered in fondant icing." She looked at Sienna's father.

He nodded, saying benevolently, "You should have whatever cake you want."

Bron clasped her hands in prayer. "Thank you, thank you, thank you." Then she tapped Sienna's arm. "I've made an appointment at the bridal shop. We'll all meet there tomorrow at ten. I know it's awfully early to choose, and they won't fit my dress until a couple of weeks before the wedding, once I've lost as much baby weight as I can. But I really want everything settled before I get foggy baby brain." She tapped her head. "Can you make it?"

It thrilled Sienna to be in the wedding. She really believed Bron liked her, that she wasn't just sucking up to the new stepdaughter.

Dad cleared his throat. "About that." When both Sienna and Bron looked at him, he shifted in the chair as if he was nervous. Except that her dad was never nervous. "I believe we should rethink the bridal party."

Sienna understood why he was feeling nerves he'd never felt before when Bron said with a hard edge to her voice, "What do you mean 'rethinking the bridal party?'"

Dad spoke to Sienna, not even looking at his fiancée. "Having you in the wedding looks bad to your mother."

Sienna's stomach sank, and a fist tightened around her heart.

Her father knocked on the table as if demanding attention. "I don't know how she knows, but she called me."

Sienna actually felt her jaw drop. Luckily, she caught it before it hit the table. "Mother *called* you?"

As far as Sienna knew, her parents had barely talked since signing the divorce papers.

Her dad went on, no longer nervous, meeting her gaze steadily. "She understands you'll be at the wedding, but having you walk down the aisle is unsettling for her."

"But she didn't say a thing to me on Wednesday when I met her for lunch." Not wanting any friction, she rarely talked about her dealings with her mom. But what her father said was utterly bewildering.

"But that's not fair," Bron spluttered. "It's my wedding."

Dad finally looked at her, a woebegone light in his eyes. Dad didn't do woebegone any more than he did nervous. But he was doing it for Bron. "We need to consider her feelings. With Sienna in your bridal party, everyone will think she's taking sides against her mother."

"No one's going to think that," Sienna snapped.

"That's why your mother came to me, because she didn't feel you would understand."

He reached out, then dropped his hand to the table, as if he thought touching her was a bad idea. "I probably should have told you it was my idea, but now you know—" He shrugged, sadly, wearily. Falsely? "—we should honor her wishes."

"But we won't have an even number of bridesmaids and groomsmen," Bron groused.

"I'm sure you can find someone else."

Sienna saw a sheen of tears in Bron's eyes.

As if seeing them too, her dad said, "I'm so sorry. But Angela could make the divorce much more difficult. She could go back to the courts to ask for more money, even try to take the Atherton house. I should never have bought it before the divorce."

Sienna looked at him, shock making her voice low. "You bought it *before* the divorce?"

His jaw ticked. "You know your mother and I hadn't been good for years. I needed a quiet place to go. I was thinking with a damaged heart—" He held his fist over his chest. "—instead of thinking about my financial well-being."

Sienna looked at Bron. "Did you know about the house?"

"Absolutely not." Her blue eyes were watery with her vehemence. "Your father and I didn't start dating until after the divorce. I only knew he was unhappy." Then she added quickly, "But not because he ever said anything."

"But the divorce is done. Mother can't do anything."

"It's not only about the trouble she can cause," her father said. "It's about her feelings. We don't need to hurt her unnecessarily, don't you agree?" He looked at them both beseechingly. "I should have thought about this before." He covered Bron's hand. "When you first said you wanted Sienna in the wedding. My bad."

Bron looked at Sienna. "I guess you're right," she mumbled. "I wasn't thinking how your mom would feel."

Sienna fumed. Mother should have said something on Wednesday, but she'd gone to Dad behind Sienna's back, just the way she always had, getting Dad to do her dirty work.

Sienna muttered ungraciously, "Okay, whatever you want."

Her mother offered her a fabulous vacation to Santorini

with one hand while with the other, she'd stabbed her in the back.

She'd never been so angry. There was absolutely no way she was going on any damn trip.

Right now, she couldn't even stand the thought of her mother.

ANGELA DIDN'T CRY. SHE HADN'T CRIED FOR YEARS. BUT Sienna's words had crushed the fragile hope inside her.

I can't go.

Just that, no apology, no question of making the trip later, no opening for Angela to beg, with Sienna's tone adding the words *not now and not ever*. Then her daughter had hung up with a curt goodbye.

That had been Friday evening, and as much as Angela wanted to call back, she didn't. Not on Saturday or Sunday either. She'd thought about calling Teresa to ask if Sienna had said anything to her, but she didn't do that either.

By Monday, she'd accepted that she would never have a good relationship with her daughter. She'd lost that chance years ago. They might have lunch occasionally, but they would never be close.

Still, when the doorbell rang midmorning on Monday, her heart leaped.

It wasn't Sienna on her doorstep. It was a statuesque blonde the same age as Angela's daughter. Donald's new flame, the woman he'd be marrying at the end of September. The woman who was having his child.

"Hi." The blonde raised her hand and gave a little wave. "I don't know if you remember me. I'm Bron."

Angela remembered. Bron had been Donald's executive secretary for two years before the divorce. She'd talked to the woman on the phone and seen her the few times she'd stopped by Donald's office. Not that she'd ever dropped in out of the blue to take him out to lunch.

"Um." Bron rolled her lips together, her lipstick remaining unsmudged. "Can we talk?"

Realizing how rude it was to keep the woman standing on the doorstep without even saying a word, Angela opened the door wider. "Come in." Then she asked out of politeness, "Would you like coffee?"

Bron waved her hands as if warding Angela off. "I don't want to take up too much of your time."

Japanese pots of orchids, philodendrons, and African violets filled the marble entryway. Two steps down from the foyer, the rarely used living room had a wall of windows with an expansive view of the meadows and mountains that lay beyond the backyard pool. "Let's have a seat." She flourished a hand for Bron to precede her.

She'd chosen the Los Altos house twenty-five years ago when she still had a marriage that didn't feel like a war zone. Maybe Donald let her keep it because it had never been as ostentatious as he would have liked. It didn't scream of wealth the way his Atherton home did. She'd driven by out of curiosity. Already planning his exit strategy, he'd bought it in the firm's name before the divorce.

But she didn't want to dwell on the past. She was free, and her life was good. Except for the loss of her children's love.

A hand protectively on her belly, Bron perched on the edge of the sofa as if afraid the cushions would swallow her if she sat back.

Angela couldn't begin to guess what this was about. "What can I do for you?"

"Well, Mrs. Walker." Bron stopped as if unsure of what to call Angela. She and Donald weren't married anymore. And now he was marrying this beautiful young woman who would give him beautiful babies.

She helped her out. "Call me Angela."

Bron nodded, her fingers curled around the edge of the sofa cushion, and finally got to it. "I can understand how upsetting the wedding must be for you."

"It's not upsetting at all," Angela said sincerely. "And congratulations on the baby."

Bron blinked as if she didn't believe her and had no clue how to answer the bold declaration. "Oh, well, thank you, I'm sorry," she stammered.

Angela put her out of her misery. "You don't have to apologize. I'm perfectly fine. We've been divorced for a year." She didn't say she'd been happier in the last year than in the previous thirty.

"I'm so glad to hear that." Then Bron rushed on as if she'd prepared a speech she had to deliver. "I want you to know I wasn't having an affair with your husband before the divorce. Not even a thought or a look."

Surely there'd been an attraction, but what counted were actions.

"I understand completely. You don't owe me anything." Though Donald did for the terrible way he'd treated her for so many years. But she knew instinctively this girl was innocent. She was a young thirty, sweet, and Angela mourned the death of her innocence when she found out what Donald was really like.

She urged the girl on. "But that isn't what you came here to tell me."

Bron shook her head, her silky blonde hair caressing her perfect cheekbones. "I don't want there to be any animosity or for you to think I have an ulterior motive."

Everyone had an ulterior motive. It didn't make Bron a

bad person. "No worries. I don't have even a scintilla of animosity." She smiled reassuringly.

"Thank you. And I want you to know that I really, really like your daughter."

Angela barely restrained her eyebrow from rising. What did Sienna have to do with anything?

"I know there's a huge age gap between Donald and me, and I feel like Sienna's a sister."

That meant Angela was more like this girl's mother. She'd been twenty-three when Sienna was born. "I'm glad. She works so hard, and she can always use more friends." Someone who could help her see that work wasn't the only thing in life.

"Well, then, I..." Bron was stammering again. "You can see why I'd like to have her in my wedding."

"Sienna told me you'd asked her to be a bridesmaid. It's kind of you to include her."

"So I'm asking your permission," Bron said. "It's not meant as a slam against you."

Angela interrupted so the girl didn't have to keep apologizing, "It's a wonderful idea."

Bron didn't seem to hear her. "Sienna and I would've been friends even if I'd never fallen—" She stopped, looking at Angela as if saying the words aloud terrified her. Then her eyes went wide as she suddenly understood what Angela had said. "You do? Think it's a good idea, I mean?"

Angela confirmed with a nod, wanting to put the girl at ease. She *was* a girl, so young, so hopeful. Angela hated the thought of what five years of marriage to Donald would do to her. She wondered if he'd make her get a paternity test for the baby she was protecting in her womb. "Sienna needs friends. I'd love for you to be close to her. Being your bridesmaid doesn't bother me in the least."

Bron shook her head as if she was trying to clear it. "Then why did you—" She stopped again.

"Why did I what?"

"Why did you tell Donald you didn't want Sienna in the wedding?"

It didn't surprise Angela. It didn't even raise her blood pressure. "I don't know why he would've told you that. I haven't talked to him in weeks."

Bron's brow furrowed with mystification. "But he said you called, that your feelings were hurt, and you thought Sienna was choosing sides. He said that you could get vindictive if we pissed you off. You could go back to the courts for a better settlement or make trouble about the Atherton house." She closed her mouth abruptly, realizing she'd said too much.

Angela couldn't hold back, asking with a sudden hardness, "Did he say this just to you? Or to Sienna as well?"

"To both of us," the girl whispered. "While we were at the caterers on Friday." She put a finger to her lips. "Right after I asked Sienna to come to the bridal shop to pick out dresses."

Donald had found the perfect opening. It didn't hurt that Sienna was in the wedding. It didn't hurt that she'd helped choose the wedding menu. But it crushed Angela to realize Sienna had called her almost immediately afterward and turned down the Santorini trip.

She sat straight and stiff. "I didn't call Donald. I have no problem with Sienna being in the wedding. I have no problem with you marrying Donald. Or having his child."

She felt sorry for the girl, but there was nothing she could do to save this beautiful, fresh-faced young woman who didn't deserve what Donald would do to her if she disappointed him. Which she inevitably would.

"I don't understand," Bron whispered.

Angela made excuses just as she would have done for

Sienna. "Maybe he's just uncomfortable with what people might say."

"But you really don't mind if she's in the wedding?" Her voice had the pitch of a teenager who needed comfort when the boy she liked asked another girl to the prom.

"I don't mind at all."

Donald had told this terrible lie while they were choosing the menu and talking about bridesmaid dresses. But that wasn't a surprise. He was an asshole.

"I hope it's not too late to go back to Sienna. You haven't asked someone else to fill the spot, have you?"

"I wanted to talk to you while Donald—" She cut herself off again.

While Donald was at work and didn't know what she was doing. Which meant Bron didn't completely trust him. It also meant she wasn't working for him anymore, that she was busy getting ready for the baby, the wedding, and fixing up their magnificent Atherton house.

How Angela wished she was that young again, still living with her illusions and her hopes. Before she'd made all her bad decisions.

"You should absolutely have Sienna in your wedding."

"But what am I going to tell her about you?"

"Just tell her that Donald changed his mind."

It wouldn't do any good for Bron to tell Sienna that her father had lied. Sienna wouldn't believe her. And it certainly wouldn't solve Angela's problems with her daughter.

She was the one who'd have to figure out how to fix the damage Donald had done for all these years.

And she'd start right now by paying him a visit.

※ 5 ※

Angela seethed from the moment Bron had, whether by accident or on purpose, revealed Donald's excuses for why Sienna shouldn't be in the wedding.

First, it was that Angela's feelings were hurt. Then it was that she'd think Sienna was choosing sides. She could let all that go. But when he claimed that she'd make the divorce settlement disagreeable, that pushed Angela over the edge. Sienna would assume her mother was a vindictive bitch who would use her own daughter to make Donald pay.

No wonder Sienna had curtly rejected the Santorini vacation. Angela couldn't abide that Donald was still trying to turn Sienna against her, even after he'd divorced her.

She jumped in her car after Bron's departure. The woman wasn't a bad person, quite the opposite. She could be a good friend for Sienna.

But Angela had to deal with Donald. She had no illusions that it would change him, but it would restore some of her power to call him on his dishonesty.

Donald's anteroom was decorated in muted colors with a sofa, two chairs, and a one-cup coffee machine on a sideboard. His replacement secretary, seated at a desk outside his door, was a battle axe of indeterminate age. After Bron, maybe he thought he needed real protection.

She glanced at the nameplate. Heather. The name was completely incongruous with the woman's wide shoulders, thick neck, short gray bob, and steely gaze.

But Angela wouldn't be cowed. "I'm Angela Walker. Please tell Donald I'd like to speak with him."

"You aren't on Mr. Walker's calendar." Her voice was as thick as the rest of her body and as steely as her eyes.

"That's because I'm his wife. I don't need to make an appointment." She couldn't quite make her voice as steely as Heather's.

"He never makes an exception, not even for family." Heather raised her nose as if she smelled something bad. "And as I recall, you're the *ex*-wife, not the current wife."

Angela smiled at the slam Heather had hoped to deliver. "I am the *current* wife because he doesn't have another one yet. He has an ex-secretary who will *become* his wife in the next few months. I'm sure he's told you all about me and that I have an axe to grind and that you should never let me in."

Her little speech surprised a raised eyebrow out of Heather. "He hasn't told me you have any ax to grind. He hasn't even told me not to let you in."

Odd. Maybe it meant that Donald didn't consider her a threat. Then she spied the pictures on the desk, two families with children, obviously Heather's grandchildren. "I'm just here to talk about our daughter. Sienna. I'd really like Donald's advice. I'm worried about her, and he could always handle her better than I could."

It wasn't a lie. She was worried about Sienna. And Donald had always gotten on better with her, mainly because he was the master manipulator.

Heather's demeanor seemed to soften, the corners of her mouth rising slightly.

Angela added, "If he's not in a meeting, that is. I don't want to break up anything important. But this is about his daughter."

Heather picked up the phone as if she'd gone through these same kid problems herself. "Let me check. If he's not on the phone, I'll slip you in."

"I'd be ever so grateful."

It took several long moments of quiet back-and-forth conversation, but when Heather hung up, she pointed at the door. "He's only got a very few minutes." She gave Angela a hopeful look, as if between the two of them, they could solve all Sienna's problems.

Donald was seated behind his massive desk, two large screens in front of him and a magnificent view of the San Francisco Bay behind him.

He waved her into a chair. "You hate driving into the city. This must be important."

At fifty-five, he was a handsome man, the gray rapidly taking over his brown hair and adding to his distinguished demeanor, steady, knowledgeable, his suit impeccably tailored, giving the sense that everything was well-toned beneath the bespoke material. Even if it wasn't.

"It's about Sienna." She came to the point. "You lied to her."

He raised one eyebrow. If his hair had been dark, he would have looked like Spock. Or the devil. "What makes you say that?"

"You told her I didn't want her in your wedding, that I was afraid she was choosing sides. And that I could be a vindictive bitch who would make things difficult for you, especially about the house you bought while we were still married and didn't include in the settlement."

His hazel eyes turned flinty. "I never said you were a vindictive bitch. And the house was purchased in the company's name, so it wasn't part of any property settlement."

"That's my point. I couldn't get it from you even if I took you to court. You just told Sienna that to make me look bad."

He allowed himself the smallest of smiles. Though he didn't want to appear to be gloating, he was enjoying the fact that she'd come here. "Sienna doesn't need any more ammunition to think badly of you. She's had her whole life to do that."

"All because you've been feeding her lies since she was eight years old."

His eyes gleamed with triumph. He manipulated everyone around him with his lies. Maybe her daughter didn't recognize it, maybe Bron didn't either. But Angela knew him so well.

"I didn't need to tell lies," he said smoothly. "You simply showed your true colors."

The only true color she had was in the love she bore her children. The love Donald had torn to pieces. "I want you to let her be in the wedding."

He held up his hands, spreading his fingers as if he were surrendering to her whims. "It's Brianna's decision, not mine. You see, she actually had a thought for your feelings. She only made me bring it up because she didn't want to sound like the bad guy in front of Sienna."

He lied so easily, without an insincere line on his face. But if she wanted to call him on this latest lie, she'd have to reveal that Bron had come by to see her. Lacking even an ounce of animosity toward the woman, she couldn't bring her into the discussion. At least not with the truth. "I'm sure you browbeat her into it."

He smiled widely, showing little of his teeth. "I don't have to browbeat her. She knows the right thing to do. Besides, she adores me."

"How long do you think that's going to last once she finds out what you're really like?"

His smile didn't falter at the insult. "I can't believe Sienna actually called you about the matter. I know about your lunch with her and how you're trying to make everything up to her, but she still doesn't trust you."

"You'd be surprised who Sienna talks to."

He laughed softly, snidely. "Ah, so it was dear Teresa."

"It could be anybody," she told him. "Our daughter talks, your fiancée talks, their friends talk. You'd be surprised at all the talk."

"I'd be surprised if your daughter told *you* anything." Donald had made very sure of that.

"I want you to put her in the wedding."

His jaw ticked. "Or what?"

She had nothing she could hold over him. All she said was, "Both Sienna and your fiancée are going to figure out exactly who you are. They're going to see through your lies and recognize how you manipulate people."

He stood then, as if he suddenly realized his lies might be traceable. "If you're considering making trouble, you better think about what you have to lose, my dear *ex*-wife."

"I have nothing to lose. You already stole my daughter and my son."

He wagged a finger. "But you're hoping for a reconciliation."

"You've made very sure that won't happen."

She stood too, slowly, sliding the strap of her handbag up her arm. Calmly, almost serenely, she said, "What if Sienna were to learn that Bron never said anything at all, that you were telling yet another lie?"

"Her name is Brianna, not Bron." Except that he was the only one who refused to call her by the nickname she preferred, another of his power trips. "And neither of them will ever believe a word you say."

She turned, saying over her shoulder as she walked away. "Maybe Sienna would."

"Then I'd have to tell her the truth. That she's not actually my daughter, but I raised her anyway. Out of the goodness of my heart."

Angela didn't falter even a single step.

Teresa was right. She needed to tell Sienna the truth sooner rather than later.

And put an end to Donald's power over her before he made sure Sienna found out in the worst possible way.

HER JOB SEARCH HAD FALLEN APART. SIENNA DIDN'T WANT to jump ship for something worse. She wanted a smaller but more prestigious firm with the opportunity to move up and make partner, and she didn't mind proving herself. She was tired of the bureaucracy and the backstabbing in a faceless, unfeeling corporation.

But there was nothing out there right now.

Maybe her weariness was why, when Bron called for lunch on the Wednesday after that terrible tasting party, Sienna signed out of her computer with a punch of her mouse and decided this would be a long lunch. Just because her mother had been cruel about the wedding didn't mean she would give up her friendship with Bron.

They met at an exclusive café on Market Street, with booths that had seats she could relax into and where the patrons dressed elegantly in business suits and designer clothing.

All except Bron, who hadn't received the message that the fiancée of the managing partner at Walker and Walker shouldn't wear leggings and a blowsy shirt that could have come from any department store. But Sienna liked how down to earth Bron was. She hadn't forgotten her roots in the secretarial pool, and she'd truly fallen for Sienna's father.

Bron had already ordered a champagne cocktail for her even though Sienna shouldn't drink at lunch. But what the heck. She lifted her glass. "Here's to a lovely lunch." They tapped flutes, Bron's filled with sparkling apple juice.

The champagne wasn't the best, but the cocktail was good. Before the baby, Bron stocked the cheapest champagne she could find, hiding it in the back of the pantry in the multimillion-dollar Atherton house. Sienna's father would have popped all the tops and poured every bottle down the drain if he'd found them, but Bron claimed the cheaper the champagne, the better the champagne cocktail. They'd even taste-tested one evening when Dad was working late. Just as Bron said, the cheap stuff made the better cocktail.

That was another reason she enjoyed Bron. She knew what she liked, and she didn't care if it was cheap. She even bragged that she'd found this or that adorable outfit at a consignment store or even a thrift shop. "You can't go looking for something specific," she always said, "because you'll never find it. It's while browsing that you come across incredible deals, some stuff still with the tags on it."

Sienna had taken a few shopping trips herself and found some amazing buys.

Eventually her father would break Bron's habits. He couldn't have his wife appearing in second-hand clothing.

Their starters arrived, Bron having ordered them already, and they told the server to come back once they'd decided on their main course.

"Let me tell you right away why I asked you for lunch." Bron licked the salt off her fingers after tasting the tempura shrimp.

"You've got me intrigued." Sienna relished a crispy shrimp.

"Here it is. I want you in my wedding. I love all my other girlfriends. But I want you too."

Sienna felt herself blush. "Thank you. I like you too." They sounded like they had girl crushes on each other. "But I think my father is pretty set."

"I've talked to him." Bron snipped the tail off a shrimp, savored the meat, then added, "Don't get mad, but I went to see your mom."

Sienna couldn't get a word out. She was stunned, even a little angry.

"I just wanted your mom to understand that we're friends, and I want you in my wedding because you're a special person and not because I wanted to stick it to the ex-wife." Bron waved her hand. "Not that I said it exactly like that."

"I wish you hadn't done that." Sienna didn't want the wedding to turn into a big deal and set the tone of their relationship. As always, her mother said one thing to her, then another thing to her father. It had been going on for years, her mom letting Dad be the grunt.

"She never told your dad that she didn't want you in the wedding." Bron leaned in close. "And she doesn't want me to rescind the invitation." She touched Sienna's hand. "She wants us to be friends. And she doesn't think you're choosing sides."

"You have to understand my mother," Sienna started to explain.

Bron rushed on, not letting her finish. "That's what your dad always says, that she tells one thing to one person and another to someone else. I get that," she said in an airy voice. "And that's why I asked your dad about it too."

Shock coursed through Sienna's body. "What did he say?"

Bron sighed. "That he knows what she's like, and he was

making a preemptive strike. He was afraid she'd do something after we'd made all our plans when it would be so much harder to change everything."

Sienna heard only one thing. "Are you saying my dad never talked to my mom? That he lied?"

Bron shook her head, her hair flying. "No, no, no. He didn't *lie*." She stressed the word. "He just..." She seemed to search for a more pleasant term. "He fabricated a story that was supposed to save us all in the end."

"Isn't fabricating," Sienna said with deliberateness, "another word for lying?"

Bron shook her head again, then tucked her hair behind her ear. "It's like little white lies that you tell to save someone else's feelings. Don't tell me you've never told a little white lie?"

Of course she had. Everybody did. You wanted to stay in and binge the last season of *Game of Thrones* instead of attending a party, so you sighed woefully and said you'd already made another date.

Bron went on. "He did it to save me. Because he didn't want me to be hurt if you couldn't be in the wedding later on down the road."

Sienna cut to the chase. "Why are you telling me this?" She raised a hand, fingers spread to wave away all the other crap.

"I want you in my wedding. So I told your father that your mom was fine with it."

The shocks just kept coming. "You actually told him you talked to my mom behind his back?"

Nobody went behind her father's back.

"He was a little upset." Bron shrugged. "But then he finally understood how I felt, that it was like he was choosing his ex-wife's feelings over mine." She put her hand on Sienna's. "Not that your mom's feelings aren't important. That's why I talked to her, to make sure." She leaned back in the booth and threw up her hands in a who-cares gesture. "It didn't bother her."

"What if my mother was the one telling the lie?" Sienna asked with all the bitterness she'd felt since she was eight years old.

Bron shook her head as if she didn't hear Sienna's tone. "I'm good at telling when people are lying, and she wasn't. And your dad admitted to fabricating the story. So it's all okay."

She thought of what her father said when she confronted him about the birthday party, that it wasn't Matthew who didn't want Mother there, it was Bron who was uncomfortable. Was that yet another fabrication? Most likely. If Bron was really uncomfortable around Sienna's mom, she would never have gone to see her. But even if Sienna mentioned it, Bron would probably write it off as inconsequential.

"Please tell me you'll do it," Bron begged. "It means a lot to me. I swear it's not that I want everyone to think I'm besties with my future stepdaughter." She put a hand to her chest in a solemn oath. "I'm not fabricating. I'm not telling a white lie. I want this or I wouldn't have gone to your mother behind Donald's back and risked his wrath."

At least Bron knew there was a wrath.

Happy for the second chance, Sienna smiled. "All right, I'd love to be one of your bridesmaids."

Bron's squeal of delight echoed in the ultra-quiet restaurant. She threw her arms around Sienna, hugging her tight. "Thank you, thank you, thank you."

Sienna didn't doubt her sincerity one bit.

It was her father who gave her doubts.

6

Though Sienna could have confronted her father, she'd already done so over the other "fabrication" with Matthew and her party. Dad would just tell her he wanted peace in the family. She hadn't called her mother either. Even Aunt Teresa wouldn't know the full truth.

Bron had canceled the previous bridal appointment, and in the two weeks since their lunch, Sienna and the other girls —four bridesmaids in total—had chosen a sexy, strapless number that hugged the chest, then flared in pleats to the floor. It was usable for any fancy occasion, or she could have it hemmed later and turned into a cocktail dress.

She'd had another interview but decided the firm wasn't right for her. Once Smithfield and Vine had turned her down, the best fit in the city of San Francisco was her father's company, where she absolutely couldn't go. She didn't want to leave the city, but it was looking more and more like she'd have to go to San Jose. Or farther afield.

But she wouldn't think about that on this gorgeous spring morning as she ran through the Presidio, then out along the water and down to Fort Mason. Being a Saturday, the path was awash in people walking their dogs, runners, speed walkers, leisurely strollers, parents with kids in tow, and dog walkers with six or seven leashed pets. She dodged through people as if they were an obstacle course, smiling at everyone, giving a low-waisted wave to other runners, a signal they were in the same class. She waved at an older man as he passed at a fast pace.

Then she heard her name. "Sienna Walker?"

She turned to see the man heading back, lifting his feet high to keep his heart rate up.

She recognized him then, Mr. Smithfield of Smithfield and Vine. He stuck out his hand, and she gave it an obligatory shake.

"How are you?" he asked, then added before she could answer, "I've seen you out here before. You keep a good pace."

"Thank you." Now that he'd said it, she remembered seeing him, though she hadn't put it together when she'd interviewed. People were harder to place in their running gear.

"I'm really sorry the position with us didn't work out for you."

A surge of resentment welled up that he hadn't given her the third interview. And she certainly hadn't thought he'd had the nerve to bring it up. But she remained polite. Never burn a bridge by being bitchy. "So am I."

He was still running in place, and she did too. "You really were the perfect candidate. I'm sure we hired someone with good potential, but I still believe you would have been a great asset to the team."

She didn't gape even though she wanted to. But since he'd mentioned it, she asked, "If I was so perfect, why did you cancel my third interview?" She punctuated with a shrug of her shoulders.

He stopped jogging then, cocked his head. "Quite frankly, it would have been a waste of time since you'd already decided my firm wasn't for you." There could have been a slight edge to his voice, but she didn't know him well enough to say for sure. "Your father gave me to understand that you'd decided to work for him."

She was floored, even worse than that lunch with Bron when she'd learned her father had lied about the bridesmaid thing. She blurted out, "I'm not going to work for my father. I want to make my own name."

But if that was completely true, why had she asked her father to put in a good word with Mr. Smithfield? She couldn't even remember how she'd justified that to herself.

"But your father said—" Mr. Smithfield cut off the sentence. "Ahh. You were using us to get him to make an offer."

She couldn't let Mr. Smithfield believe that of her. "I absolutely wouldn't do that. Your firm is the best in the city, exactly where I wanted to be. I won't work for my father because I don't want anyone to think there's nepotism going on." Her shoulders rose defensively.

Mr. Smithfield regarded her a long moment from beneath bushy gray eyebrows. "Then I'm sorry you and your father got your wires crossed." He started jogging in place again, getting ready to take off.

Sienna rushed to ask him, "When did my father call you?"

"The evening before your interview." He put his fingers to his wrist. "My heart rate is off pace."

"I'll let you go. Thanks for stopping. I'm sorry about the misunderstanding."

He took off, then turned, once more running in place. "If

we have a new opening, I'd still like you back for that third interview. Now that I know we were your first choice."

Then he turned and raced away, leaving Sienna mute and flabbergasted in his wake.

❀

SIENNA TOOK TWO DAYS TO COOL DOWN BEFORE confronting her father. Then another two days to decide whether to go to his house, his office, or make a lunch date.

She opted for lunch and called him. "Lunch today? I'd like to talk about a job."

"Absolutely, sweetheart." The rare use of a term of endearment meant he was terribly pleased with himself.

She didn't tell him which job. Maybe he thought his ruse had worked, and she'd decided he was the only game in town. Maybe that was his plan all along, to push her into a position where she'd be in his control.

Her father was always classy and distinguished, and today he wore a navy pinstripe suit with a silver tie and a pocket square.

Sienna slid into the circular booth. He'd suggested an exclusive restaurant atop one of the city's leading business buildings. It wasn't listed on any tourist sites, designed for the upper echelon of business people, the cream that rose to the top of San Francisco Bay Area elite. The waitstaff, male and female, were impeccably dressed in suit and tie. The tables were draped in damask, the flower arrangements fragrant and low-slung to afford conversation without obstruction.

She'd been here only once, when Matthew joined her father's firm. Dad had invited her along for the lunch, flaunting the perks Matthew received and once again making her feel unwanted.

His smile was perfect, veneers he'd put on a year ago. Just

after the divorce. As if he wanted to make sure the deduction didn't go on their joint tax return.

Her skin was no longer livid with anger. She'd banked her rage. If she'd gone to him right after seeing Mr. Smithfield, she would have lost her cool and come out the loser.

"I'm so glad you called," her father said, his voice amiable.

He hadn't risen to kiss her cheek. They weren't that kind of family, never had been. She hadn't known her paternal grandparents well. They'd both died when she was young. But she had an impression of austere natures and the need to be quiet when she was around them. Her father, the only child of those somber people, was the least demonstrative man she knew, even with Bron, though he tolerated her touches and hugs and kisses. She wondered how long that would last after the wedding. Maybe he thought she'd be too busy with the new baby to care.

"Thank you for meeting me." She kept her voice upbeat, not wanting to give him time to form a strategy to deal with her.

She ordered a champagne cocktail while her father liked Campari and soda. Maybe the bitterness agreed with him. And maybe that was her bitterness talking. They ordered when the drinks arrived, and her father continued when they were alone again.

"I know Brianna has asked you again to be in the wedding." She hadn't thought he'd address it, but she nodded for him to go on. "I'm sure it seems like I told a lie, but I didn't want a big mess on our hands on the wedding day." He reared back slightly to look down his nose. "You know how your mother can be."

She couldn't resist saying, "No, I don't really know how my mother can be in this situation."

He nodded, blinking a long moment, like an animal with

double lids. "Let's just say that she's volatile and likes to play games. I wanted to avoid that. I hope you understand."

Sienna smiled. "Oh, Dad," she said in a gentle, almost playful tone. "I think you know how to play games better than anyone."

He smiled with her. As if he had no clue what was going on in her head. Maybe she was that good an actress.

"I'm terribly sorry about the job as well." He reached out, stopping a scant inch from where her hand was fisted on the table. "There's always a place for you at Walker and Walker."

She dipped her head so he couldn't see her eyes. "If I came, would you change it to Walker, Walker, and Walker? Or Walker and Family? Or maybe just..." She trailed off, shrugged. "Maybe you want to keep Walker and Walker, the good old boys' club."

His smile faded over his pearly veneers. "There is no good old boys' network at Walker and Walker. You should know that."

"But there is a good old boys' network between all the top financial firms in the city, isn't there." She said it flatly, turning it into a statement, not a question.

The hazel of his eyes steeled into something close to gray. "Of course. Isn't that why you had me call Smithfield? To give you a leg up?"

"That's exactly why I asked you to talk to him." She smiled without a hint of her inner feelings, and it seemed to make him relax. "I'm sure Matthew told you they hired some nimrod he knew in university."

He drummed his fingers on the table. "He couldn't be a nimrod if Smithfield chose him over you. He must have had *some* redeeming qualities. Although I can't understand what." The veneers popped out again.

"Did you know that Mr. Smithfield likes to run along the marina down to Fort Mason?"

He stumbled at the abrupt change in topic, his mouth slightly ajar. "He's quite trim, but I thought he was more a gym man."

"Like you?"

He nodded, his eyes hooded as he tried to gauge where she was going. "And you'll be free to use our gym anytime. We've also got a pool, a sauna, a whirlpool tub, and a masseuse on staff. All perks of being on the Walker and Walker team."

She didn't let the perks distract her. "I often like a run out to Fort Mason too."

The drumming on the table stopped as he contemplated the implications. Their entrées arrived, and she smiled at the waiter as he set her lobster salad in front of her.

Her father had grilled salmon on a bed of steamed vegetables. At fifty-five, with a fiancée young enough to be his daughter, he was looking out for his weight. No more strictly meat and potatoes for him.

"How interesting," he said without inflection. His fork sliced through the salmon, and he speared a broccoli floret as well.

She savored a bite of lobster, then said, "I wouldn't have recognized him. You know how it is when you see people out of context." She waited for that to sink in, but her father's gaze didn't flicker. "But he recognized me. I have no idea why. Maybe it was because of your phone call." Her smile felt stretched across her face.

"You can quit the games, Sienna," he drawled. "I know where you're going."

"Good," she said with a calm she didn't feel. "Then maybe you can clarify for me why you told him I'd changed my mind and didn't feel that Smithfield and Vine was the right firm for me. Which then prompted Mr. Smithfield to cancel my interview."

Her father didn't break out in a sweat. He was the coolest cucumber in the salad. He finished another forkful of salmon, this time topped with rice pilaf, only then saying, "You know the best place for you is Walker and Walker, where you have me to guide you. I let you go off on your own to a huge corporation. But even when you realized your mistake, you went to Smithfield." His face pinched like a spinster detecting a bad smell. "It was my duty to help you see that Walker and Walker is far superior. And where you belong."

So that was it. He couldn't have his daughter going to his biggest competitor. "And you screwed me over because you knew what was best for me?"

"I don't like your tone or your language, Sienna." His voice dipped to a growl.

Softly, without all the animosity rising in her, she said, "I don't care what you like, *Father*." She said it the way she used to say Mother when her mom made her so angry she could scream. "There's no way I'm ever going to work for you. Even if I have to leave the city and move to L.A. Or Chicago or New York. And I'm only a member of your wedding party because I like Bron. She's a friend. Which is why I call her Bron, because that's what she likes, not Brianna."

She ate more of the delicious lobster. She wouldn't walk out on this fabulous meal. Especially since lobster had been the most expensive thing on the menu.

He sighed wearily, as if she were an annoying thirteen-year-old who no longer showed respect for her parents. "You're young, Sienna. You don't know what's good for you. One day, you and Matthew could run my firm."

She wanted to snort. "I don't think so. You'll make Matthew the senior partner, expecting him to lord it over me. You want me under your thumb to keep me from rising up the ladder. Why? Because I'm a woman?" Her words were heartfelt, her thoughts tearing a hole inside her.

"You make it sound as if I hate you, Sienna. If I did, I'd never make you an offer at all. Instead, I'm giving you the biggest opportunity of your life." A blaze sparked in the depths of his gaze. "Just like I offered your mother when I married her. But she didn't know what was good for her either." The fire in his eyes chilled her.

"I know you two didn't have a great marriage. But I shouldn't have to pay for that." When he opened his mouth to speak, she rushed on, "I just wanted you to know that Mr. Smithfield offered me another opportunity. And this time, I don't need you to call him."

"You're going to regret it, I promise you. It's the biggest mistake of your life, and it's going to bite you in the ass." He smiled, an ugly, wolfish grin, and for the first time ever, she believed she was seeing the real man.

He lowered his voice to a harsh note. "And tell your mother it'll bite her in the ass too."

Then slowly, methodically, his meal only half finished, he folded his napkin and laid it on the table. Sliding out of the booth gracefully, he rose to his feet, signaling the waiter with a snap of his fingers. "Put this on my tab."

Sienna smiled. "Thank you, Father. The lobster is delicious." She looked at the waiter. "Do you have a doggy bag?" she asked, pointing to her father's salmon. "I'd really hate for that to go to waste. And another champagne cocktail would be nice too."

7

"He's so manipulative," Sienna ground out between gritted teeth. Two days after that lunch, she was still angry with her father.

"That's the nature of the beast," Aunt Teresa quipped.

Sienna was taking another long lunch, this time at Aunt Teresa's house. She was starting to love long lunches and didn't even feel guilty. They were seated in her aunt and uncle's gorgeous sunroom filled with light and green plants and blooming flowers all year round. Aunt Teresa called it her indoor garden.

Uncle William was one of the top attorneys in the Bay Area. The house in Saratoga was a showpiece, with a formal living and dining room, because Aunt Teresa and Uncle William entertained often. Despite their wealth, Aunt Teresa was down to earth, a mother figure, and the only person Sienna could run to with her troubles.

"He's become so controlling since the divorce. And it's not Bron's fault. Maybe he's just worried she'll leave him because he's so old."

Aunt Teresa patted her hand. "Did you ever consider that

he was always manipulative and controlling and you just didn't see it?"

Knowing her mother was coming to lunch as well, Sienna had arrived early to do a data dump on her aunt. She told her about the birthday party when her father lied about Matthew, compounding it with a "fabrication" about Bron, then the lie about her mother not wanting her to be in the wedding, and finally about Mr. Smithfield and the complete *lie*, not *fabrication*, that lost Sienna the job. All because he *supposedly* was looking out for everyone's feelings and knew what was best.

"I'm not saying he hasn't always liked to have things his way. He's a man, after all," Sienna said. She'd worked with a lot of men, and most of them liked things their way. "But this is different," she insisted. "He deliberately sabotaged the job because he didn't want me working for his competitor." She shook her hands as if she could shake out the agitation. "Sure he offers me a job, but I know how it would play out. I'd be under his and Matthew's thumb doing all the grunt work. But I want my own clients to service. I want to be a partner."

"I know how hard it is, sweetie," Aunt Teresa sympathized. "But now you can see what it was like for your mother."

Sienna shook her head, her hair flying. "I'm telling you, he is so much worse."

"Maybe you finally caught him at it."

Sienna pursed her lips stubbornly. "I would have caught him long ago if he was doing this for years." She looked at her aunt. "I worry about Bron. What's she getting herself into?"

"Bron's a big girl. She worked for him, and she knows what he's like. She'll be able to figure out if he's not the right man for her."

"Sure. But she's already pregnant."

The doorbell rang through the house. Her mother. The

heart-to-heart was over. She hadn't even gotten around to asking Aunt Teresa's advice.

The sisters hugged when her mother entered. They couldn't be more different in personality, but they both had the same beautiful deep brown eyes, silky dark hair now streaked with gray, and figures that men would have drooled over in their younger days. Not that either of them had lost their shape. It was just that they were, well, older.

It was a fact of life that men going through a midlife crisis —like her father—wanted a younger woman. It was truly sad that older women became invisible no matter how beautiful they were. Luckily, Uncle William would never cheat on Aunt Teresa.

She thought over her aunt's comment. Had her dad always been controlling, but just better at hiding it before? Sienna didn't know. For so long, she'd thought all the problems were her mother's fault.

And what about her mom? She was broken by the divorce. Or maybe thirty years with a man like Donald Walker was enough marriage for any woman. She'd probably never marry again.

She and her mother gave each other awkward air kisses on both cheeks. It had been like this for years. She didn't think it could ever change.

"Let's eat," her aunt said. "I know you have to get back to work, Sienna." She waved them over to the linen-draped table as if they were dining in a five-star restaurant. Salad plates had already been set out.

"I'm so sorry about that job you wanted," her mother said. Aunt Teresa must have told her. Not that Sienna minded.

"Thank you. I'll find something. Maybe even another opening at the same company."

"But do you really want to go there if they've already

passed you over?" Her mother obviously didn't realize how insensitive that was.

"They didn't pass me over." Sienna did her best to keep the irritation out of her voice. "They were just looking for someone with a different skill set."

But why had they hired Jeffrey Deck? Maybe Matthew was overstating his objections. Jeffrey couldn't be that bad if he made it into Smithfield and Vine.

Her mother smiled. "I'm sure they couldn't find anyone better qualified than you." She seemed to try too hard.

Sienna recalled what her father had said as he walked away, that her choices would come back to bite her in the ass just the way her mother's choices would bite her in the ass too.

She tried to look at her mom with fresh eyes. Mother kept Sienna from going on all those outings, saying her brother and dad needed male bonding. She'd shut Sienna out of that relationship, as if being a girl meant she wasn't good enough. And she wasn't wanted.

As she listened to her aunt and mother chat about charities and garden clubs and Nonni and Poppa, she realized again that it was always her father saying things *for* her mother. As if he was her voice.

She closed her eyes, bringing those times to mind, her father saying she should stay with her mother and keep her company while he and Matthew did their bonding thing. As if he was trying to save her mother's feelings, just like he'd told that lie about Matthew to save Bron's feelings, or the so-called fabrication about the wedding and how it would save her mother's feelings. And the lie about Smithfield and Vine, which was supposed to save her from making the biggest mistake of her life.

It was always her father saying the things she'd blamed her mother for.

She opened her eyes again. Words came unbidden to her lips, and she let them out. "I'm sorry for the way I turned down the trip you'd planned, Mother. I was angry about something else, and I took it out on you."

Her mother gaped, but Aunt Teresa's smile brimmed with approval.

"It's okay, honey," her mother murmured, as if a louder voice would ruin the mood. "I understand. About the wedding, I mean. But I would never stop you from being a bridesmaid. And I'm happy that you're friends with Bron."

Sienna tried to detect an ulterior motive, even a lie. But the only look on her mother's face was hope.

Maybe it was her father's recent lies. Maybe it was the way he'd sabotaged her interview in order to get what he wanted. Maybe it was the yearning in her mother's eyes. Whatever it was, Sienna did the most spontaneous thing of her entire life. "I've got a lot of vacation time saved up." She shrugged as her two mothers stared at her. "I think I can swing it. When did you say you wanted to go?"

Her mother's voice was quiet with surprise and awe. "The middle of June."

Sienna pulled out her phone and checked her calendar. "That's over two months away, certainly enough notice for the company to handle my absence."

She didn't have accounts anyone else couldn't handle easily, but she'd give her clients advance notice. If one of them needed her, she was only a phone call away. Hopefully the market wouldn't crash while she was gone. "I'm sure I can handle it, but I'll confirm with my boss."

Her mother clapped her hands, her mouth an *O* of delight. "That would be wonderful. I'd love for you to come."

Sienna stopped short of making a promise she might have to break. "I'll do my best to make it work."

If her mother's goal was to fix the relationship, then Sienna could give her a chance.

"SHE'S SO SERIOUS," ANGELA SAID AFTER SIENNA RETURNED to work. "I wish she could lighten up a bit."

Teresa snorted a laugh. "She's just like you. When did you ever lighten up?"

Angela flattened her lips, flared her nostrils, and crossed her eyes in an attempt to lighten up. "Point taken. I hate that she's so unhappy with her job. Although I'm not sure she'd be any happier at Smithfield and Vine."

"She just wants to build a life that your ex-husband doesn't have a hand in."

Angela let out a long sigh, wrapping her hands around the warmth of her coffee cup. "Did she tell you how he tried to use my hurt feelings to boot her out of the wedding?"

"The bridesmaid thing?"

Angela nodded. "He had the nerve to tell her I'd called him—" She put her hand to her chest in affront. "—and that I'd said I was uncomfortable with her being in the wedding."

Teresa gaped. "Asshole. How do you know all this?"

"His fiancée came to see me. She wanted to change my mind. Sienna didn't tell you?"

Teresa put her hand flat on the table. "I don't like to reveal what Sienna confides to me." She eyed Angela as if afraid of her reaction, but Angela was well aware her daughter preferred talking to her aunt over her own mother. "I'm going to tell you anyway. Because I think he's escalating."

There was a hitch in her heart rate as if she'd suddenly developed an arrhythmia. "What did he do this time?"

"Sienna asked him to call Smithfield and put in a good word for her."

"Oh God," Angela muttered.

"And instead—" Teresa's voice seethed with outrage. "—he told Smithfield that she didn't think the job was the right fit for her."

Angela covered a gasp. "What the hell was he thinking?"

"That he could push her into working for him so she didn't work for the enemy." She air-quoted.

"God forbid she ever works for him." Angela put a hand to her forehead like a swooning romance heroine.

Teresa waved her fingers. "She won't. But here's what I have to say about your ex-husband." Teresa had never liked or trusted Donald. "His manipulation and underhandedness used to be more subtle. Now he seems to think he can lie with impunity, as if no one's going to challenge him." She leaned closer. "You need to tell Sienna the truth before he does. I think he's planning something."

Angela felt that arrhythmia again. "He said something like that when I confronted him about the wedding. I told him I didn't like him using my name to spread his lies." She breathed in slowly, let the air slide out again. "And he made a crack."

"About telling her?"

Angela nodded.

Teresa nodded too. "He'll slap her with it and make you look as bad as possible."

Angela bit down on her inner lip. "I wanted Sienna to come to Santorini with me and feel what it was like to be young and free and on the trip of a lifetime. And how things could just happen. I've already decided it's the perfect spot to tell her the truth."

"That's a couple of months away. You better hope he doesn't get to her first."

"I'm certainly hoping. Once she knows, it'll give me a whole new sense of freedom," Angela whispered. "Even though I'm worried about how Sienna will react, Donald can no longer hold this secret over me."

Teresa brought her brows together. "You're not going back to Santorini to find *him*, are you? Or introduce Sienna to him?"

Angela didn't need to ask who Teresa meant. "I was supposed to meet him in June." But she hadn't gone back to Santorini. Everything changed, and she'd never seen him again. This trip was like a pilgrimage to the mistakes of her past.

"You're thirty years too late." While the words were harsh, Teresa's tone was gentle.

"I'm too late, period," Angela said.

"Then why go back and torture yourself?"

She didn't know how to explain it. "I just want to remember how it felt. To be young. To be in love. To have hope." She dipped her head, focused on the cooling coffee in her cup. "I want to believe that it's possible to experience that feeling again, now that I'm divorced."

Teresa snorted. "I wish Donald was out of our lives forever. He's like a bad smell that keeps hanging around."

It was such an apt description that they laughed. Donald was the bad smell that had everyone looking around to see who'd done it. Only they can't figure it out.

Teresa sobered. "I just don't think you can go back to a place where you've lost everything and expect to feel better. If you want to start over, do it here."

"I don't expect to feel better," Angela insisted. "But I also don't think I lost everything there. I gained Sienna. And I learned what genuine love was."

Teresa tutted. "You knew him for three weeks. That's just starry-eyed lust. And because you didn't love Donald when you married him, you turned this guy into a fantasy that no one can live up to. Even if you found him, he wouldn't be the man you dreamed him into."

She'd certainly had her fantasies. Even with Donald, she'd been caught up in the romance of being the sole focus of his attention along with the glitter of his lifestyle, just like her mother was. It was only on Santorini that she saw how she mistook being desired for true love.

"You'll never be able to understand, Teresa, because you've been with the man you love for so long. But love can happen just like that." Angela snapped her fingers.

She'd seen him, and she'd fallen. Hard. Never to recover.

"Have you ever Googled him?"

Angela poured herself another cup of coffee. "An internet search would be like looking for a needle in a haystack."

"Seriously? How many Xandros Daskalakis can there be?"

Xandros. His name slipped off her tongue when he touched her. Tall and muscular and beautiful, with dark wavy hair and the most piercing blue eyes she'd ever seen. She'd always thought black hair meant brown eyes, but his eyes reflected the Santorini blue of the water. When he looked at her, it was as if he knew her soul. And she knew his. It wasn't some tawdry romance between a girl on vacation and her tour guide. She didn't truly believe Xandros picked up a new woman every tour, despite what her mother had convinced her when she was young.

Teresa, on the other hand, had always believed Angela when she said that his love was true. She'd just never thought it could last.

Angela could still hear her mother's voice all those years ago. "You stupid, stupid girl. How could you let this happen?"

She'd whimpered like a lost child. "But I love him, Mama."

"You sound like that idiot girl in *West Side Story*." Mama put her hands together in prayer. "I love him," she mocked

Angela in a high falsetto. Then she jammed her hands on her ample hips. "I will not let you throw your life away on a beach bum."

"He's not a beach bum, Mama. He's a tour guide."

Her mother had glared. "Even worse. He probably picks up a new girl every tour."

"He wouldn't do that."

Mama had laughed. "You're a silly girl. What makes you think he'd even want that little baby?" She poked Angela's stomach. "You think you'll fly over there in a year, and he'll welcome you and the bambino with open arms? You're even more stupid than I thought." Mama shook her finger. "You will not embarrass me. Not one month away from your wedding. You will not think about that boy again. You will not write to him. You will marry Donald Walker and let him think that baby is his, do you understand me?"

"How am I supposed to make Donald believe it's his baby?"

Mama narrowed her eyes. "Don't think I don't know what you've done out in that boathouse. And don't give me that innocent look."

She couldn't deny it. She'd slept with Donald, even the night before she left on her trip. If only she'd waited until she'd met Xandros.

Her mother kept on at her. "Go over there tonight and seduce him. Before your holiday and after your holiday, he must sleep with you."

What would her life have been like if she hadn't surrendered to her mother's browbeating? Would Xandros have been waiting for her in that small café on Santorini? Would he have welcomed Sienna? She had only the dreams she liked to tell herself, but she would never know the truth.

Her mother's voice stayed with her. "Make sure Donald thinks that baby is his."

Angela had, and they were married. She had a daughter and then a son. Then Sienna had her accident, falling out of a tree, a branch stabbing her leg. A doctor had pulled Angela aside to say that Donald's blood didn't match. They'd used her blood for a transfusion. Even then, she thought she might get away with it. Until she'd overheard a nurse telling Donald as well.

He'd made her pay from that day forward. He hadn't divorced her, but he'd made sure the children hated her.

Teresa reached across the table to fold her fingers around Angela's. "Maybe we should tell Sienna now. We can do it together to soften the blow."

Teresa, though always supporting her, had believed Mama might be right. Xandros wouldn't be waiting for her. He wouldn't want a baby. And Teresa encouraged her to marry Donald for appearances' sake, telling her it wouldn't be so bad, that he had pots of money, that her life would be comfortable, and her kids would be her solace. The first years had been comfortable, if not loving. Angela loved both her children with all her heart. Her mother, however, never became the toast of Silicon Valley the way she'd wanted, even with her son-in-law's connections.

None of them had found their dreams except Teresa, who'd fallen in love with a great guy and never made a wrong step.

"I appreciate the offer. But I'll tell Sienna on Santorini."

"Then I'll to go to the church every day and light a candle, praying Donald says nothing before you leave."

Angela hadn't been to church in years. But she was grateful for Teresa's candles.

8

"I'm not even tired," Sienna said as they stepped into their Santorini home for the next two weeks.

Angela had never been happier than when Sienna said she'd worked out the trip with her boss, and over the following two months, they'd planned everything, booked the perfect villa, and she'd encouraged Sienna to shop for swimsuits and summer clothes.

Donald hadn't acted on his threat, thank God. Maybe he didn't believe Angela would ever tell and that he could still hold all the cards.

It had been a long flight, with a stopover in Athens, then the hop to Santorini. Angela had thought about staying a couple of days in Athens, touring the Acropolis and other ancient sites, then taking the ferry over. But Santorini was the only place she wanted to be. They could stop in Athens on the way back.

They'd flown first class, and she and Sienna had slept much of the way. Despite the time change, neither of them felt jet lag yet. It was early evening, the heat of the mid-June day dissipating. Angela wanted to stay up until at least ten o'clock to get fully acclimated to the time.

Sienna dumped her bags in the villa's living room. "This is amazing. I love it."

Angela was glad she'd done something right.

The villa was built into the hillside with views of the turquoise Aegean from lounge chairs on the deck. Gorgeous pink and red bougainvillea climbed trellises along the white walls. Inside was a living room, half bath, and kitchen on the first level, and two bedrooms plus a shared bathroom upstairs. Villas surrounded theirs on either side, as well as above and below. That was Santorini, the houses stacked on each other, climbing up the steep hills.

Angela planned to make this an idyllic holiday where she could undo the damage Donald had done to her relationship with her daughter.

After checking out the downstairs and testing how comfortable the sofa was, they carried their bags up to the bedrooms.

Rather than shelves, there were niches in the walls for books or an alarm clock, a tray on the bureau for jewelry or vitamins. The same was true of the bathroom, niches for makeup and other sundries, the walls curved rather than straight. With the villa fit snugly into the hill, there were no windows in the back rooms, only along the front. But that was enough light beneath the bright Santorini sun and blue sky.

Angela gave Sienna the queen-size room while she took the double bed. The bathroom was equipped with a large stall shower and pedestal sink.

Without bothering to unpack, she trotted back downstairs to scope out the kitchen supplies. The small euro-style refrigerator was empty except for ice cubes in a tray, but the cupboards revealed cinnamon, salt-and-pepper, and several typically Greek spices. There was a coffee machine and filters, but no coffee.

When Sienna joined her, Angela suggested, "Let's find a grocery store that's still open and get a few things, coffee, milk, and bread, something for the morning. Maybe some butter too." They'd eaten a meal in Athens, and she wasn't hungry right now.

"It'll be all mom-and-pop places nearby," Sienna said. "Will they be open past six?"

"Let's walk and find out. We'll see the sunset too."

"Can't we watch the sunset from the patio?"

Angela laughed. "Yes. But you really have to see what the town is like, the narrow cobblestone alleys, the stairs, the blue domes. The towns of Santorini are like nothing you've ever seen. All the best places are built on the hill."

Sienna groaned. "I might do the bike in the gym, but it's not like climbing up and down stairs on the side of a mountain."

Angela wrapped her in a quick hug, even though she probably shouldn't. "Being on Santorini, you'll get used to hills and stairs."

Sienna whipped out her phone and typed. "I found a market here." She pointed. "They're still open."

Angela flourished her arm. "Then lead on." Purse slung over her shoulder, she locked the terrace door and opened the blue gate that led to a narrow pathway between the houses.

There was no parking on the road, as they'd found out when their taxi driver had lugged their bags down the steps to the villa. If this wasn't Santorini, she would have felt cramped. But on the island, where the towns perched on the hillside overlooking the caldera, few roads would fit large cars. There were bicycles and scooters and quad bikes as well as the occasional small car, and foot traffic was heavy. Even from their gate, they could make out tourists taking the stairs to restaurants or shops.

Santorini had been formed thousands of years ago when the volcano exploded. The island was only eleven miles long, and the principal towns of Oia and Fira were constructed on the caldera side, with a view across the crater. The blue Aegean Sea had long since filled in the volcano, creating the smaller islands. They'd chosen a villa in Imerovigli, within walking distance of Fira.

As they headed to the steps, Sienna let out a laugh, louder than her normally restrained humor. "Look at that sign." She pointed, reading aloud. "Don't step here. This is a church." She laughed again. "It's in English, as if Americans are the only ones who would dare to step on the roof of a church."

Angela didn't care that they might be loud, noisy Americans. She was simply glad for Sienna's laughter, hoping that Santorini would be good for her daughter. As they turned, looking for stairs, she noticed a young man on the terrace above and slightly to the right. He waved when he saw her looking. Angela waved back.

Though the sun hadn't set yet, it cast long fingers of color over the clouds drifting across the sky. It was going to be a gorgeous sunset, as all Santorini sunsets were.

"We'll go to Oia," she told Sienna, following her down a set of steps. "It's the best place to watch the sunset."

On her first trip, she and Xandros had gone there on many evenings. They hadn't minded the crowds taking up every available space, but he'd always gotten them there early, setting her in front of him, his body blocking anyone from ruining their view. The crowds were as bad as the sunrise watchers on Hawaii's Diamondhead, where she'd honeymooned with Donald. He'd never wanted to go in the early morning, claiming the Japanese tourists were a nuisance. But Angela had always enjoyed joining the tourists. Just as she'd loved every moment in Oia, watching the sunset with Xandros's arms around her.

They wandered the narrow streets until her daughter stopped in front of a small grocery, planting her feet wide and spreading her arms. "And you doubted me."

"I didn't doubt you for a second."

Near closing time, the store was almost empty. They walked past baskets of fruits and vegetables and an assortment of goods they'd find in any mini-mart back home. In a small refrigerated section, she picked out milk and butter. Coffee was down another aisle, and she plucked a loaf of bread from a basket by the counter.

A wizened old woman seated on a stool spoke in a flurry of Greek.

"I'm sorry, I speak only English." Angela pushed everything across the counter, showing the lady what she wanted.

The woman answered in English. "We bake daily. You come tomorrow. Fresh." She shook the loaf of bread. "Not now. Too old."

Angela wondered how to explain that she wanted it for toast and freshness didn't matter.

But the lady squeezed the bread, saying, "No charge for old bread. You come tomorrow and pay full price for fresh." Then she tapped numbers into a handheld calculator. There was no cash register or credit card reader.

The lady beamed with all her teeth as Angela counted out the euros. She'd exchanged some dollars at the bank for purchases like this.

Plopping the goods in a string bag, the woman handed it to Angela. Back home, they would have paid extra for the bag and the day-old bread wouldn't be free. "Thank you so much.

We'll be back tomorrow for the fresh bread." Hopefully she could find her way.

Outside, the sun was setting like fire over the volcano, reds and oranges and yellows splashed across the sky. They leaned against a wall to watch with the other tourists along the cobbled street. When twilight finally descended, they headed back up the hill.

"I hope you can find our way," she told Sienna.

"I've got an app that retraces our footsteps."

"You're amazing." Passing a wine shop, Angela stopped. "Let's get a couple of bottles. I'd like a glass of wine tonight."

The store was closing in ten minutes, but the proprietor didn't rush them through their choices, even making recommendations. They came away with four bottles, including *Vinsanto*, a sweet dessert wine.

Back at the villa, she poured two glasses of the *Vinsanto*, and they carried them out to the terrace. June was a warm month on Santorini. July and August were hotter, but they were also more crowded. Now, with the sun behind the volcano, the evening was fabulous.

"I'm surprised both shopkeepers knew English," Sienna said. "I know a lot of young people in foreign countries are taught English, but generally the older generation isn't fluent."

"I'm sure they get a lot of English-speaking tourists, especially from the cruise ships."

They sat in companionable silence, and yet the silence pointed out how much they didn't talk. She knew about Sienna's life mostly from Teresa. When they were together, they made small talk, and if Angela asked questions, Sienna revealed little. She saved all her heart-to-heart conversations for her aunt, not her mother.

Maybe on this trip, without Teresa a buffer between them, Angela could change that.

Angela woke early the next morning. It was probably the time change. She looked in on Sienna, who was still sound asleep, and decided on a walk by herself.

She'd brought good walking shoes and headed out along the path from Imerovigli to Fira. It wasn't even a mile and a half, and she'd be back in an hour, probably long before Sienna woke, though she left a note just in case.

The path meandered up and down, and the sun was rising, bathing the white houses of Santorini in a golden glow. She was alone on the walk, and she had plenty of time before the cruise ship passengers swarmed the town.

She could make out Skaros Rock and the blue belfry of the church at its base. In all the world, there was nothing like Santorini blue, and the view along the path was breathtaking. She and Sienna should make the hike out to Skaros Rock on one of their day trips.

Drawing closer to the town, she passed the Three Bells of Fira, the old Catholic church, its blue domes and bells the most photographed site on Santorini. She climbed the steps for a better view of both it and the luxurious Santorini Palace Hotel, only a stone's throw away.

She'd toured all these places with Xandros, but it had been over thirty years, and many of the images had faded in her mind. But as she walked, she recalled every moment of her time with Xandros, never tripping on the stones or steps as some invisible thread seemed to draw her to the terrace café where, if things had been different, she would have met him that long-ago June.

Xandros had been the tour guide for her first five days on Santorini. He possessed a wealth of information about the island and its history, and she'd relished every site, savored every word, and cherished Xandros. He'd introduced her to real Greek yogurt drizzled with honey. She'd bought a lot of grocery-store Greek yogurt since then, but nothing tasted like the yogurt she'd shared with Xandros.

And nothing had ever been like those weeks with him. When the tour was over, he'd become her personal guide, watching every sunset with her, walking the Karavolades Stairs from Fira down to the old Port, taking the cable car back up, and vice versa. They'd hiked every trail at Skaros Rock, and he'd driven her to all the island spots the cruise ships didn't take their passengers.

In the nights, he made love to her, the most amazing love-making she'd ever known.

She'd promised him she'd come back one year later on the same date she'd left, meeting him in their favorite café.

Only she'd returned to San Francisco to discover she was pregnant. Even then, she might have gotten away with canceling the wedding if her mother hadn't found the sticks in the trash. Her wrath had been merciless, her insistence that Xandros wouldn't want the baby insurmountable.

Would she have believed that now with her thirty extra years of wisdom?

She wanted to think she wouldn't. She wanted to think she'd have been stronger. But who really knew? For eight years, she'd convinced Donald that Sienna was his child, but she couldn't say she'd ever been happy with her decision.

Angela wiped a tear from her cheek as she left the path to head into Fira. It was hard to tell exactly where the towns of Imerovigli and Firostefani ended and Fira began. They were a maze of narrow streets, steep stairways, and white houses with blue fences. Bougainvillea hung from the balconies and climbed trellises. The restaurants and shops weren't crowded with tourists yet, but people were out for a stroll like she was.

She wondered if Teresa would be right, that the café was

long gone, that this was a fool's errand. It didn't matter. Angela would know the spot by the view across the sea. They had gone there every day, until she left on the ferry. She could still see Xandros standing on the dock waving her away, a solitary figure surrounded by people, until he was only a dot on the horizon.

She never saw him again. Never talked to him. Never kissed him.

From the path, she found a set of stairs and from there turned right two blocks, left along another stairway and to the right again, hoping her directional sense was good. When she found it, the café's gate was still blue and recently painted. The arbor of bougainvillea was of bright red, faded pink, and extraordinary coral. Blue-checked tablecloths covered the small café tables, the folding chairs softened by matching blue cushions. The white terrace wall surrounded the patio, a short wrought-iron railing atop it painted the vivid blue of the sea.

The waitress signaled her to take any table. Only a few were occupied by other early risers, a couple so in love they shared the same coffee and couldn't stop looking each other, an older man and woman entranced by the blue sea, a man with his face buried in a newspaper, another gentleman taking photographs, editing each right away.

Angela chose a table by the wall so she could see the sea as the sun rose from the ridge behind her and sparkled on the water.

How many times had she gazed out from this spot with Xandros? Every morning they ordered strong coffee and shared a *bougatsa*, a flaky pastry filled with custard and topped with powdered sugar and cinnamon, its dusting all over her fingers, its taste melting on her tongue.

She wondered if he'd been here thirty years ago. The anniversary was two days away, and she would come again as part of her pilgrimage. Not that he could possibly be here too.

And yet with her arrival, she was telling the universe, telling him, *I made a mistake thirty years ago, but I'm here now.*

When the waitress came, she ordered café au lait and a *bougatsa*. When the coffee and treat arrived, she savored every mouthful and licked the crumbs and spices and sugar from her fingers. She closed her eyes and imagined she was that twenty-two-year-old girl again, madly in love with her amazing Greek lover. She imagined a do-over.

When her cup was empty and the *bougatsa* devoured, she opened her eyes to the blue Santorini waters. She understood that people never got a do-over. Sometimes there were second chances, but you could never erase the mistakes.

And she still had to tell Sienna who her real father was.

HE WATCHED HER OVER HIS NEWSPAPER.

She was the most beautiful woman he'd ever seen. She wasn't young, but the lines at her eyes showed her wisdom, and they made him appreciate her more. Most older men went for the young ones, as if to prove their prowess. But this woman, with her short, curly hair, her fine-boned features, kissable lips, and beautifully full figure, was a sight no self-respecting, red-blooded man could ever ignore. Even if he was young and foolish.

But he hadn't been young in years. And he hoped he was no longer foolish.

As she licked the custard and powdered sugar from her fingers, everything inside him tightened. Her profile was like a Roman statue, the slope of her nose graceful, the rise of her cheekbones chiseled. She was a work of art.

He could imagine her in his bed, a breeze off the Aegean,

fluttering curtains over her naked body. He imagined he could breathe in her scent, the sweetness of a sugary dessert, and the light fragrance of bougainvillea.

She was the woman of his dreams.

But she had come back thirty years too late.

9

"**I** made fresh coffee," Sienna said as Angela laid the new loaf of bread on the counter.

She'd promised the old lady she'd return, and she'd been happy to support the locals. "How did you sleep?"

Sienna retrieved a mug and poured for Angela. "I woke up at two and couldn't get back to sleep. But I must have zonked out again around five."

Though she'd already had café au lait in Fira, Angela took the mug. "Thanks for this." Then she added, "I slept most of the way through, but by five-thirty, I was wide awake. So I took a walk."

They carried their mugs out to the terrace and sat in the loungers, Sienna still wearing her shortie pajamas.

"We can find a bigger grocery store to do the rest of our shopping," Angela said, gazing at the gorgeous blue Aegean. It was nine now, and boats were cruising the waters.

"They actually have bigger grocery stores here?"

Angela smiled indulgently, the way Xandros would have when she'd sounded as if Santorini had no amenities. "Yes, they have supermarkets where we can get whatever we need.

In fact, I passed one on my walk. It's not that far. Or we can take a bus." She hadn't rented a car, primarily because of the parking issue, and she figured they could take taxis or the bus wherever they wanted to go. Santorini wasn't that big.

"What about all the groceries we'll have to carry back?" Sienna looked at her with skepticism.

"Not to worry." She winked at her daughter. "I found a wheelie basket in the kitchen."

Sienna pretended to choke on her coffee. "A wheelie basket, like we're little old ladies?" She grimaced.

"I *am* an old lady."

Sienna waved her hand. "You're not *that* old. Old is over sixty."

Heh. To Angela, the cutoff was now seventy-five. When she turned fifty-five, that would climb to eighty.

"Let's walk to Fira this afternoon," she said. "It's only a mile and a half. We can take the cable car down to the old port before all the tourists start back down to their ships. Then we'll walk back up the Karavolades Stairs. There's only 588 of them. And by that time, most of the tourists will already be up top."

Sienna stared at her for fifteen seconds, her expression one of pure horror. "You want to walk up 588 steps in the heat of the day? Are you crazy?"

"It's only supposed to be eighty-two degrees today. Not that bad." Angela smiled, one eyebrow peaked. "We could take a donkey ride up."

Sienna snorted. "That's even crazier than walking. Can't we just take the cable car down and then back up?"

"It's no worse than hiking some of the steep hills in San Francisco."

"I don't walk hills, Mother." Sienna rolled her eyes. "I work out in the gym."

Angela let her smile sparkle in her eyes. "This will use all new muscles then. It'll be perfect. You'll love it. Hills are my favorite hikes."

Sienna gazed at her in awe. "You hike?"

"Every day. It's not called the Los Altos Hills for nothing." She snorted softly. "There's lots of trails back there, some of them only locals know about."

"I didn't know that."

"I belong to a hiking group. We sometimes go to the Fremont Hills or the Santa Cruz Mountains. Even down to Pinnacles National Monument. It's amazing the number of places to hike in the Bay Area."

Sienna said, "Oh," as if she had no clue who or even what her mother was. "No wonder you can climb 588 steps."

Angela laughed. "I plan to rest at each switchback."

"Thank God for that." Then all signs of horror and humor faded from Sienna's face. "I'd really like to stay here today, catch some sun. My legs are pasty." She looked at Angela. "Is that okay with you?"

"That's fine. I don't mind doing the shopping." Truly, she didn't.

But she wondered if this was how the whole vacation would go, with Sienna turning her nose up at anything Angela suggested.

Would they spend any time together at all?

HER MOTHER WORE CAPRI PANTS, A BLOWSY TANK TOP, sunhat, and oceans of sunblock. The wheelie cart was fold-able, and she left with it tucked under her arm.

Sienna lay on the lounger in her bikini, soaking up the sun's rays. It was only eighty degrees, just as her mother said it would be, and yet it seemed hotter, as if the sun shining on all the white walls increased its intensity.

She couldn't imagine walking up all those steps. Going balls to the wall for the last two months completely exhausted her. Her elderly clients needed more handholding, and she'd met with each one, making sure she'd prepared them for her vacation. Mother didn't work, so she couldn't understand how hard it was planning for vacation.

She hated being a bitch, sending her mom out to do the shopping. She felt bad about refusing to climb 588 steps, but she certainly wasn't riding on the back of a donkey. That was even crazier than walking. But she had a newfound respect for her mother. A hiker, who knew? Sienna would work up the energy for those steps in a couple of days. Or maybe a week. For now, she wanted to lay on this lounger, her sunglasses blocking the sun, her visor shading her face.

She didn't want to think about her father either. Yet the moment the thought hit, she couldn't stop thinking about him. Did he really believe the only place she could make it was at his company? Maybe he was afraid she'd make it big somewhere else and show him up. Her blood started to boil again, but she didn't want to work herself up, not while this gorgeous sun was leeching the aches and pains from her body.

There was absolutely no way she'd tell her father that Mr. Smithfield had called her for another interview. He had a new position, but he didn't want any leaks and didn't want to say too much until he saw her. As if she would tell anyone. Not this time. Mr. Smithfield hadn't balked when she said she'd have to meet him in two weeks, once she'd returned from vacation. His amazing response had been, "It'll give me a chance to get my ducks in a row."

What the heck did that mean?

But she'd probably say yes to whatever he wanted. As long as it was a win-win for both of them.

A blast of music snapped her out of a doze, followed by loud voices and laughter, some even louder than the music.

The thumping began as if they were all dancing on the terrace above.

When had she last been to a good party? Even her birthday party had been a whirl for her, making sure everything went well. She'd barely gotten a chance to enjoy it. She shouldn't have to host her own birthday bash. Someone else toasted you, someone else celebrated you, someone else cleaned up the mess. How perfect that would be.

Her mind drifted with the music. The thumping, the laughter, the voices, and even the occasional shrieks of young women didn't dampen her vacation mood.

She was here to relax and regain her equilibrium so that when she interviewed with Mr. Smithfield, she'd know exactly what to do with any offer he made.

Maybe she needed to think about her mother too. Was there any way they could end up being friends the way she was with Aunt Teresa? Sienna didn't have a lot of friends. There were work acquaintances and the girls from her sorority, but somehow, she'd always felt guarded. She hadn't even told Aunt Teresa about the interview with Mr. Smithfield. And she admitted why. She didn't want her aunt telling her mother. She didn't want this vacation to turn into a question-and-answer game.

All she wanted was to lie here and enjoy the sun.

From above, a female voice screeched, "Carter, this drink sucks."

Then freezing liquid and chips of ice rained down on Sienna's chest, splattered her face, plastered her hair, and slid down her arms.

She shrieked as if someone was murdering her.

Sienna opened her eyes, glaring at the next-door balcony one level up.

The man leaned over his railing. "Holy hell," he called down in a voice of abject misery. "I'm so sorry. We didn't know you were down there."

A pretty young woman with a straight brunette bob leaned over with him. "I'm sorry." She put her hand over her mouth and giggled, which turned into hysterical laughter.

"Shut up, Tamryn, or she'll think we're not sorry at all."

Sienna sat up, brushing off the ice cubes. After the first shock, the ice actually felt good on her overheated skin.

Tamryn laughed, then wobbled, forcing the man to grab her arm to steady her. "Get a soda instead of a margarita," he said in a harsh undertone Sienna heard.

Alone now, he turned back. "I really am sorry." He leaned with both arms on the terrace railing. "I had no idea she'd throw it over the side like that."

Sienna thought about scolding him, but with his surfer blond hair, blue eyes reflecting the Santorini sea, and a beautiful mouth, he made her think about kissing.

She hadn't thought about kissing in months.

"That's all right," she called up. "I was getting a little hot in the sun, and the ice cubes cooled me down." She put her hands together. "But the margarita is sticky."

"Don't move," he said, waving a hand. "I'll be right down."

After what seemed like forever, he stepped through her bright blue gate carrying a tray, a steaming cloth folded on it like something old-time barbers used on men's whiskers. There was also a glass along with a plate filled with something emitting delicious odors.

Close-up, his eyes were almost turquoise, his hair short and pleasantly rumpled, his face made up of strong lines and a chiseled jaw. He was clean-shaven, none of the scruff that, in her opinion, looked messy.

83

"Again, I'm so sorry." His accent was a flat American that didn't give away what part of the country he was from. "I brought you a drink." He pointed at the blended margarita, salt around the rim, then he laughed. "I know we should drink something very Greek like ouzo or retsina, but this bunch—" He hooked a thumb over his shoulder. "—they love their margaritas." Then he nudged the plate. "And I brought a few appetizers too."

Setting the tray on the table beside her, he lifted the cloth. "And a steamed towel to wipe away the stickiness."

She stood, leaning over the lounger, finding the cloth still hot to the touch. Looking at him, she wiped down her shoulders and arms, her chest and stomach, the swipes of the cloth sexy in a way she hadn't felt in a long while. Obviously, work was taking up too much of her time.

Patting her face, she said, "Thank you. It really wasn't necessary."

"I assure you it was. I'm afraid Tamryn was a little drunk." Then he laughed. "Actually, I think most of my friends are drunk."

She tossed the cloth on the tray. "They start early."

He laughed again. "We're doing a cruise this afternoon, and I thought we'd have something to eat and drink before we go down to the dock." He rolled his eyes and raised his hands. "That was a mistake." Just as quickly, he smiled, completely sober. "Why don't you come with us?"

It was on the tip of her tongue to say yes. He was handsome and polite, and she hadn't been on a party boat since college. But there was her mother. "Thank you for the offer, but my mom's doing the shopping. It's our first full day here, and I can't leave her alone."

He spread his hands expansively. "She's more than welcome too."

"That's really nice of you." Did she want her mother along?

She realized immediately what a horrible question it was. Her mother had paid for the entire trip, and this morning Sienna had refused to climb the Karavolades Stairs or go shopping.

She decided for both of them. If her mother didn't want to go, then that was on her. "That's really generous. I'm sure my mom would love it." She waved a hand toward his terrace. "If your guests don't mind having someone older with them."

"My guests are so tipsy they won't even notice a couple of extras. Let alone that one of them is your mother. The bus is picking us up at one o'clock." He smiled again, deliciously sweet and hot too. "I'll lean over the balcony and call down to you."

"Thank you." It could be the best way to spend their first day here, a party boat. As long as her mother brought a lot of sunblock.

Before he left, the man stuck out his hand. "Carter Ellis." His grip was firm.

"Sienna Walker. Nice to meet you."

He smiled, deep enough that dimples peeped out at the edges of his mouth. "Even though we doused you with ice cubes?"

"You're making up for it with a margarita and food."

He pointed at the plate. "There's spanakopita. And that's tzatziki, a creamy yogurt-and-cucumber sauce for the veggies." He'd added carrot, cucumber, and red pepper sticks. "And these are *tomatokeftedes*."

"What exactly is that?"

"A Santorini specialty, tomato fritters. Hopefully they're still warm. There's nothing like them. Dip them in the tzatziki." He backed toward the gate. "I better get back up there to make sure nobody else dumps a drink on you."

She called after him, "Make sure you don't step on the church roof either."

His laughter floated to her even when he was out of sight. "I would never step on a church roof."

She collapsed on the lounger. More sunblock, Greek appetizers, or a margarita?

The choice was easy. She went for the fritters.

Held together by bread crumbs, or maybe flour, then fried, they melted on her tongue with the sweetness of tomato complemented by feta cheese and spearmint. So good. The spanakopita dipped in the creamy yogurt sauce brought out all its flavors. Licking her fingers, she sipped the margarita. It was just to her taste, not overly sugary, a little tart, the blended concoction giving her a momentary brain freeze.

Carter Ellis seemed nice enough. Even if his friends were huge partiers. Was Tamryn his girlfriend? Not that it mattered. Sienna wasn't interested in a holiday fling, even if he had pretty blue eyes. But she would enjoy the party boat.

A noise on the stairs leading up from the cobblestone road announced her mother's return, and her short curly hair appeared. The cut suited her, making her look at least five years younger. She wasn't even winded as she opened the gate, pulling the wheelie basket behind her, smile radiant as if she was happy for the first time in years.

Obviously, Santorini was good for her.

"You should've come with me. I went totally crazy." Mother held up her hand, palm out, sounding like a teenager. "We've got champagne and ice cream and—" She paused when she saw the margarita on the table beside Sienna, along with the appetizers Carter Ellis had brought.

Sienna felt completely magnanimous. "I've got some appetizers too. And a margarita. We can share."

The offer seemed to delight her mother, her smile growing. "Wonderful. I'm famished after the walk. Let me just put the perishables in the fridge." She wheeled away, not the least embarrassed about looking like an old lady with a wheelie cart. Not that her mother actually looked old. She seemed almost young right now, with a bounce in her step.

Sienna gulped the margarita and gave herself another brain freeze. She plowed down a fritter to counteract the sensation. There were still plenty for her mother, who was back in less than five minutes.

Sienna fluttered her fingers at the plate. "You absolutely have to try these tomato fritters. They have an unpronounceable Greek name. But they're delicious."

Her mother sat down on the lounger, the table between them. "Where did you get all this?"

Sienna pointed to the terrace above. "Someone doused me with a margarita, and the host brought this down as an apology."

"He can throw a margarita on me anytime if that's what we get." Her mother bit into the fritter, chewing, her eyes closed, a beatific smile on her lips. "I haven't had *tomatokeftedes* since before you were born." The Greek name rolled off her tongue.

"Why didn't you ever make them at home?"

Her mother's expression shifted subtly, as if a wistful memory had crossed her mind.

"It was too difficult. And you really need Santorini tomatoes. There's something in the volcanic soil they grow in that makes them extra special."

Her mother was an amazing cook. They'd had money for a maid, a cook, and a nanny. But Angela Walker had always made their meals, most of them gourmet, and never had help around the house, certainly not a nanny.

"Maybe I'll try again when we get home," she said, the reminiscent look fading.

"I have another surprise." Sienna pointed once again up to the neighbor's terrace. "Our benefactor has offered to take us on a cruise this afternoon. He's got a party boat."

Frowning, her mother put a finger to her lips. "I'm sure it's a young person's party. They don't want an old lady hanging around."

A twinge of guilt twisted Sienna's stomach. She'd said exactly the same thing, and it was Carter who'd said he'd loved to have her mother. "His name is Carter Ellis. He sounds American, and he said he'd adore having you along." She leaned forward to tap her mother's knee. "It'll be fun."

She didn't know why she was pushing. Her mother's presence might make her feel inhibited. And yet it was rude not to ask her. "Come on. You haven't sailed on the Aegean in thirty years."

Her mother laughed with her hand over her mouth, covering the bite of spanakopita she'd just taken. "All right. You're on."

"And you have to bring a bathing suit," Sienna told her. "I don't want you hanging around in capri pants."

"You know me so well."

She didn't know her mother at all. Her smiles always seemed a bit forced and her laughter a second too late, as if she wasn't sure she should laugh. Her mom always let her dominate their conversations. Sienna hadn't even known she was a hiker, for God's sake.

This vacation was a chance for them to become closer than mere acquaintances.

10

The catamaran loped over the surface of the Aegean beneath a glorious sun. The music was loud for Angela's taste, with a beat she couldn't get into. But then she was older, and it was tradition to hate the music of the younger generation. It had been happening since the Beatles, or maybe far longer. It seemed as if everyone on the boat, even the crew, was thirty or younger. The captain, who appeared to be in his mid-twenties, reminded her of Xandros, the height, the smile, the dark hair, the olive skin.

She sat under an awning shading half the boat, while the three women in Carter Ellis's group had climbed up top to sunbathe. The men, four including Carter, clustered around the back of the boat, talking, laughing, drinking, eating. Angela had been out there for a while, but despite her sunblock, her skin had started to sizzle. Sienna had joined her in the shade.

The food and drink were excellent. They'd indulged in spanakopita and *tomatokeftedes*, Greek meatballs, fried goat cheese, tzatziki with toasted pitas, and on and on. Margaritas weren't a Greek drink, but they were delicious.

The day was warm, but the wind off the Aegean and the shade of the overhang kept her comfortable. She'd worn shorts over her swimsuit. Her usual capris would have been unbearable out here on the water.

"Tell us about yourself, Mr. Ellis," she said as he joined them under the awning, whether out of politeness or to get away from the blast of music, she couldn't be sure. "Married, engaged, kids?"

Beside her, Sienna squirmed. But Angela was older, and she could ask the important questions. They'd settled in comfortable canvas chairs, drinks in hand, the platter of appetizers on the table between them. Angela nibbled while he answered.

"Call me Carter. No wife, no fiancée, and no kids. I'm twenty-nine. I'm a lawyer out of San Jose, California."

Angela wasn't sure who gasped first, her or Sienna. "You've got to be kidding. This is far too big a coincidence. Sienna is in San Francisco, and I'm in Los Altos Hills."

Carter laughed, glancing at Sienna. "Serendipity. We were meant to meet."

"And I suppose your girlfriend up top was meant to throw her drink on me," Sienna drawled. Angela couldn't read the look in her eyes, whether it was pleasure or annoyance.

Carter laughed again. "Absolutely. Or we wouldn't have met." Then he added with a smile, "And she's not my girlfriend."

The girl in question teetered on high heels as she maneuvered down the ladder from above, grabbing another drink before climbing back up. There was so little material in her bathing suit that it could barely be called a bikini. If she was thirty years younger, Angela might have had the courage. But at fifty-three, she was strictly one-piece. Sienna wore an attractive tankini which, as she moved, showed a strip of midriff. The high-cut hips showed off her long legs. Angela couldn't tell if Carter Ellis looked at them behind his sunglasses, but she'd be surprised if he hadn't.

"I'm a tax attorney," Carter went on. "Sounds boring, I know, akin to being an accountant." Then he leaned forward as if he had secrets to share. "But it can be fascinating matching wits with the IRS."

"I didn't know IRS agents had wits," Sienna said smoothly.

Carter guffawed. "Good point. But like any profession, there are the dimwits and the ones who have more wits than are good for them. Or, I should say, good for me."

They all laughed. "Do you have your own firm?" Angela asked, not to gauge his net worth or consider him for son-in-law material, but to keep the conversation going.

"It's my dad's firm. A family affair. My two brothers and sister work there as well."

Sienna raised one eyebrow behind her sunglasses. "Now that's a family business."

Once again Angela couldn't read her, whether that was sarcasm or admiration, or even a comparison to Donald's family business, Walker and Walker.

Not wanting the conversation to falter, Angela asked, "Someone mentioned you're here for three weeks. How long have you been on the island?"

Carter gazed out at the water a moment. "Two weeks. We're flying out a week from Monday."

"You've been enjoying yourselves?"

He nodded. "Swimming, taking out mopeds for day trips. You'd think we'd have done more in two weeks, but now we're trying to pack stuff into the last week." Then he asked, "What do you do, Angela?"

The question surprised her. She would have thought he'd ask Sienna. "Just a housewife," Angela answered, then corrected herself. "At least until my children grew up." She smiled at Sienna, who kept a poker face. "Now I'm a divorcee, and I spend my time volunteering for different organizations. I work at the SPCA feeding and grooming the animals."

Sienna seemed to startle. "You clean litter boxes and wash out kennels?"

Angela laughed, though she would have done whatever they needed. "Just feeding and playing with the kittens. Some of them need bottle-feeding. Some puppies do as well. And I walk the dogs. It's a real cushy job."

"Sounds like it," Carter said. "But you can't do that full time. What else do you do?"

She pondered how to bring Sienna into the conversation. It would be too blatant to blurt out that her daughter was a financial advisor.

"I drive for a great organization that provides rides for seniors. I had to get rid of my SUV and buy a car with a lower chassis to accommodate them. But seniors are wonderful and chatty and some of them are very lonely. I take a ninety-two-year-old woman to the community pool three times a week where she does water exercises."

Worried about her instability, Mrs. Brandt's daughters had recently asked Angela to get into the pool with the elderly woman. She even helped the lady in the shower. It wasn't part of the drive service, which was only supposed to be door-to-door, but Angela didn't mind. She wanted to keep Mrs. Brandt active for as long as possible. She often carried in groceries, putting everything away, helping her seniors as best she could. It was worthwhile work, and she loved it.

"The elderly are a delight when you get to know them," she added.

Sienna looked at her as if seeing her in a whole new light, a real person instead of Mother.

"But enough about me," Angela said. "I don't want to take you from away from your friends."

He showered her with a winning smile. "I've known these guys forever. We went to university together. Every year we get away in the summer for one big trip. My father believes that after a year of hard work, you have to let loose or go crazy. So he lets me out of my cage for three weeks to get wild. We've done the beaches of Brazil, the Caribbean, London and traveling around England. But the girls—" He hooked a thumb, indicating the top deck. "—wanted more beach and sun. So this year we decided on Santorini."

"Wow," Sienna said. "This is my first vacation in three years."

Grinning, Carter asked, "Does that mean you're going stir crazy?"

Sienna's smile was genuine this time. "Yes, I am."

"That's why I wanted to get her away for a two-week holiday." Angela couldn't resist taking credit for getting Sienna here. It made them sound like they were close, that she'd been working on her daughter for years to get away, when the reality was that Angela didn't even know Sienna hadn't taken vacation in three years.

"Good on you for bringing her to Santorini. And rather than hanging out with these guys—" He shrugged at the noisy group in the sun. "—I'd rather know more about you two." He jutted his chin at Sienna. "What keeps you from taking a vacation?"

Sienna leaned forward for another canapé, saying before she took a bite, "I'm a financial advisor. With the ups and downs in the market, my clients need a little extra handholding." She popped the fritter into her mouth.

"It sounds more like they need a lot of handholding."

She nodded, swallowed, and said, "I work with a lot of elderly clients, and whenever there's a dip, they're afraid they're going to lose all their savings. I have one sweet old lady—" She gave an inner-directed smile as if she was picturing the woman's face. "—who grew up in the depression, and she's terrified of ending her days as a bag lady living in a cardboard box. Every time there's a downturn, even a small one, I always call her right away and reassure her."

"That's good of you," Carter said, his head tipped as if examining Sienna. "Most people would find that annoying."

Sienna smiled, punctuating with a little snort. "My colleagues dump their elderly clients on me. I have no problem with that at all." She looked at Angela. "It's like you driving the seniors. Most of them are really sweet." She shrugged. "But they need TLC."

Angela felt a kinship with Sienna that she hadn't known in years. It was wonderful to hear how caring Sienna was.

"That's what keeps me at my current company. I don't want to leave my clients."

And yet Sienna did want to leave. "Would it be unethical to take those clients with you?" Angela wanted to know.

Sienna frowned. "Well, it's not exactly kosher. Then again, it would be unethical to leave them in the hands of colleagues who don't want to bother with them."

"Technically, aren't you allowed to give them your cell phone number when you leave? And if they choose to call?" Carter let the sentence hang.

"We'll find out," Sienna said with a sudden smile. "I have an interview with a group called Smithfield and Vine when I get back."

Wasn't that the job Sienna had been so upset that she *hadn't* gotten?

Hearing the question Angela hadn't asked, Sienna explained, "I saw Mr. Smithfield while I was out jogging, and I mentioned that if he ever had another opening, I'd be interested. He called me just before we left."

Why hadn't Sienna said anything? But Angela knew why. Because Sienna didn't talk to her. She should be used to it by now. "I hope you get the job. I know it's what you really want."

"I know Smithfield and Vine. Great outfit," Carter added. "We've often worked with them. But if you're interested in staying in San Francisco, you might try Walker and Walker, another good company up there." He stopped, cocked his head. "Walker." He raised one finger. "You couldn't possibly be part of the family or you'd already be working there."

"That's my father." Sienna's lips thinned. "My brother works for him. But I wanted to strike out on my own."

As if realizing it wasn't a subject Sienna wanted to discuss, Carter clapped his hands. "I wish you all the luck at Smithfield and Vine, and being able to bring along your elderly clients who adore you. And while I have you as my captive audience, I'd like to invite you to go with us tomorrow to climb the Karavolades Stairs. We plan to go around noon. That way all the adventurous tourists coming from the old port will have already made their way up the stairs or taken the funicular." He waved a hand. "We'll ride the cable car down and climb back up."

She was about to say that Sienna wouldn't climb the steps, but her daughter jumped in before she got a chance. "My mother's been talking about walking those stairs. It'll be fun with a group."

Angela barely stopped her jaw from dropping. When she'd asked, Sienna preferred to sunbathe, but when Carter Ellis offered, Sienna immediately said yes. All right. That was fine. Angela knew where she stood. She wasn't hurt, she wasn't even upset.

It just meant she had her work cut out for her.

HER MOTHER LEANED AGAINST THE BATHROOM DOORJAMB as Sienna removed her makeup.

"It was a good day, don't you think?"

"Yeah." She scrubbed a little too hard at a mascara smudge under her eye. "They sure are a hard-drinking group."

Her mother laughed. "They're on vacation. And they're young."

"Not *that* young." Sienna washed her face and came back up for air to find her mother still standing there.

"What did you think of Carter?" her mom asked.

God forbid Mother should start matchmaking. She wasn't sure about Carter. How could someone take off every summer since he'd graduated from law school? Lawyers, just like financial advisors, had to work their way up the ladder. And that didn't involve taking off three weeks every summer. If his friends were any indication, she wasn't sure how any of them had graduated. He'd said two of the guys were lawyers, another was an accountant, so was one of the girls, all of them on the partner track at large firms. Another of the girls had become an interior designer. And Tamryn was in marketing. But they were all partiers. Carter was handsome, and he seemed polite, but she had to consider the company he kept. Maybe the fact that Carter worked for his father said it all. He didn't have to work hard. He already had it made.

"And he lives and works right in San Jose," her mother went on. "How's that for serendipity?"

"Coincidence," Sienna said. There was a world of difference between the two. Her mother was definitely matchmaking. "Please don't get any ideas about Carter and me. He's not my type."

Her mom arched a brow. "You're both in high-stakes careers. You both work hard. You're both career-oriented."

Sienna put a hand on her hip. "Really? Didn't you see how much those people were drinking?"

"Yes," her mother said calmly. "But Carter didn't drink any more than we did. Besides, if you work hard eleven months out of the year, you deserve to let loose for three weeks."

Sienna had expected agreement from her mother. "Anyway, I'll never see him once I'm back home. I'm too busy. Especially if this interview with Smithfield and Vine goes well."

"I hadn't realized you had another interview with them."

Sienna felt a stab of guilt as she smoothed on her moisturizer. They'd been out in the sun all day on the boat, then gone to dinner with Carter and his group, dining on calamari, moussaka, and dolmades, delicious stuffed grape leaves. The others had dug into the ouzo to the point where she was sure it was oozing out of their pores. But her mother had a point. Carter hadn't imbibed nearly as much as the others.

"I'm sorry I didn't tell you," Sienna said. "I wanted to keep things close to the vest in case it goes south like the last time." She shouldn't have even mentioned it, but she'd been making conversation with Carter.

"It went south because of your father," her mother said softly. There wasn't reproach in her voice, just something wistful.

Sienna gasped. "Did Aunt Teresa tell you?"

"She didn't mean to. I dragged it out of her. I couldn't understand why you weren't the top pick, and I kept saying you should have gotten the job. So she had to tell me about Donald."

She wondered how much of what she told her aunt made it back to her mother. Did it matter? If she really wanted a relationship, maybe she needed to talk more.

Instead of pushing the conversation, though, her mother changed the subject. "I've decided not to climb the stairs with you guys tomorrow."

Letting her hair out of the elastic she'd pulled it back with while she washed her face, Sienna gaped. "But you wanted to climb the steps."

Another twinge of guilt squeezed her. She'd refused to walk the stairs with her mother, yet she'd jumped at going with Carter and his friends. She hadn't wanted to look like a stick in the mud. But there was a bigger question here. Why did she care what Carter Ellis thought?

It couldn't be because she liked him. He was a playboy with good looks and a winning smile, but he wasn't a hard worker. He was a year younger than her, unmarried, and he should put his career first.

She tried to explain. "It's just that since I didn't join in with the sunbathing or dancing or drinking or being with his friends, I didn't want Carter to think I'm..."

"A stick in the mud," her mother finished for her.

She smiled at her mother's use of the same cliche. "Yeah. They're having fun and doing all the touristy things, but the first thing you want to do, I say no. I'm sorry. I was just tired. The last couple of months have been busy getting ready for this trip." She sighed.

"And you wanted a day or two to relax in the sun and acclimate. I understand."

She squirted toothpaste on her toothbrush. Maybe her mother understood a lot more than Sienna had ever thought. Especially about her dad. "Yes. But—" She held her toothbrush aloft. "I feel like I can make it tomorrow." She truly wanted to have fun with Carter, even if he wasn't as career-oriented as she was. Maybe she'd even get to know his friends. If they weren't drinking so much, they might be okay.

"I'm not offended at all. And I hope you're not offended if I don't go."

Another wave of guilt turned her face pink. She'd been mean to her mom today, and she didn't like that about herself. "Then I won't go either. We'll do it together another day."

Mother shook her head. "Absolutely not. Go have fun. They're having breakfast out too."

Sienna groaned, thinking of the climb up all those steps on a full stomach. "I'm sure as heck not eating a lot. Or drinking."

Smiling, her mom leaned in to touch her arm. "I won't act like a mother and tell you to drink lots of water and rest regularly and put on suntan lotion and wear your hat." They both laughed. It felt good to laugh.

"Anyway, it's way too late in the day for me. I like to go early. And we've got two weeks together to do whatever we like."

"I don't want you to feel left out."

Her mom shook her head, her short curls bouncing attractively. "I'll go for a walk while you sleep in and have a coffee at a café I found yesterday. And if you're gone when I get back, I just might lie in the sun and read a book."

"Are you sure?"

"Absolutely. Now brush your teeth, dear." She blew a kiss and went off to her room.

Her mother was beginning to amaze her. All her volunteering, her understanding of how fulfilling working with the elderly could be, just the way Sienna felt.

There was so much more to her than Sienna had ever imagined. She'd thought her mother went out for coffee chats or brunches with her friends and spent the afternoon watching *Dr. Phil* and *Judge Judy*. How ridiculous. Of course her mother would be hiking, volunteering at an animal shelter, and driving old people around. Nonni volunteered her time too, but she excelled at organizing five-hundred-dollar-a-plate galas and auctions that benefited this or that group. But her mom was hands on. Sienna liked to think she gave a lot to her clients: confessor, advisor, friend, a shoulder to cry on if they needed it. Was there that much difference between what she did and what her mother did?

If she moved to Smithfield and Vine, she'd have to find a way to bring her clients with her. She absolutely could not leave them in the hands of indifferent colleagues who were only out to make a buck and didn't care how they affected the lives of the people they advised. It was only about the commissions they could make. And the company rewarded them for that attitude. That's why she needed to leave.

For the first time, she felt like her mother understood her goals.

11

Despite the day on the boat, the sun, and the alcohol, Angela once again woke before dawn. She got ready quietly, so she didn't wake Sienna. The sun was just rising above the ridge as she closed the blue gate and headed to the Fira trail. The café was her destination, no detours, no sightseeing today.

Last night's conversation with Sienna occupied her thoughts. Though it wasn't necessary, she appreciated her daughter's apology. It was nice to know that Sienna had no ulterior motive for turning her down yesterday. Her daughter had never explained her actions before, at least not to Angela. She wanted to be the confidante Sienna had never allowed her to be, but she accepted she had a long way to go to make up for all the distance between them.

At the café, the same table was available, and she relished the view of the blue Aegean, the red bougainvillea hanging overhead. With only half the tables filled, the waitress attended to her almost immediately, bringing her the same café au lait she'd ordered yesterday. "Would you like *bougatsa?*"

"Absolutely." Having the young woman recognize her made her feel like a regular, the way she'd been with Xandros.

There were other regulars, the man behind his newspaper, the photographer. She sipped the sweet coffee brew, inhaling its scent, tripping once more down memory lane.

Xandros would have left Santorini years ago, when he tired of being a tour guide. Just the way she was sure the young man captaining the catamaran today would eventually leave. He'd reminded her of Xandros at that age, the curly black hair, the aquiline nose, the Mediterranean complexion deepened by the sun.

That's what she wanted from this trip, to remember how she felt, to remember how good they'd been together, even if it had been only three weeks.

She wasn't stupid, even though her mother thought she was. She'd long since outgrown that pregnant young woman's fantasies, wanting to believe he'd welcome her and her baby. He wouldn't have wanted to be tied down by a child he'd known nothing about. He would have moved on to better things. Maybe he was a businessman in Athens now. He would have married and had children.

And she would be a distant memory, if he even thought of her at all.

Her mother was right.

But she was wrong about Donald. Donald wanted a pretty doll he could dress up and impress people with. He'd picked out her clothes, told her what to wear, sent her down to the salon to get her hair and makeup done. But he'd never loved her.

He was relentless, always telling her what to say, how to act, how to make an impression that looked good on him. He might have gone on like that for years. And she might have been fine because the children made up for everything.

Until the truth came out with Sienna's accident.

The most chilling thing was that he'd only mentioned it once. *I know what you did.* His threats were oblique. *You wouldn't want the children to know what you're really like.* He relentlessly turned them against her. Everything Sienna wanted to do, he refused, saying *Mother* wouldn't allow it. Every time he went off with Matthew in tow, he told her son that his mother couldn't be bothered. And there was nothing Angela could do about it. The threat hung over her, that he would tell the children the truth. And she'd lived knowing that he would make sure they hated her for what she'd done.

But that wasn't the trip down memory lane she wanted to take now.

Her *bougatsa* arrived, and she relished the flaky pastry, the sugary sweetness of the custard and the powdered sugar making her taste bugs twang. Her marriage was done, that part of her life over. Now she wanted to indulge in memories of her three weeks with Xandros, the touch of his hands on her, the taste of his lips, the feel of his hair beneath her fingertips.

When she raised her cup to soften the sweetness of the cream with the delicious bite of coffee, she noticed the man had lowered his newspaper and was looking at her.

A little older than her, he was still extremely attractive, his black hair salted with silver, his mustache thick, his face a little weather-beaten as if he spent much of his time outdoors.

She imagined this was the kind of man Xandros would have become.

He stood then, a tall man, maybe close to Xandros's six foot three. Folding his paper, he laid it on the table and reached in the pocket of his cargo shorts for some coins to throw down. His trim, muscular body spoke of hard physical work, his calves corded as if he did a lot of walking or hiking. His chest was broad and his stomach flat beneath his T-shirt.

This man could have worked a fishing boat, or hauled rocks up the steep slopes to make the paths and stairways that allowed tourists to walk so easily in Santorini villages.

When he looked at her again, she turned away, not wanting him to catch her ogling.

The waitress breezed onto the terrace again, calling out to him in Greek. He replied in a deep, toe-tingling voice. It had been a long time since she'd felt the magic of a man's attention, and it was natural that she'd be so aware of a handsome man who reminded her of Xandros.

She sipped her coffee, dipping her index finger in the crumbs of flaky pastry and sugar and licking it off. Then a shadow fell across her table, and she looked up.

The sun behind him created a corona around his head as he spoke in a rich, seductive voice. "I believe you're thirty years late, Angelika."

Her heart stopped, her ears roared, and her hands went numb. Her cup slipped from her fingers, hitting the saucer, and splashing coffee over the table as the cup fell on its side and rolled to the edge, where he deftly caught it.

It couldn't be him.

But she looked into those penetrating blue eyes and knew this was no lookalike.

This was Xandros, the man who'd occupied every dream she'd had for the last thirty years.

He hadn't meant to startle her. He'd seen her watching him and thought she knew. But when he spoke, it was obvious she didn't. To her, he'd been a nameless man sitting in the corner of the *kafeneío* terrace.

It wounded him. Yesterday he'd watched her from behind his newspaper, but today he'd put the paper down and let her examine him. Yet the shock was obvious. Until he'd said her name, she hadn't recognized him at all.

"May I sit?" He waved at the seat opposite her.

She choked out a reply which might have been yes. He would have taken the seat anyway.

"Why are you here, Angelika?" It was what he'd called her, a variation of her name, but she'd always basked in its glow. "It's not the fifteenth until tomorrow." Thirty years to the day when they were supposed to meet again. "You were here yesterday as well. Just scoping out the clientele?" he asked, using the American colloquialism.

Eleni rushed from the cool interior of the *kafeneío*, a cloth in her hand to mop up the mess. "I am so sorry," she said, as if it was her fault.

Finally, Angelika spoke. "I was clumsy. I'm sorry. At least I didn't break the cup."

She'd avoided the drips off the table, which would have stained her white knee-length pants.

"It is no problem," Eleni said. "I will bring you a new cup." She rushed off again, leaving him alone with Angelika even as tourists began filling the *kafeneío*.

"Why have you come?" he murmured.

She blurted out, "I envisioned you moving to Athens and becoming a businessman. I didn't expect you to be here."

He laughed, a big sound that echoed across the terrace. "You should know I would never leave my Santorini."

She dipped her head, as if she couldn't meet his eyes. "Yes, I should have known that."

He had so many questions. What had she been doing for thirty years? There was no ring on her finger, so she wasn't married. Divorced maybe. She would be fifty-three now, three years younger than him. And those years had been good to her, her figure lush and curvy, exactly the way he remembered. The lines at her eyes and her mouth only added to her beauty, and her skin was still peaches and cream the way it had been all those years ago. He'd seen older American women here, sunblock gathering in the lines of their leathery faces, hats with floppy brims on their heads. Her hat was now sitting on the table beside her, splatters of coffee on its khaki rim. But there was nothing leathery about her.

He said what was in his heart. "You are still beautiful, Angelika,"

Her skin flushed, so very visible on her peaches-and-cream cheeks. "I'm just old."

He laughed, softly this time. "You think only the young can be beautiful?"

Her gaze roamed his face for long moments in which it felt as if her fingers were on him. "No. Beauty isn't only for the young." She blinked, looked down. "But age suits men better than women."

He bowed his head slightly. "If that is a compliment, I thank you."

What to say now? Should he ask her all the questions running through his mind? What she'd been doing, if she had lovers, if she had children, was she a career woman? There were so many things he wanted to know about her.

And so many things he was afraid to know.

HE WAS SO BEAUTIFUL. SHE WANTED TO RUN HER FINGERS through his thick hair, feel the silkiness against her skin. She wanted to stroke his full lips, put her mouth to his, feel the soft tickle of his mustache, taste him again.

She hadn't known what she truly wanted when she came here. Was it a pilgrimage and a place to discover a closeness with Sienna where she could finally reveal the truth?

Or had she been hoping to find him again?

As she looked at him now, his strong, handsome face, the lips she wanted to feel against her skin, she admitted this was what she'd prayed for, hoped for, wanted, needed.

For him to find her again.

Her gaze dropped to his hand. He saw the look and answered her question. "Divorced."

She couldn't help the sigh that whispered from her heart. "I'm also divorced."

"But do you have another man back in the States, Angelika?"

She loved the way he said her name, but she laughed, softly and a little bitterly. "There's only been my husband. He divorced me a year ago. I haven't wanted anyone else." Except Xandros.

"I've been divorced for ten years."

She didn't want to know, yet it was the only thing she could ask. "In ten years, you must have had other women in your life. Is there one now?"

It was a yes or no answer. She didn't want to know all the women he'd been with since his divorce. She wanted only to know about this moment.

"There is no other woman."

It was all she needed to hear.

But it wasn't all she needed to say. "I'm sorry I wasn't here that day." She didn't ask if he'd come. There would be too much pain, too much loss either way.

Their pretty young waitress arrived then, bringing her a second café au lait and a deep black coffee for him.

He smiled. "Thank you, Eleni." Then he said, "I came here that day."

Angela closed her eyes. She didn't want to see the pain in his or feel the sorrow in her own heart for what she'd done.

"But I was engaged to another woman."

Her world crashed and burned, her heart squeezing tight

until she was afraid tears would leak out. She'd dreamed of a joyous reunion that day even as she'd told herself it could never have happened. Her mother was right. He had a girl in every port. And he'd come to this café already engaged to another woman. Oh, but she'd dreamed.

"Why did you come then?" she asked.

He smiled gently, his eyes closing in a slow blink. "I was hoping you'd save me from a marriage I didn't truly want. It was a business deal." He shrugged. "Her parents, my parents. If you were here, I thought I'd find the courage to break my engagement."

"But I wasn't here," she whispered, wrapping her numb fingers around her hot coffee.

"But you weren't here," he echoed. "And I married her." Then he added softly, "I have no regrets about that. I have four beautiful children I adore."

"I have two children. I love them with everything in me." Even if they didn't feel the same way. But she didn't tell him about Sienna. She wondered if he would hate her. She wondered if in telling him, she would hate herself.

"Did you marry him?"

She hadn't lied to Xandros back then. She'd told him about the engagement, about Donald, that she'd realized she wasn't in love with him, but that her mother was a forceful personality with high hopes. "I married him. I couldn't stand up to my mother."

He nodded, a slow, knowing move of his head. "It seems that neither of us could stand up to our parents. I suppose that is the way of things. But because I did not have courage, I have four children I love, a business I enjoy, and after twenty years of marriage, I have my freedom." He reached out, didn't touch her, and finally withdrew. "That's when I started coming back here every June fifteenth." His chuckle was soft music. "Though I come here often for my morning coffee. It is the most relaxing way to begin the day." His smile faded. "But every fifteenth of June, I look for you." He held her gaze a long moment. "And finally, you are here."

"I'm sorry I didn't have the courage to come back."

"I'm sorry I didn't have the courage to fly to the States and find you." Then he grinned, his mustache twitching. "I once saw an old American movie called *The Graduate*. I imagined running up the aisle on your wedding day, just like Dustin Hoffman."

"But what would your life have been like, cut off from your family?"

He shrugged, very Greek, very nonchalant, what will be will be. "Neither of us will ever know."

"I only know what my life is like now. Even though I've been divorced for only a year, I've been alone for thirty-one." She'd never learned to love Donald, not even before he'd learned about Sienna.

"But you are here now." This time when he reached out, he pulled her fingers from her coffee cup, linked them with his. "Do you think thirty years have changed us completely?"

"Absolutely."

He squeezed her fingers. "Yet you came back."

"Yes." The problem was the same as it had been all those years ago. Sienna. She couldn't tell him he had another daughter before she'd even told Sienna.

But once Sienna knew, Angela would have to tell Xandros too.

And that was the second problem. Could he ever forgive the fact that she'd stolen his child from him? That she was pregnant and still hadn't come back, that she'd let another man raise his child? If the tables were turned, she didn't know if she could forgive.

But he was smiling, unaware. "I am not that twenty-five-year-old boy anymore. I am a man. I run a corporation. And I have learned courage."

"Before I saw you, I thought I was a woman with courage. Now I'm afraid I'm lacking any at all."

"I have courage for both of us."

She was afraid it wouldn't be enough.

As if still blaming herself for the spilled coffee, Eleni wouldn't bring a bill when he asked so Xandros left a pile of euros on the table.

He looked at Angelika. "May I walk you to your hotel?"

She had come a year after her divorce. She'd changed her life to get here. And even if she claimed she lacked courage, it took courage to return to the place where they'd lost each other.

He had no intention of losing her again.

She looked at her watch. "Don't you need to get to work?"

He understood it for the stalling tactic it was. "I am my own boss. I make my own hours. And I would very much like to walk with you."

She stood, brushing nonexistent crumbs off her pants. "I'm with my daughter."

"I'd like to meet her."

"I don't think I'm ready to explain who you are."

He put a finger beneath her chin and tipped her head, making her look at him. "I've been coming here for ten years. I am a very patient man. But now that I've found you again, I cannot let you walk away."

He leaned down to touch his lips to hers. It was barely a kiss, but somehow it made him dizzy in a way he hadn't felt since the last time he'd held her in his arms. He asked the all-important question. "Do you want me to walk away?"

She put her fingers to her lips, as if she could still feel his warmth. "I don't think I could bear it if you did." She paused, looking down, eyelids shuttering her gaze. "I just need to adjust and consider how to deal with this."

He slid his hand down her arm, laced her fingers in his, and led her from the terrace. Walking the cobbled streets, which were filling with cruise ship tourists, he said, "You came here after thirty years. You and I both know that means something. This town, this date, our *kafeneío*."

"It's the day before," she said.

God, he wanted to kiss her, deeply, thoroughly. She wasn't as easy as she'd been all those years ago. He didn't mean easy in the demeaning American colloquial sense. It was just that she had known almost from the moment he had that they were meant to be together.

But thirty years had taught her wariness.

He compromised. "I promise not to invite myself into your hotel. I will only walk you there and give you my number. And I will wait for your call."

For her, he didn't use contractions the way the Americans did. Though in his business dealings with English speakers, he spoke as they did. But for this moment, he wanted her to understand the importance of his words.

"I'm not staying in a hotel. We rented a small villa."

He smiled then. "Even better." He stopped, stroked a hand down her cheek, savoring her soft skin. "I will see you again." There was certainty in the way he emphasized the words. He would see her again, without a doubt.

They stood in the street overrun with tourists from the cable car and the intrepid souls who'd walked the stairs or ridden a donkey.

Her gaze roamed his face, and finally she said, "I'll see you again. It won't be like the last time. I promise."

They had both promised before and look how that turned out.

She pulled out her phone. "Call me. Then my number will be in your phone and yours will be in mine."

He laughed softly. "What if you never pick up?"

"I'll pick up." She recited her number, he called, and she answered the ring, ending it quickly. He watched as she opened her contacts list and added his name. "I need to see what my daughter has in mind. Then we'll plan something. I promise."

He had such plans for her. "How long are you here?"

"Two weeks. We flew in a couple of days ago."

All those years ago, she'd seduced him in less than a week. And he would seduce her in less than that now.

He wouldn't let her go without a fight.

Angela walked faster the closer she got to the villa, her anxiety rising as she checked over her shoulder to see if Xandros was following. He was nowhere in sight.

He had come back for her on the day they were supposed to meet. But she'd already been married, with his child in the cradle.

Once his divorce was final, he'd come back again, still waiting for her.

It had taken her thirty years.

What horrible thing did that say about her? Maybe just that she was a frightened twenty-two-year-old girl engaged to another man, the wedding only a month away, and her mother's words ringing in her ears. *He won't want you, he won't want the child, he's busy seducing another girl on another tour, and he's forgotten all about you.*

But he hadn't forgotten. He'd come for her. Even if he'd married the next day.

She raced through the cobblestone streets and up the narrow stairs. She'd been fooling herself, thinking she could tell Sienna on this trip. Maybe all along, even as she was planning the trip details and telling herself she'd finally reveal the truth, it was just an excuse not to do it when Teresa urged her to. But Teresa had never understood how much Sienna hated her. She'd poured out all her secrets to her aunt and kept the truth from her own mother.

Just the way Angela had kept the truth from Sienna.

How could she tell her daughter now? She risked losing all the traction she'd made. Sienna would never forgive her for letting her think her father didn't love her when the truth was that her mother had lied about who her real father was.

And now she had to add Xandros into the mix.

She dashed up the last set of stairs, tore open the terrace gate, and could only breathe again when she saw the French doors were open. Sienna hadn't left yet. Rushing in, she stood on the terracotta tile and called her daughter's name. "Sienna, are you still here?"

Her daughter loped down the stairs, dressed in a tank top, shorts, and sturdy walking shoes. Her bag was hooked over her shoulder, and sunglasses dangled from her fingers. "You're back. I'm just about to meet Carter and the others, and we're heading out to breakfast."

The need came over Angela, so strong she could barely breathe. "I changed my mind. I'd like to come with you, if that's okay." She waited once more for Sienna's disapproval. Her daughter wanted to be with her new young friends. She wouldn't want her mother there.

But Sienna wrapped her fingers around Angela's elbow. "That's great. I wasn't sure about being with a bunch of people I barely know."

Angela felt the loss of her daughter's warmth as her hand fell away. "But you know them. You spent almost the whole day with Carter yesterday."

Sienna snorted. "I barely got a word in edgewise. That

man can talk. And I didn't say anything to his friends. They were hanging out at the other end of the boat or up top." She frowned. "I hate making small talk with strangers."

Angela was suddenly seeing another side of her daughter. She'd always thought Sienna was invincible, in control of any situation. But maybe that was just in a work environment. "Then I'm glad I'll be there with you."

Sienna shrugged. "Besides, I have nothing in common with Carter. I mean, really, who takes three weeks off every summer when he's supposed to be growing a law career?" She rolled her eyes and huffed out a breath. "He works for his father, and that says it all."

Disdain laced her voice, and Angela felt the need to defend him. "I'm sure he works hard the rest of the year. It's good for him to let off steam." She smiled. "Just like I'm so happy you're here letting off steam with me."

"I probably wouldn't have come if I wasn't already planning to leave the company." She didn't notice Angela's wince. "The timing was perfect." Then she looked at Angela's shoes. "You're ready for the stair hike, but where's your water?"

"I'll grab my day pack." Angela took the stairs two at a time, as if Sienna would leave without her. Sunblock and tissues already in her fanny pack, she added some money, a credit card, her ID. Downstairs she grabbed two water bottles out of the fridge and shoved them in the pack's holders before swiping her sunhat off the chair where she'd tossed it. "I'm ready."

"We're meeting at a little taverna, then we'll walk to the cable car."

As they closed the terrace gate behind them, Carter's group was already trooping down their villa's steps.

"You decided to come with us," he said with a wide grin, briefly taking Angela's hand. "Great." Then he touched Sienna's arm, turning her slightly and heading her down the stairs. "I'm glad you both wanted to come."

"It'll be a lot more fun climbing the stairs with a group," Angela said.

His entourage passed them by and Carter called out, "Don't step on the church."

Two of the girls rolled their eyes, saying, "We can read, Carter."

Of course, they weren't girls but somewhere in their late twenties. These days, anyone under the age of thirty-five was a girl to Angela.

The alley was wide, and Carter held out his arms, allowing both Sienna and Angela to loop a hand through his crooked elbows. "It's nice to escort two beautiful ladies."

Sienna laughed. "You're such a schmoozer."

"It's not schmoozing if I mean every word."

Sienna bumped his hip, and he swayed slightly against Angela.

They made a couple of turns, separated to go down a set of steps, and finally arrived at a terrace taverna with a beautiful view of the caldera and the sea. Carter had obviously called ahead as the wait staff had already pushed three tables together for their group of nine, making enough room for Angela too.

She didn't remember a single name between the three men and three women, having barely talked to any of them yesterday on the catamaran.

The waitress stood by the table, ready for their drink orders. Despite the drinking they'd done on the boat and at dinner, the girls asked for mimosas and the guys ordered Bloody Marys.

"I'll have a mimosa, too," Sienna said when it was her turn, Carter ordering the same.

Hadn't Sienna said she wouldn't drink before the walk?

But Angela was glad she was lightening up. For herself, however, she thought about having to go to the bathroom on the climb if she had alcohol, but when she asked for water, Sienna said, "Come on, Mother, live a little."

"Yeah, Mom, live a little," Carter added.

She couldn't say why it felt good, except that it was almost like having both her daughter and son with her.

"All right, a mimosa too."

Carter clapped, and Sienna joined him.

SHE WAS GLAD HER MOTHER WAS LETTING LOOSE, ALTHOUGH Sienna had to admit she didn't know whether or not that was new for her mom.

The breakfast was yummy. Topped with honey and walnuts, the *tiganites*, Greek pancakes, were thinner and lighter than American pancakes, their edges scalloped. Her mother ordered Greek yogurt drizzled with honey and sprinkled with fresh berries.

"You could have that at home, Mother," Sienna leaned close to say.

Her mom shook her head. "Real Greek yogurt is to die for. So much better than the stuff at home." Then she sighed and smiled. "I confess I stopped for a latte and a *bougatsa* earlier. It's a delicious pastry with custard on the inside and powdered sugar on the outside."

Listening in, Carter gasped. "You had *bougatsa* without us?" He put a hand to his chest. "I'm shocked and dismayed."

"You have to get up with the sun to have *bougatsa* with my mom. She's out walking by six."

Carter tucked his chin and flat-lined his lips, which might have been his version of a pout. "I'll have you know I was awake by at least seven."

"That's far too late for Mother," Sienna said, laughing. It felt good to laugh. Carter actually made her want to laugh more.

"The early bird catches the worm," her mom quipped.

"How many worms did you catch today?" Carter wanted to know.

Her mother's face flushed as if she had a guilty secret, but she said primly, nose in the air, "A lady doesn't discuss her worms."

That was interesting. Maybe she'd met a handsome gentleman on her walk. Wouldn't that be crazy? And weird.

They didn't linger over coffee. It was going to be hot enough on those stairs as it was.

When her mother pulled out her wallet to pay for their meals, Carter waved her away. "My treat."

"Thank you, but you don't have to do that."

He patted her hand. "I want to." And he paid for everyone.

Sienna couldn't figure him out. He brought his friends along on a fabulous trip, but he didn't drink with them, didn't party with them, he didn't even seem to talk to them much. He'd paid far more attention to Sienna's mother.

Finally out on the path to Fira, Tamryn complained, "Carter, honey, don't tell me we have to walk all the way to the cable car. Isn't it enough that we're climbing up the stairs?"

"It's only a mile," Carter told her. "Angela has already walked there and back today."

Tamryn didn't acknowledge the achievement. "Come on, sweetie, let's call a taxi."

With all the endearments, she acted like Carter's girl-friend. And yet he'd said she wasn't.

"Yeah," one of the guys agreed. "Let's taxi it." Sienna couldn't recall his name. She only remembered Tamryn because yesterday she'd dumped her drink over the side of the terrace.

Carter shrugged. "Sure, go ahead. But I'm walking. What about you, Sienna?" He jutted his chin at her. "I know your mom wants to walk."

"I'm walking." She couldn't let her mother—or Carter—outdo her.

He turned back to his friends. "We'll meet you at the cable car."

They began walking while Tamryn and the others veered off the path toward the road.

Watching, Carter smiled. "We'll probably beat them to the cable car if they can't flag one down. We should have rented mopeds. We've done that several times since we've been here."

"That's how we got around when I was here in the olden days," her mom said, poking fun at herself.

"You make yourself sound ancient," Carter scoffed.

Her mom laughed. "Old enough to be your mother."

Then, acting like a mother, she got out her sunblock and slathered her neck, shoulders, arms, and the backs of her knees and calves, offering the tube to Carter and Sienna as well.

The path was pleasant, but Sienna was glad for a hat, good walking shoes, and the sunblock.

Acting as the tour guide, her mom pointed to a big rock on the cliff. "That's Skaros Rock. There's a few hiking trails around there, and a small church." A little while later, she added, "And that's the Three Bells of Fira with the big blue dome you always see in pictures of Santorini. It's an island icon."

The path wasn't completely flat, and sometimes there were steps, but the small towns seemed to run into each other, just like Bay Area suburbs, but on a much smaller scale.

As Carter predicted, they beat the others to the cable car, and it was fifteen minutes before they arrived, all scrambling out of a tiny car. Sienna was sure one of the girls had to sit on a lap. But they were laughing, the mimosas and Bloody Marys having loosened everyone up.

The line for the cable car wasn't long since most of the crowd was coming up from the cruise ships. At the end of the day, the tourists would gather up top for the downhill trip.

Though the ride was barely five minutes, the view was amazing, the turquoise Aegean, the caldera against the blue of the sky, barely a cloud flitting by, the white buildings accented with the ubiquitous blue shutters, doors, railings, and domes climbing up and down the hill.

There were small restaurants at the bottom, as well as stores, duty-free shops, and kiosks for booking volcano and caldera tours. The cruise ships were out in the sea, and the small dock was teeming with tourists being ferried over in small launches. They lined up for the cable car or donkey rides up the Karavolades Stairs.

"ETA," her mom read on one of the nearby tour kiosks. "Isn't that the same company that did your catamaran?"

Carter nodded. "They're a mainstay on the island. Exotic Travel Adventures. They do boat tours to the island of Nea Kameni, where you can hike around the volcano. Or you can take a helicopter ride and see the caldera from the air. They even have cruises around the Greek islands and tours on the mainland. But anything you want to do on Santorini, they've got it. Zip lining, wine tasting, bus tours, moped tours. Or you can just rent mopeds and quad bikes from them and go on your own."

"We should definitely rent mopeds," Sienna said to her mother.

A beatific smile creased her face. "I'd love it. It'll be just like when I visited before."

She should have known her mother would be up for it. A hiker, she had a lot more get-up-and-go than Sienna had given her credit for. This vacation wouldn't be a slog, with her always waiting for her mother. It would probably be the other way round.

After slotting her mom away as an older woman, she was now discovering how vital she was. Her mother was the poster child for the saying that sixty was the new forty.

"Touring the island on mopeds is great," Carter agreed.

Sienna wondered if Carter would keep inviting them on the sojourns he took with his friends. It didn't bother her. He made things more fun. But she needed to discuss it with her mom. After all, this was supposed to be a mother-daughter trip.

But her mom beat her to it, saying, "Everything's more fun when you go as a group."

Tamryn jammed her hands on her hips, either annoyed at the idea of Sienna and her mother horning in on all their excursions or the fact that they were taking too long. "Are we going to stand here all day admiring the port, honey? It's going to get mighty hot if we don't start." With a huff, she asked, "Can I take a donkey?"

Donkeys lined the stairs, wearing colorful blankets and docile expressions.

"Whatever you want, *dear*," Carter emphasized. He was easy, adaptable, never upset with a change in plans.

But as Tamryn approached a donkey, she wrinkled her nose, giving an exaggerated, "*Ewwe*. They stink. All right, I'll walk."

Not wanting to offend the Greek donkey minders, Sienna lowered her voice. "It seems cruel to make the donkeys walk all the way in this heat."

Carter shrugged, shaking his head. "In the olden days—" he glanced at her mom with a smile. "—donkeys were used to cart everything up from the port. That was how their owners earned a living. It's part of life here on Santorini."

"I remember being told the same thing when I was here," her mother added. "Even in the *olden* days." They all laughed with her.

Carter raised his voice. "Let's get this show on the road. Everyone have their water?"

They answered him, "Yes, Dad," and "We're not stupid," and laughter.

Sienna wondered just how *fun* this walk would actually be. 588 steps. Good God.

Closest to the bottom of the stairs, Sienna's mom led the way. She didn't take off in a sprint, but climbed the stairs at a steady pace. The three guys raced past her, as if they couldn't let an older woman outdo them. Tamryn and one of the girls followed them, but the other walked with her mother, Carter and Sienna right behind them.

The stairs were wide, especially at the switchbacks, with most of the foot traffic going up versus down. At each switchback, there was room to step aside, rest, take a drink, and to get out of the way of any donkeys.

"I'm sorry, but I forgot your name," the girl said, a frown of embarrassment marring her forehead.

"Angela," her mom replied. "And you are?"

"Irene."

Now Sienna remembered.

"Irene." Her mom smiled. "That's an unusual name for this day and age, isn't it?"

Irene's laugh tinkled in the air. "It was my grandmother's name. My mom adored her."

Sienna eavesdropped on their conversation.

"It's a lovely name. I bet you adored your grandmother too."

Irene nodded, and Sienna thought that might be the glimmer of tears in her eyes. "She was the best. When I dropped out of law school to become an interior designer, she was the only one who supported me. My dad said I'd never make enough money as a decorator and that I'd probably end up working in some department store measuring people's blinds. My grandma said I would be the next Dorothy Draper and get my designs into *Architectural Digest*. They don't just do the home itself but all the furnishings, you know."

"I'm sure your grandma was very proud you went after your dream."

Sienna remembered her mother asking if she really wanted to go into finance, or if there was another career that stirred her heart. Sienna hadn't even listened, thinking her mom had believed she'd never be as good as her dad. For the first time, Sienna wondered if the concern had been about making sure she loved the path she'd chosen. And she did. She loved talking with her clients, learning about their children, their grandchildren, then helping them reach their goals. Her boss said she wasted time with all the chitchat, but that proved to Sienna that she'd chosen the wrong company, not the wrong career.

She tuned into the conversation again when Irene said, "She died last year. And I miss her so much."

Sienna's mom squeezed Irene's hand. "I'm so sorry." Then she asked, "What's your favorite memory of her?"

Irene brightened immediately. "Her house at Christmas when I helped her make her Christmas cakes." She laughed. "It's fruitcake and it's god-awful. But the rest of the family loved it, so Grandma and I slaved away. She wouldn't use a mixer because she said it needed to be hand-mixed. But she couldn't turn the dough anymore, arthritis, so I did. We blanched the almonds to go on top. We could have bought skinned almonds, but no, we had to blanch them and peel them all ourselves because that's how she'd always done it."

Even a few steps behind, Sienna heard the smile in her voice.

Carter leaned in to say, "Her grandma died a few weeks before Christmas. It devastated Irene. But she had to make those Christmas cakes because it's what her grandma would have wanted."

Sienna felt a wave of respect and admiration for Irene, who she'd barely spoken to. She'd judged her because of the partying, but she had far more depth than Sienna credited her with.

As if by agreement, she and Carter walked side-by-side and eavesdropped.

"And when the cakes had cooled," Irene went on. "We drilled holes into them for the sherry." She moaned, grabbing Mother's arm. "Angela, she more than tripled the sherry we poured in. I swear, people got drunk on her Christmas cake." Irene's smile grew, her memories loving. "She wrapped them in tinfoil and put them in the cupboard to sit for a month. And on Christmas Day, before we could open any presents, she brought out the Christmas cake and different cheeses. We each had a bite and had to say which cheese went best. It was a ritual."

"I'm sure you loved it."

"Oh, I did, even if I hated Christmas cake. And last Christmas I made the cakes, and we did the tasting as if Grandma was there."

"I'm sure you're going to do it every year."

Irene nodded, her blonde ponytail swinging. "For the rest of my life. I might even start liking Christmas cake."

The two of them giggled like little girls.

Something twisted around Sienna's heart. She'd never been this free and easy with her mother. And somehow the story spilled out in soft words to Carter. "My mom seems so different here on Santorini." She held his arm as they climbed. "She was always so anxious when I was growing up. I fell out of a tree when I was, like, eight. All this blood was gushing because I stabbed myself on a branch. I probably would've bled to death if my mother hadn't wrapped a tourniquet around my leg. I still have the scar. They gave me a transfusion too." She breathed in deeply, watching her mother's camaraderie with a girl she barely knew. "After that, she never let me do anything or go anywhere. As if she was afraid I'd make another mistake."

"It sounds like you scared the bejesus out of her that day."

Without intention, she slowed down, her mom and Irene pushing ahead.

"She probably was. But then she stymied me."

"Can you blame her?" Carter asked gently.

She didn't want to look at him. He probably thought she was a terrible person. "I can see her doing it for a while. But for the rest of my life? Whenever Dad and Matthew were going somewhere fun, the zoo or the Exploratorium or a camping trip—or even when Matthew got to go to summer camp, Dad would always say—" She deepened her voice. "You need to stay with your mother. She doesn't want you going on this trip."

"And you always felt left out," Carter interpreted.

"Yeah. And she always made my dad into the bad guy because he was the one who had to say I couldn't go."

"But you blame your mom anyway."

She nodded. Her feet felt heavy on the steps, but maybe that was just her heart. "I did. There were so few outings with Dad because he was always busy, going on business trips and working late. So it really hurt that I didn't get to go." She laughed then, suddenly feeling self-conscious, as if she was revealing all her silly childish feelings, and she changed the subject abruptly. "What about you? How can you take three weeks off every year when you're trying to build a high-powered law career?"

Carter's laugh was loud enough to turn both Irene and her mother. He waved them on. "I'm not the high-powered type. But I work damn hard during the year, and my father practically forces all of us to take a long summer vacation."

She remembered he had two brothers and a sister, all working at their dad's law firm.

"We all take a three-week vacation at different times. Dad says people need to blow off steam, that we can't be all work and no play."

Yet this was her first vacation in three years. She'd been working her vocal cords down to their nubs, but was she where she should be in her career? That's why she needed to move to a company who valued their employees, a company where she could grow and be respected.

"My mom's a homemaker," Carter told her. "And she insisted my dad be home for dinner every night. He had a drink and a bowl of nuts before dinner, then we ate together. It instilled in all of us the belief that working harder, climbing the ladder, and making more money couldn't be at the expense of family."

Besides not really trusting men's motives, here another reason Sienna didn't have a boyfriend. She didn't have time. And maybe it wouldn't have been fair either. She was kind of a workaholic.

"And yet, even with that philosophy, Dad's firm has flourished. We have over seventy-five attorneys," he told her proudly.

"Wow." After Carter mentioned the name, she recognized his firm, but the number of lawyers surprised her. It was small compared to firms in cities like Chicago or New York, but in San Jose, that was more than midsize.

"My brothers and my sister and I all came up through the ranks. Dad didn't countenance slackers. I've never wanted to do anything else." He smiled at her endearingly and her heart leaped. "But I love my three-week vacations, and I don't think about work while I'm gone."

"But if you're so into family, how come you're not married with a passel of children?"

He laughed again, not so loud, and she looked up, realizing Irene and her mother were at the next switchback. They hadn't even stopped to rest.

Carter's smile crinkled the corners of his eyes. "Maybe I haven't found the right woman."

She waved her hand up the stairs. "What about Irene or Tamryn or—" She couldn't remember the other girl's name.

"Alyssa," Carter supplied for her.

"Alyssa," she repeated. "Why not one of them?"

He shook his head. "We're all just good friends."

She wondered how he could be friends with Tamryn. She was a complainer. But then again, Sienna was judging her without knowing her. Just like she'd judged Irene before hearing the story about her grandmother.

She revealed a little more about her family. "My dad worked and traveled a lot. My mom was a homemaker too." She smiled then, remembering the story she and Matthew had shared a couple of months ago. "She always made our favorite things when he was gone because he didn't like them. We had lasagna and homemade pizza and tacos, chicken fingers and pasta with meatballs. She was a good cook."

"So you have some good memories."

She'd given him the impression that she and her mother didn't get along at all, which wasn't what she'd intended. "I have a lot of good memories," she uttered the lie, wishing she had more. She wished she had stories about her mother like Irene had about her grandmother.

His mouth close to her ear, Carter murmured, "Maybe you can make this trip a fabulous memory too."

He might be right. This trip could be a new beginning for her and her mom.

As they turned another switchback, Sienna's breath felt labored, and she tried to hide it from Carter, who didn't seem to breathe hard at all. Donkeys lined up for those who couldn't make it another step. At the top of the next switchback, her mother was laughing and talking without a single wheeze while the guys, Tamryn, and Alyssa balanced their hands on their knees as they gulped air. They'd been walking so fast, they had to have been at least two switchbacks ahead of her mother. Yet she'd caught up while they were still recovering.

"Your mom is amazing. She blows them all away." Carter laughed, looking at Sienna.

"She blows me away too," Sienna said, feeling a little wheezy and hiding it with a slug of water. "She surprises me all the time." She returned Carter's look and finally answered the question in his eyes. "You've probably already realized we're not all that close. We came on this trip to repair our relationship."

He puffed out a breath. "I thought you two were besties."

Sienna shook her head. "I was much closer to my father." She didn't say that she'd recently learned how good her father was at lying.

Maybe some of those lies were about her mother. And they were the reason she and her mom had grown so far apart.

THEY HAD A LATE LUNCH AFTER THE HIKE UP THE Karavolades Stairs, feasting on *horiataki*, Greek salad of homemade feta, cucumbers, red onions, Kalamata olives, and the delicious Santorini tomatoes, with an accompanying plate of toasted pitas and tzatziki. As she'd told Sienna, the volcanic soil gave the tomatoes a taste like no other in the world.

Angela excused herself for the restroom and used a little extra time to text Xandros, arranging for a meet the following morning. Was it a bad idea? Probably. She'd been fearful this morning. Yet now she didn't care. She had to see him again. Even his typed words on the phone screen made her breathless.

Afterward, they trooped up to Carter Ellis's villa with its terrace pool, which wasn't deep but enough to cool off after baking in the sun. By dinnertime, they were all tipsy on margaritas, the Greek beer Mythos, and retsina, a Greek wine Angela had never been fond of. Instead of going out again, Carter ordered a light dinner comprised of appetizers.

"We were supposed to view the sunset in Oia. There's a perfect spot, though it's crowded as the sun goes down." He waved a hand at the group behind him. "But I don't think we're in any shape to get there. I'd planned on walking." He snorted a laugh. "These guys haven't recovered from the stairs the way you have."

"I hike a lot at home," Angela said. "Hills in the morning get the blood pumping."

"I need to climb the San Francisco hills." Sienna crossed her eyes dramatically. "Because I certainly couldn't take those stairs the way you did. I'm impressed, Mom."

Angela barely stifled a gasp. She hadn't been *Mom* since Sienna was a little girl. Maybe it was the Mythos beer.

"Tomorrow will be easier," Carter said, grinning. "We're

renting mopeds. You can each ride on the back with one of us, or we can rent a couple more."

Angela looked at her daughter. Her eyes were shining and her smile sweet as she looked at Carter like he was a chocolate truffle she'd love to savor.

She noticed Tamryn looking too, a frown marring her otherwise pretty face.

"I'd love to," Angela said. "But despite how easy you seem to think that climb was for me, I'm exhausted." And she had a date at the café. "I'd like to rest and read." She touched Sienna's arm. "But you go." She smiled at Carter. "She can ride on the back behind you."

It wasn't precisely matchmaking, but if something developed, there'd be no long-distance impediment.

"You must come with us, Angela," Carter coaxed.

Even Sienna added, "Yeah, come."

Angela shook her head. "Mopeds are for the younger generation." Though she could have done it easily. She and Xandros had gone everywhere on mopeds.

"You can always change your mind in the morning." Carter winked.

"Thank you." She gave him a quick hug. "Now, it's been a long day with all the walking, the sun, and the delicious food, and I'll take my leave." She put her hand on Carter's cheek. "Thank you for a wonderful day. And take care of my daughter tomorrow."

"Night, Mom," Sienna called as Angela left through the terrace gate that led to her stairs.

Hours later, she heard the French doors close a little too sharply, then a loud curse. Sienna had obviously indulged in a few more drinks. Angela could only hope it loosened her up a bit. She was so staid back home, so career-oriented. She rarely dated, and she'd never had a long-term boyfriend. Angela didn't want her daughter to be alone. Carter Ellis could be a good influence, especially with his father's edicts about vacations and leaving work in time for dinner.

The door opened and Sienna called softly, "Mom?"

Angela pretended to sleep. Not that she didn't want to talk to Sienna, but she knew in her mother's heart that she would start pushing her daughter toward Carter. And Sienna would resent it. No, it was better to say nothing at all and let the matter take its course.

As soon as Sienna closed the door with a loud snick, Angela wondered if she should have taken the opportunity for a heart-to-heart. This morning, she'd wondered all over again if she could actually tell Sienna the truth. It was the shock of seeing Xandros. But despite her fears, she knew the only way through was to tell Sienna everything. She just had to find the right time.

And hope her daughter didn't hate her more than she ever had.

❧ 14 ❧

Sienna had left fifteen minutes ago with her new friends, who'd planned an unusually early start to make sure they got mopeds before the tourist crowd snagged them all.

It was a gorgeous day, and wearing a sleeveless teal blouse and black capris, she set out later than her customary time. She was jumpy, worried Xandros had changed his mind. Maybe seeing her yesterday had turned him off. For thirty years, he'd thought of the young girl she'd been, not the middle-aged woman she was.

And he was in his prime.

She made it through the maze of alleys and steps to the café, breathless. It was the anniversary of the day she'd let him down. She'd let Sienna down too, because by then she'd allowed Sienna to believe another man was her father. What would their lives have been like if she'd made another choice?

But then there would have been no Matthew.

It was too late for rethinking as she pushed through the gate onto the terrace.

Xandros stole her breath all over again.

The café was full of tourists getting their first taste of delicious Greek coffee and licking *bougatsa* powdered sugar off their fingers. But Angela didn't have eyes for the tourists or the sky or the sea. She saw only him, the strong lines of his face, the toned muscles of his body, and the deep Santorini blue of his eyes.

He smiled when he saw her, rising from his chair in a courtly gesture. His hand on her arm was warm as he seated her, saying, "Eleni is bringing your coffee and pastry."

"Thank you." And she admitted, "I wasn't sure you'd be here."

He raised one dark eyebrow. "Why would I not be?"

"I was afraid." She stopped, wondering how to put it without forcing him to soothe her ego. "We all have images that stay in our minds. Maybe the reality wasn't the same."

He put his hand over hers on the table. "The reality is far better."

She'd forced him to compliment her, but she liked it, especially when he added, "I'm so glad that you texted me."

Eleni trotted out with café au lait and a *bougatsa* to share, leaving them with a smile.

Xandros asked, "What did you do yesterday after you left me?"

He made it sound as if she'd left him alone all over again. "We took the funicular down to the old port and walked back up the stairs."

"Intrepid. Just the way you always were."

She laughed softly, feeling at ease now that they were talking about mundane things. "I shocked my young companions when I made it up the stairs without needing a cane." Her smile grew wider. "Or a donkey."

"Young companions?" he asked. "I thought you were here only with your daughter."

She licked sugar off her fingers. "There's a group of young

people in the villa above ours. They've taken us under their wing. Our first day, they invited us to go on a catamaran they'd rented, then yesterday we did the stairs." She smiled, punctuating it with a chuckle. "We've had most of our meals with them as well, and today, Sienna, that's my daughter, is on a moped trip around the island with them."

"And you're not going?" He turned his coffee cup on its saucer.

She shrugged. "I'm not sure I can handle a moped."

He laughed, and she remembered how much she'd loved his laugh. It sent tingles through her belly, and now it made her think of her nights with him, the touches, the kisses.

"You handled a moped well before. You can still do it."

She ignored all those tingles, all the long-ago thoughts. "I like this young man. His name is Carter, and I think he's sweet on Sienna. So I thought I'd give them time together without Mom hanging around."

He winked. "A summer romance."

That's what theirs was supposed to be, a holiday romance. It became so much more. It became Sienna. "It doesn't have to be. He lives in San Jose, near San Francisco."

He nodded, his expression suddenly grave. "She doesn't have a young man at home?"

She shook her head, adding a little snort. "Sienna thinks only of her career. She doesn't have time for relationships. I could barely get her to come on this vacation."

"Hard work is admirable."

"I think so too. But a person also needs a life outside of work." Then she added. "Like you do. Taking time for coffee in the morning, enjoying the sunrise, reading the paper."

His smile was heart-stopping. "I have never been what you Americans call a workaholic. As you will remember, my job was more fun than work."

"Do you still work tours?" She knew very little about his life now.

He shook his head, tapping the rim of his coffee cup. "I leave that to my children."

"You still run your father's company?"

A frown formed between his brows. "Sadly, my father passed away fifteen years ago. So it is now my company."

She wanted to touch him, offer comfort, but she didn't know him anymore. "I'm so sorry."

Losing the frown, he said, "Thankfully, my mother is still very much with us." She hadn't met either of his parents, but he'd talked about them. His mother had been a force to be reckoned with, wearing the pants in the family. "How are your brothers and sisters?"

He'd talked about them too. He came from a big family, the eldest, with two brothers and two sisters younger than him. "They're good. My mother is happy to have many grandchildren and great-grandchildren."

"And what about your kids? Tell me about them." She wanted to know everything.

"Christos works in Athens, a software engineer, married, two children. He did not want to come into the family business. Thea has moved to France with her husband. She has three children. But Niko has stayed with me at the company." He grinned widely. "And Juliana, my youngest, attends Athens University, a business degree." His eyes shone bright with love. "She says she will run the business when I no longer want to."

"That's wonderful."

"Enough of me," Xandros said. "I want to know more about you. You have a daughter."

"And a son. Matthew. He works for his father. They're all financial advisors and managers." It was the easiest way to describe Donald's investment house.

"And your daughter works for him also?"

She ran her finger through the last bits of pastry on her plate, licked it off. "She works for another company. She's very independent and wanted to prove she could make it on her own without needing her father's help."

"Your son didn't feel that way?"

She didn't want to get into her family's power struggles. "It's different for a son. They have less to prove."

At that, he laughed. "Just like my youngest, Juliana. She would like to think she can do everything better than her brothers. And truly, she's right." He leaned close, his voice intimate. "And what of you? Did you become the teacher you wanted to be?"

She sighed. She'd been pregnant with Sienna when she got home. There was no chance for a career. But she'd never been as career-oriented as Sienna. "I had Sienna fairly quickly." She glossed over the details. "Matthew was born two years later. I stayed home to take care of the children. But I don't miss having a career," she added.

Then he asked, which she should have known he would, "With the children having their own lives now, what do you do?"

The real answer was not much. She'd accomplished nothing major in her life. But she didn't want to sound pathetic. "I'm an avid hiker, and I belong to a hiking group. I do volunteer work as well." She smiled, thinking of Mama. "My mother was always involved with good works. She could never stand to be idle, and she taught me that."

His smile was soft. "I remember that about you. You always wanted to be doing something. 'Where shall we go today, Xandros, where shall we go?'"

She was pleased he imitated her so fondly.

He patted her hand. "Let us do something together, Ange-lika, since your daughter is away with her friends."

She was surprised, even shocked, but so pleased. "I don't have any plans."

"Then let's have fun like the old days."

There was a look in his eye, a spark, saying that he'd thought of all the things they used to do. Especially in bed.

Xandros stood and held his hand out. "Come with me."

His Angelika was so beautiful she made his heart beat faster. He'd hoped he could get her to spend the day with him and learning that her daughter had made young friends on the island was a huge boon. He wondered how many days he could eke out with her while her daughter was off to play with those friends.

As she put her hand in his, he felt the burn of need deep in his belly. But there would be time enough for that. All he wanted now was to know the woman she had become. Throwing a few bills on the table, he winked at Eleni, and holding Angelika's hand, he led her out of the café and through the tangle of narrow streets. They were early enough that the tourists from the cruise ships hadn't completely flooded the roadways of Fira. They climbed steps, and he noted she wasn't breathing hard. She'd said she was a hiker, and he could believe it, especially on a narrow stairwell as she climbed ahead of him, her calf muscles flexing, her shapely bottom firm.

She was a dream come true, just the way he remembered her, though with a dusting of gray in her hair, just as he had. Her locks were short but lush. All those years ago, he'd loved running his fingers through the long silk, but this style complemented her features, the curls framing her face. He wanted to tangle his hands in her hair and never let her go.

"Take a right here," he said at the top, and they turned onto a narrow strip of road too small for cars, room only for mopeds and quad bikes. He removed a key from his pocket. "That's mine," he pointed ahead of her.

"That?" She gasped.

The quad bike was grimy. There'd been no time to wash it, but the two seats were clean.

He laughed softly. "Yes, that."

"You want me to ride on the back of an ATV?" She looked at him, one eyebrow raised, each word pronounced succinctly.

He grinned widely. "I always bring the quad bike when I come down here for my coffee. Sometimes, after I read my paper, I like to go for a ride."

It relaxed him before going into the office. The company took maintenance and planning, but he had good people working for him, not just his family. He'd always made room for family and things outside of work.

She looked from the ATV to her cutoff pants. "Thank goodness I wore black."

"I promise not to drive through any mud puddles," he said with a grin.

"You can't help but get me dusty."

Hell yes, he'd like to get her dusty. He'd like to take her to the beach, lay her down in the warm sand, and get her oh so very dusty.

But that would come later. After they'd gotten to know each other again.

He handed her an open-face helmet, and she patted her curls. "I'm going to get hat hair."

Amused, he chucked her chin as if she were a child. "That's what you always said."

He stowed her hat and bag in a pouch on the back of the

quad bike. Hopeful when he left this morning, he'd brought the two-seater and his daughter's helmet.

Climbing on behind him, she fitted her legs alongside his. He liked the feel of her surrounding him, her subtle fruity scent and the lingering aroma of sugar on her fingers.

He turned the key, held the brake down, pushed the button, and the quad roared to life, the thrum of its motor between his legs.

The back roads proved to have less traffic and no buses. She could have relaxed against the seat, but she clung to him, her breasts pressed to his back, her arms wrapped around him. Going off road, he gunned the motor to push them over a small rise, and the pristine blue of the Aegean lay before them.

Over the rumble of the engine and the wind in their faces, he heard her gasp of pleasure.

He bumped the ATV along until they reached the cliff edge. From here they had a walk down a steep path to the beach. Turning off the engine, he climbed off, helped her onto her feet. They removed their helmets, and she fluffed her hair as he asked softly, "Do you remember?"

She nodded, saying with equal softness, almost reverently, "I remember."

He hung the helmets on the back and took her hand, leading her to the cliff path.

Tourists rarely discovered this place. The only vehicle that could make it here was an ATV. An intrepid tourist could have hiked in, but this beach wasn't on any map and didn't have a name. It was a stretch of shoreline that locals reserved for themselves. There were plenty of beautiful beaches and vistas to keep the tourists happy.

He went first down the steep slope, checking back to see that she was sure-footed on the rocky path. He was glad for her good walking shoes. With only a short jump left, he held out his hands, catching her even though there was little danger of her falling.

"It's exactly the same." She scuffed her shoe in the gray sand, the white cliffs rising around them. "I'd have thought by now the tourists would have found this place and packed every square inch of it."

He led her onto the beach. "It's off the beaten track. And the cliff path can be treacherous. We locals never talk about it."

"It's as beautiful and peaceful as I remember."

The sun sparkled on the Aegean, the sky above them the deepest blue, one cloud daring to scud across. The white cliffs rising high above kept the wind from passing through. It was calm and serene down here, no one else venturing out today. Still holding her hand, he led the way to a rock outcropping, helping her to sit on the ledge.

They had come here their last night. He'd lit a fire for the glow rather than the heat and laid a blanket on the sand where they'd watched the sunset.

They'd made love for the last time.

He asked her again, "Do you remember?"

SHE NODDED, REMEMBERING EVERY MOMENT OF THAT night, their last, though she hadn't known it then. She hadn't known Sienna was already growing inside her. She'd known only that she loved him. When he asked her to come back, she'd pledged that she would.

She had been so sure of everything that night.

Seated beside her on the rocks, Xandros raised her fingers to his lips. "I'm glad."

He didn't press for how she felt in this moment, or even her feelings about that long-ago night. They simply sat in the quiet cove, the memories beautiful rather than wrenching.

Until finally she jumped down, holding her hand out to him. "Let's put our feet in the water. I haven't had the chance to swim in the sea yet."

He hopped off the ledge. "Sacrilege." He smiled down at her. "But you don't have any water shoes. The rocks will be tough on your feet."

She grinned, walking backwards, pulling him along. "I'm willing to brave it."

And brave it she did, stuffing her socks in her shoes and walking out into the waves. Closing her eyes, she let the water lap at her calves, over her knees, soaking the legs of her capris. It wasn't the warm waters of Hawaii, but cooler, refreshing.

Angela felt him beside her, creating little waves around her. She smelled his earthy male scent, and her skin tingled, her body came alive, and she opened her eyes to meet his hot, dark gaze.

Xandros wrapped his big hand across her nape, reeling her in like she was a puppet destined to do whatever he commanded.

"You came back." His voice was hoarse with emotion.

She answered softly, sadly. "Thirty years too late."

He shook his head, blinked, his eyes opening and closing slowly, as if he were looking at the image of her against his closed lids. "It doesn't matter. You're here now."

The water swirled gently around her knees, Xandros's warm hand on her. "But we both married other people," she whispered. "Had children by different spouses." And she bore him a child he didn't know about.

"Maybe that wasn't our time." He tucked her hair behind one ear, pushed another errant lock behind the other. Her hair was already short, and now she felt as if he'd bared her soul.

"I want to believe that," she said.

He smiled gently, nothing more than a twitch of his lips. "I hear a 'but' coming."

"But there's been so much time lost. We don't even know each other anymore."

"Then we must talk, tell each other everything, fill in those gaps. It's not too late, Angelika." His voice was so soft on her name, a caress, as if he'd trailed fingers across her skin.

His hand at her nape again, he pulled her in, his lips taking hers.

At first, she didn't open to him. It wasn't shock, but something more akin to fear. If she let him in, she would lose herself. The way she'd lost herself all those years ago.

But after only a second, as his mustache tickled and his tongue traced the seam of her lips, everything shifted. Fear became desire and desire became need. She went up on her toes, closing her arms around his neck, opening her mouth fully to him, taking his tongue inside as if she was taking his body.

His arms wrapped around her waist, he pulled her tight against him, tight enough to feel his desire against her belly. He angled his head and delved into her very depths.

The years fell away. They were young again, enchanted, obsessed, in love. She clung to him, and when she felt his hands on her, pressing, lifting, she swung her legs up, circled his waist, and held on tight. Hoisted above him, it was her turn to plunder his depths, kissing him wildly, as if there was nothing but this moment. No thirty years. No secrets.

If he'd carried her back to the beach, she would have begged him to take her right there.

She felt the water rising, but before she understood what he was doing, he'd plunged them into the sea.

She came up spluttering. He came up laughing. The sight of his mirth written on his face made her laugh too.

"You beast."

His smile was so wide that his teeth gleamed against his olive skin. "You say we don't know each other anymore. So come home with me. I will show you my house and tell you everything you need to know."

She'd go anywhere with him. And do anything he asked.

15

Sienna was having a marvelous time, clinging to Carter on the back of his moped, her arms around his waist, the scenery flashing by. With its dark volcanic soil and reddish dirt, even the earth of Santorini was awash in color.

The other girls drove their own scooters, but Sienna wanted to ride behind Carter.

It was strange, because she hadn't actually liked him that day on the catamaran. Sure, he was good-looking, and he'd been polite after Tamryn dumped the drink over the terrace. But talking on the open water, Sienna had seen him as a playboy who put pleasure above work. Yet now she wrapped her arms around him and held him close.

She hadn't felt this way about a man in years, maybe never. She'd had her share of flings, but only the job had been truly important. Maybe it was the freedom of vacation, the beauty of Santorini, and that her mother wasn't here to steal knowing glances at her. Not that her mom would be upset to find her clinging to Carter. Mother, all mothers probably, wanted her to find a man as if love was the only goal in life.

What she wanted right now was to tug off her helmet, feel

the wind rush through her hair, and lean her cheek against Carter's broad back.

Santorini was only sixteen kilometers long, and a circuit probably took less time than a commute back home, but they'd made stops along the way, first for pastries and coffee at a café. Now Carter led the group to a lighthouse on a bluff at the southern tip of the island.

Sienna climbed off. Carter pushed down the kickstand while she pried the helmet off her head, turning her face to the wind blowing across the promontory.

"We can't even get inside," Tamryn complained. "There's a fence all the way around."

The lighthouse was stark white in the sunshine, the way of most buildings on Santorini, and topped by a green dome, the light inside to warn sailors.

No one bothered to lock down their helmets. There were only a couple of other vehicles, a rickety old car and a quad bike beside a kiosk for drinks and food.

Carter laughed at Tamryn. "We don't need to go inside. We can walk all around." He led them all to a path Sienna hadn't seen.

"Honey, I'm going to fall and break my neck." Tamryn's voice rose as if she were contemplating panic.

Maybe the endearments applied to everyone because Bill threw an arm around her. "No worries, sweetheart, I'll walk in front, and if you fall, I'll catch you."

She laughed and cuffed him on the shoulder. But Sienna saw the reason for her anxiety as they started down the rocky slope. Tamryn wore sandals and two of the guys had only thongs, but Bill, Carter, Alyssa, Irene, and Sienna had worn shoes. Carter warned her they might do some trails. She was sure he'd warned Tamryn as well.

They made their way single file, climbing over rocks and heading down.

Sienna looked up, sucking in a gasp, and hearing her, Carter turned. "It's a pretty cool sight. Akrotiri Lighthouse, built in 1892. They stopped using it briefly in World War Two."

She liked that Carter knew something about everything. The lighthouse, with its green dome and white walls, perched atop the promontory, having weathered years of strong winds and sea storms. It still glowed white in the sunlight, its small windows like eyes and its dome like a top hat. She snapped a few photos.

"It'll get a lot busier later when people come for the sunset." Carter smiled at her. "Did I do all right on this one?"

She nodded. "You did great."

The cliff face wasn't a sheer drop, but there were enough spiky rocks to make a tumble painful. Yet Carter's feet on the rocks were as sure as a mountain goat.

They made it down to the plateau and along a path to the edge that gave them unobstructed views of the sea. The expanse of the caldera lay before them, illustrating how the islands had once formed a volcano. Boats and catamarans sailed across the blue waters, flitting between the islands. She could make out the town of Oia at the far end of Santorini.

The wind here was cool and fresh against the warmth of the mid-June day.

They made their way around, climbing up a twisty path back to the top where they'd parked. Standing on the edge, she pointed to a building in the distance. "What's that?"

"It's the old Minoan village destroyed when the volcano erupted 3600 years ago. Discovered in the 1860s, they didn't do a major excavation until the 1960s. They've secured most of the ruins inside a modern building to preserve them from rain and the elements." He looked at her, still standing close, and she could feel his body heat against her arm. She hadn't been this aware of a man in a long time. "Would you like to visit?" he asked.

"I'd love it," she said, her voice breathless. She wondered if Carter noticed.

"We'll do it another day, so we can bring your mother. I'm sure she'd like to see it."

"She probably saw it when she was here before."

His brows knitted. "Wasn't that thirty years ago?" When Sienna nodded, Carter added, "Then I'm sure she'd like to see it again. They're always excavating, so there'll be new finds."

She nodded again, her head like a bobblehead dog who agreed with everything. And for once, Sienna didn't care.

Carter raised his voice to say, "Hey everyone, let's do the Akrotiri ruins tomorrow." He pointed to the distant building.

"Sounds delightful," Tamryn drawled, shooting daggers as if Sienna had put him up to the outing.

Sienna wondered why Tamryn even agreed. She always seems so bored with everything.

But the others weren't. Alyssa and Irene echoed each other with, "Awesome." And the guys gave a resounding, "Yeah!"

Climbing back on their mopeds, they rolled off to their next destination. The road was rocky and full of potholes, and Sienna felt as if her teeth were rattling in her head. Heading along the coast, they parked once more, right next to a cliff edge, and Carter helped her off the scooter.

He removed his helmet. "Santorini has red beaches, white beaches, and this is a black beach."

They all stood on the edge, looking down at the black sand below. The sun sparkled on iridescent bits of rock as the waves rolled in and out. Others had found the place and were sunbathing or frolicking in the water. Sienna finally made out the rocky path to the beach.

"Do you want to go down?" Carter said loudly to be heard

over the wind. Everyone but Tamryn raised a hand. She grumbled under her breath, though not low enough to disguise her words. "If I'd known we'd do all this climbing, I would have worn different shoes."

Carter laughed indulgently. "I told you. But you were talking and not listening."

She wrinkled her nose at him, but they all made it down. While the rest were shod in walking shoes, Reed, Jamal, and Tamryn kicked off their flip-flops and ran knee-deep into the water. They mugged for selfies, and Tamryn asked a sunbather to take a picture of the group. The woman was delighted to do it and asked for one of her and her husband in return.

Back on the scooters, they motored out to the road, and Carter headed along the backside of the caldera. They roamed narrow dirt roads, sometimes having to backtrack if the trail didn't lead anywhere. Sienna didn't care. She loved the feel of her body against his, her legs bracketing him, her arms enfolding him while the glorious scenery flew by.

Cruising up to the higher points, they passed vineyards, the vines coiled on the ground instead of hanging on trellises. Tomato vines and vegetable fields stretched down the mountain as they roared along the top. Her mother was right, Santorini tomatoes were delicious whether topping a salad or fried into *tomatokeftedes*.

They rolled into a small village, and as with everywhere else on the island, there were at least two churches. Santorini seemed to have more churches than it did hotels and restaurants. They stopped at the ruins of an old castle, and when they got off their mopeds, Carter gave a brief history. "We're in the village of Pyrgos, and these are the ruins of a Venetian castle. Though it's still well-preserved, the 1956 earthquake caused extensive damage."

"How do you know all this?" Reed asked.

Carter huffed out a laugh. "I read guidebooks."

They clambered among the ruins, snapping pictures. Carter leaned in. "Pyrgos has the highest elevation of any town on Santorini. But the highest point on the island—" He indicated a peak behind them. "—is Prophet Elias Mountain. There's an old monastery up there too."

She gave him a smile. "You really do like your guidebooks."

It was only when he was standing close enough to hear Sienna's stomach rumble that he called out to the group. "Let's get some lunch."

All agreed, with hands on their stomachs and great groans.

They followed cobbled streets, past shops, cafés, and tavernas, until they found a little place that was to their liking. Seating themselves at three small tables on a wide patio, a towering tree shaded them from the midday sun while bougainvillea climbed a trellis behind them.

With no tables for a group of their size, Carter sat with her, the others nearby. Gyros were the specialty, but they were nothing like the gyros she'd had at home. The meat was tastier, the pita fresher, probably homemade, the spices more pungent. She bit into the gyro after dipping it into the small bowl of tzatziki. It was to die for. She'd ordered pork along with Jamal. Reed and Irene tried the lamb, and the rest had beef. All except Carter, who'd taken his with goat meat.

"Gross." Tamryn grimaced, looking at his plate.

"Goat is a staple in Greece. Try it."

Tamryn wrinkled her nose, but Sienna said, "I'll try." Carter held out the gyro, feeding her. "Hmm." She wiped her mouth. "It's a bit like lamb, but maybe gamier. With the spices, it's yummy."

She was about to tell Tamryn to try it, but the girl glared at her and pointedly turned to her beef gyro.

As everyone tucked into the meal, Carter said, "So tell me more about you."

She licked the drizzle of tzatziki from the corner of her mouth and saw Carter's eyes following the action. She liked the way he looked at her, as if she was something to savor. "I told you everything, about my job and all of that."

"What were you like growing up?" He laughed. "You must have been a tomboy since you enjoyed climbing trees."

She put a hand over her mouth, saying, "I was always climbing the trees in our backyard." She swallowed the bite. "And my mother was forever telling me to get down." She shrugged. "I guess I proved her right when I fell."

He pushed a lock of hair behind her ear. "Poor Sienna."

She thought again of the accident. Everything was different after that.

"What's wrong?" Carter asked, reading the emotion on her face. Most people didn't want to hear about a sad childhood, but not so with Carter. "Tell me," he urged.

She looked down at her gyro. "I already told you most of it. It wasn't just my mom. It was like my dad didn't want a tomboy anymore. Whenever I wanted to go with them, he'd say, 'oh no, your mother doesn't want you to do that.' And then she'd offer something like baking cookies or girly stuff I didn't want to do. Like it was a consolation prize." Then she said slowly, softly, "She just seemed so needy."

She stopped then, looked at Carter, and clapped her hand over her mouth. "Oh my God," she exclaimed. "I sound like a whiny little kid." She tried to smile away her embarrassment.

"You don't need to be embarrassed. It helps me know you better."

She snorted. "Yeah, like a pathetic little girl lost." She took a big bite of her gyro so she couldn't say anything else.

He trailed a finger along her jaw, leaving tingles in the wake of his touch. "You're not whiny. You're a very capable woman. It explains why you're so capable, because you felt like you had to prove yourself."

His understanding made her heart stutter. She'd complained so often to Aunt Teresa, thinking that was all she needed. But telling Carter was different. He empathized with her, yet admired her at the same time.

Swallowing a bite of gyro, she said, "Thank you."

Even his eyes smiled. "For what?"

"For understanding. And I'll tell you another big secret. I always wore shorts under my dresses so the boys couldn't see my underpants when I climbed in the trees."

He laughed, loudly. And Jamal called out, "You two are having way too much fun over there." He pulled a chair over to join them, even if it crowded the small table.

"Why don't you all pull over your chairs?" Carter called.

They did, bringing the tables too, and the rest of the lunch passed with a lot of laughter.

It hit her then. She was smitten with Carter Ellis, an old-fashioned word because this felt old-fashioned. Not lust, just something pure and sweet.

And she wanted more.

16

His home was spectacular.

Thirty years ago, Xandros had lived in a small cave house built into the hillside in Fira. A large sofa separated the kitchenette and small living space from his bedroom area. But it had been perfect for the two of them, cozy, romantic, with floor-to-ceiling front windows that opened to a view of the caldera and the Aegean.

But this was a whole different world.

After he helped her off the quad bike, she set her helmet on the seat, gazing at his home sitting on a promontory just above Fira. She counted four levels, each with a balcony draped in bougainvillea and flowering plants. He'd built the house of the same bright white as most island homes, its gates, doors, and shutters all blue.

He was far from the beach bum her mother had said he would be all his life.

Xandros held out his hand, and she took it, saying, "Your home is amazing," as he led her through the blue door framed by a bougainvillea vine.

"I built it for the best views." He smiled as they stepped

into the interior. "I wanted a room for each of my children. And now there are my grandchildren." His eyes twinkled with fondness for his family.

They entered on the top level. A huge family room with French doors at one end opened onto a large balcony. The sun sparkled on a sea that seemed to stretch forever.

She had only one word. "Wow."

He threaded his fingers through the hair at her nape. "Remember how we talked about waking every morning and sitting on our balcony to watch the sunrise?"

"And the sunset too," she added.

"I built my home for both views. I could have been higher on the southern end of the island, but it's windier up there."

She laughed. "It's windy everywhere." The sea always whipped up the winds on Santorini. She'd grown used to it.

He opened the French doors for her, and she stepped out, hit by the full heat of the sun. Though it was mid-June, and July and August were the hottest months, the day was still warmer than she was used to back home. Below them were the stacked buildings of Fira, and to the north was Oia. The balcony wrapped around to the view of a small vineyard, the vines coiled on the ground to minimize the heat and wind that ravaged the grapes.

She turned to him. "You make your own wine?"

He shrugged eloquently. "It is small. I don't sell the wine. I use it only for giveaways to friends, guests, and clients of my company."

He ushered her back inside to show her the rest of the house. Beyond the living room, sunk into the cliff, was his kitchen. Copper pots and pans hung from a wire rack over an island with a state-of-the-art cooktop and pop-up fan. Cubbies along the back wall held every appliance imaginable, a built-in microwave and double oven, cupboards, glass-fronted cabinets with dinnerware, glasses, and mugs. The dining area was in the northeast corner, where the sun would bathe it in morning glory.

"You still cook."

Xandros had always loved cooking, making all the Greek specialties for her.

"I like nothing better than hosting parties and preparing all the food myself."

He'd done that back then, cooking for his friends. So many things had changed and yet so many had not.

He curled his fingers around hers. "Let me give you a tour."

A spiral staircase led to a lower level that housed a rec room with a pool table in the center. Two bedrooms set into the rock shared a large bathroom between them.

She sent the cue ball flying into a stack of colored balls. "This is a new pastime."

He grinned at her. "There was no room for a billiards table in my tiny home. But I played a lot in Athens while I attended university. And the children enjoy it."

She tried to keep the surprise off her face. "You didn't tell me you'd been to university." They were together for three weeks and he'd never mentioned it.

He turned and walked to the French doors, blue again, and stood looking out of them. "I attended after you left. My wife preferred Athens," he added as if he needed to explain. "I took a business degree, like my daughter. I felt I couldn't expand my father's business unless I learned." He turned to her once again, his arms folded. "Learning the business from the ground up." He smiled, his teeth gleaming even with his back to the window.

"I got my university degree and did nothing with it except become a mother and head charity committees."

His smile faded, and the sparkle in his eyes seemed to die.

She couldn't bear to hear what he might say, rushing on

with, "It's so cool in here." She held up her hands. "Despite those floor-to-ceiling French doors."

"The white building reflects the heat, and with the back of the house built into the hill, it stays cool. Like the old cave houses." He put a hand on the glass. "I also used the most heat resistant technology in the windows."

He showed her the two bedrooms, both with single beds. "For the grandchildren." He winked at her. "Adults can use them and sneak into the other bed in the middle of the night."

Another circular stone staircase led to a lower floor, this one with three bedrooms, two bathrooms, and a cozy sitting area with a fireplace. "The flue goes to the balcony above, the heat rising for cold winter nights, almost like a fire pit."

She couldn't help laughing. "I think our definition of cold is probably different."

"You would be right, but a fire pit is always welcome."

The rooms on this level all had queen beds. She wondered where he slept.

Xandros opened an outside door and stepped onto stone stairs that led down. He pushed on the blue gate, glancing over his shoulder. "The steps are steep, and I use this as a child-proof gate. With the pool and hot tub down here, the children shouldn't go down on their own."

He held her hand as they took the steps, as if afraid she might fall. A gate set into the wall at the bottom led out to the drive.

Down here, bougainvillea hung over the white walls surrounding a vast stone patio with a narrow lap pool, a kidney-shaped pool, and a hot tub.

Without her noticing they were there, he opened glass bifold doors, revealing a massive bedroom with a sitting area before a white stone fireplace. A king-size platform bed filled the back wall, its bookcase headboard stacked with books, some on their sides, some upright, one open as if he'd just set it down.

"Wow," she said on little more than a breath.

Xandros turned on recessed lighting in the ceiling and waved her to the bathroom door. The walk-in shower was big enough for two, with dual rain showerheads, and despite the hot tub outside, there was a large jetted tub made for two. And two sinks in a long marble vanity.

A prickle ran up her arms as she imagined his wife living here with him.

He seemed to read her mind. "I built this home for myself. My wife preferred Athens. She enjoyed the nightlife. While we have nightlife here on Santorini, it was never to her tastes."

It felt odd getting this insight into his marriage. She didn't want it, and yet she did. It actually buoyed her to know that in many ways they had lived separate lives, just as she and Donald had after Sienna's accident.

She smiled, needing to ease the tension. "I can see why you want the gate up there, especially if you leave your curtains open to the night."

He didn't smile. "I bring no one down here except to use the hot tub and the pools. There are three levels above for partying."

She didn't know what that meant. He didn't bring other women down here? He'd never brought women to this house? Or that he always entertained his women upstairs?

His expression changed, lightened. "You must be famished. I'll make salad for lunch."

He led her out of the room across terrazzo tiles intricately laid with mosaics between them. Pushing a button, he closed the doors and a set of blinds. "It keeps the room cool."

They climbed the stairs once more to the kitchen level, and there he prepared a delicious salad of fresh shrimp, greens, avocado, olives, and Santorini tomatoes. She'd at first found the olives too salty, but she'd learned to love them. Back home, they'd become a reminder of him.

She was enjoying a delicious tomato spiked with vinaigrette and a tasty shrimp when the front door burst open. A young man rushed through, skidding to a stop on the tile entry when he saw his father with a woman he obviously didn't know.

Xandros rose to his feet. "Niko, I thought you had a tour today."

"I did," the young man said. "Earlier this morning. But I left the house without my phone. It was too late to come back or I would've been late for the catamaran." He spoke in English, perhaps because Xandros had.

He looked familiar, and his voice resembled Xandros's when he'd been young.

Then she registered the word *catamaran*. This was the young man who'd piloted their catamaran. He wore the same blue shirt with the logo and the name of his company, Exotic Adventure Travels.

He'd looked familiar even then, with his resemblance to Xandros.

She thought she might choke on her shrimp and swallowed hard.

Xandros held his hand out, forcing her to stand. "Angelika, meet my son, Niko."

Niko came forward to pump her hand. "Nice to meet you." Then he bounded down the two steps into the living room. Looking at his father, he said, "I can't stay. I have another tour this afternoon."

"You said you wanted no more than one a day."

Niko shrugged, a gesture so like his father's. "They came in at the last minute, and Lorenzo already had another one booked." He was turning, dashing for the spiral staircase, his feet pounding on the stone. "It's probably downstairs," he called, disappearing into the stairwell.

"Niko stayed over last night," Xandros explained. "He wanted to have a party with his friends, and his home is too small."

"I've already met him, though I don't think he remembers me. He was the captain of our catamaran."

Xandros beamed. "I'm glad you chose Exotic Travel Adventures." The pride in his voice had her putting all the pieces together. "You own Exotic Adventure Travels."

"I expanded from what my father and I used to do, so we gave it a bigger name. We are now the busiest tour company on the island."

She shook her head in wonder. "Not just on Santorini. Exotic Adventures Travels is all over the Mediterranean. You even have cruise ships." Carter had told her all about the company.

He nodded. "Yes. My daughter Juliana is running a cruise this summer, in training I suppose you'd call it, before she goes back to university in the fall."

"No wonder you have a house like this." It was far beyond her imaginings. Far beyond anything her mother could have dreamed of.

Niko pounded back up the stairs, throwing out a flurry of Greek. Xandros pulled out his phone, tapped an icon, and somewhere in the living room, a phone rang.

Diving beneath the couch cushions, Niko came up triumphantly with the ringing phone. "So nice to meet you, Angelika." He dashed for the door. "Gotta run," he said just like a young American.

"He's a whirlwind, isn't he?" Finally, she looked at Xandros.

His smile was full of such love that it brought tears to her eyes. This was how she looked at Sienna and Matthew. But she would never feel the ease with her children that Niko and Xandros seem to share, especially not after Sienna learned the truth.

Or maybe the truth would eventually heal the wounds.

"They're all a whirlwind." Xandros stepped down into the living room, moving to a sideboard with a row of photos she hadn't noticed.

In only a few steps, he changed her world. He held out a frame. She had to take it, and she saw exactly what she expected. Despite the emotions rising up her throat, she smiled. "You have such beautiful children."

She remembered all their names. There was Niko, the image of Xandros. She picked out his son Christos, another Xandros clone, surrounded by a gaggle of beautiful children all under the age of ten, and, she presumed, his dark-haired wife clinging to his arm as she gazed up at him adoringly. The woman next to them, children clinging to her skirts, had to be Thea, her husband with the aquiline nose and long face of a Frenchman, his arm around her. Thea was a beautiful woman with Xandros's thick curling hair. Xandros stood in the middle, one hand on his son-in-law's back, the other arm draped around his son's shoulders. Seated below them in the center was his youngest daughter, Juliana.

That's who the young woman must be, and yet she saw Sienna in the long hair, the beautiful features, the pretty smile.

It was Xandros's smile too, and Angela felt as if Sienna had transported into this photo, as if she was part of this family, the way she should have been for thirty years. How much happier would her daughter have been? Angela had always explained away the likeness to Xandros by saying that Sienna had her Italian heritage, her coloring, her wavy hair. But it was clear she was Greek through and through, that she belonged to Santorini. To Xandros.

It was painful to look at. Tears pricked the backs of her eyes, and she blinked quickly to wash them away. But Xandros saw, and he took the picture from her hands, setting it on the sideboard and cupping her cheek. "What's wrong?"

She gave him the only explanation she could. "I was thinking about all that I missed."

He added for her, "All that *we* missed." He stroked his thumb under her eyes as if a tear had escaped. "But we wouldn't change it, would we." It was a statement. "I could never give up Niko or Christos or Juliana or Thea. Could you give up your son and daughter?"

She didn't say that she'd lost her daughter and son long ago. She couldn't say that she wouldn't have lost Sienna if she'd been with Xandros. Sienna would have been *theirs*.

So softly he had to lean close to hear, she said, "And yet we missed so much."

He framed her face with his big hands, his warmth seeping into her. "Look at it another way. We won't miss anything else. You are here, we have found each other, and we can make up for what we missed."

She looked at him, his beauty, his intensity, the deepness of his gaze on her. "Can we really have it all?" she whispered.

"Yes," he said just before his lips took hers in a kiss so sweet, so consuming, that she was suddenly the young woman in love she'd been all those years ago.

SHE TASTED SWEET AND SPICY, LIKE THE VINAIGRETTE HE'D drizzled on her salad.

A deep need welled up from inside him, the desire to show her they could have everything. He opened his mouth, kissed her so deeply that he dragged a moan from her. He held her with only his hands and the heat and hardness of his body. Yet there wasn't a breath of air between them. He wanted her, with everything in him, the way he'd wanted her so long ago, the way he'd wanted her in his dreams for the past thirty years, the way he needed her now, in this moment, without question.

His lips still fastened to hers, he bent, picked her up, and carried her to the sofa, setting her on the soft cushions. Coming down on top of her, his mouth sealed to hers forever, he fumbled with the buttons of her blouse, putting only enough air between their bodies to finish the task. He didn't look, not yet, simply tasted her, breathed in her scent, and drank in her moans as his fingers found the clasp of her lingerie and popped it open.

Only when he felt her flesh beneath his fingertips did he leave her mouth to trail kisses along her jaw, down her throat, across her smooth skin to the peak of her nipple. Her beautiful breasts were still full and firm, as if the years hadn't changed a thing about her.

"You are so beautiful, so perfect." Her curves entranced him, beckoned him. He'd always loved that she wasn't the frighteningly skinny model type.

She clutched her fingers in his hair, begged, "Please." And pushed him down until he took her in his mouth.

He sucked hard, remembering the way she liked it. She rewarded him with another moan as her body arched. He brushed the other bra cup aside and played with her, pinching lightly, loving the writhing of her body beneath him.

He hadn't meant for this to happen now. They needed to get to know each other again. He wanted to tell her everything that had happened since they'd parted, to learn everything about her. Yet this was how they'd learned each other the first time, through the rhythm of their bodies, what they each liked, what made them crazy. And he craved her taste.

He crawled down her body, kissing her quivering skin.

Then he reared up to tear his shirt off, undid the button of her pants. His hands in the waistband, he hauled them down her legs. By some miracle, her panties remained in place, pure white bikinis, lace along the edges, a red bow in the middle.

That tiny red bow was his undoing.

Her chest heaved with her quickened breath, her eyes glistening with desire. "Do you want this?" he asked.

Her hands fluttered, her lips opened and closed, then she murmured, "Yes, please," along with his name on a rush of breath.

Wanting to feel her skin against his, he tore off his jeans, toed off his deck shoes, his feet bare, everything bared, all for her.

His erection was almost painful, but first there was this, his mouth on her panties, blowing warm breath that made her writhe. He stretched, reaching a nipple, tweaking her as he sucked her through the white cotton. She was as needy as she'd been thirty years ago, groaning, even growling, winding his hair around her fingers, pulling the strands tight, signaling how badly she needed his mouth. He only got as far as pulling the panties off one leg and left them dangling from her knee before he spread her legs and devoured her.

She was warm and wet and sweet, like the petals of a flower. She tensed and released, her feet digging into the sofa beneath them as she rode his mouth, his lips, his tongue. He knew her so well, even after thirty years, knew the quake and shimmy of her body, the rising keen of her voice. Pushing his fingers inside her, he glided over that spot, caressing slowly, until he felt her contractions. He remembered how her body milked him, almost forcing him to come deep inside her. She thrashed on the sofa cushions, her body clamping around his fingers, and she cried out, a deep wail, as she bucked against him. He relished her, savored her, licked and sucked her until he could almost feel her tears.

It was time. It was what she needed and what he craved.

He rose up, thrust hard and deep inside her. She cried out, and her eyes flashed open, a grimace on her lips. He feared she wasn't ready, that it had been too long for her, and he'd moved too fast, taken too much, pushed too hard.

Until she clasped his arms and wrapped her legs tight around him, holding him deep, her body grinding against him. "More. Please. Now."

He gave her exactly what they both hungered for.

SHE WAS FLOATING IN BLISS. HIS BODY LAY DELICIOUSLY and wonderfully heavy on hers, his skin warm, his breathing hard. She clenched her legs around him, her arms across his back, afraid he'd move, afraid he was a figment of her imagination.

She hadn't climaxed like that in more than thirty years. She hadn't wanted a man the way she wanted him. Never.

There had been that momentary pain, not a virgin's pain, but the ache of a woman who hadn't felt a man inside her in more years than she wanted to count. She hadn't been sure she'd ever have a man inside her again, but she'd been sure that man wouldn't be Xandros. He had been her dream, her fantasy, part of her memories of Santorini.

She stroked his skin, the dusting of hair on his back just the way she remembered. He wasn't a figment or a dream or a fantasy. He was real and he was Xandros and he was inside her.

He kissed her neck, licked the sweat off her skin, nibbled her throat, took her mouth in a soul-searching kiss. He filled her up. He made her whole.

Then he rested on his elbows to look at her. "I didn't mean to hurt you."

She shook her head. "You could never hurt me. It's just been so long."

"I'm sorry." She didn't know whether he was apologizing for the brief pain or the fact that she hadn't known sexual joy in years.

"I didn't use a condom. I lost control."

She cupped his cheeks. "It's not like I can have a baby." She told him not to worry in just a few words. "And I haven't been with anyone."

"I have been." Something dark and shameful flickered in his eyes. "I wish I hadn't. I wish I'd waited until you came back. But I am careful, and you need not worry."

She raised her head to kiss him sweetly. "I was never worried."

He pulled back to whisper the words she'd waited to hear for thirty years. "I never stopped thinking about you. Never stopped hoping for your return. Never stopped loving you."

She didn't ask why he hadn't come for her and answered with the only honesty she had. "I couldn't get here. Until now."

"Now is the perfect time. As long as..." His words trailed off.

She knew what he needed to hear. "I never stopped loving you."

"That is all that matters." He moved to pull out, and she clung to him.

"Don't go yet," she whispered. "I want you right where you are. I don't want to worry about tomorrow or the future. I just want this for now."

He didn't question her fears or ask if she might leave him. She didn't question that he might leave her when she told him the truth.

All she cared about was that he was kissing her again, trailing his beautiful lips to her ear, blowing sweet nothings, licking her neck, sliding his hands up her body, smoothing his thumb over her nipple. Then, skimming down between them, he found the button at her apex and made her tremble all over again. His touch pushed her higher and higher, until sensation shot through her, and she cried out in uninhibited pleasure.

He thrust hard and deep then, grinding against her, drawing out her climax, pushing it on forever and ever, sweeping her off into a blissful oblivion where all that mattered was his arms around her, his taste on her lips, and his body deep inside her.

17

Sienna loved the feel of Carter Ellis between her legs. She loved the feel of her arms wrapped around his waist as they flew along the road to Oia.

She found it strange the way her feelings for him had changed so quickly. As they'd all gathered round the mopeds discussing what they would do next—cliff-jumping in Amoudi Bay below Oia—she'd feasted on the angles of his face, the timber of his voice, and the animation on his features. They'd talked about walking down to the bay, but the others didn't want another set of stairs, even though Carter had insisted they'd be going *down* from Oia Castle. Irene had chimed in with the old saying, what goes down must come up, though maybe it was the other way round. Carter had given in, agreeing to ride the mopeds and pray for parking, his beautiful, amazing smile making things tingle in Sienna's belly. It made her want to touch him, even if only to cup his cheek as he smiled at her.

She felt sixteen again, watching Dylan Becker, how his body moved, how his eyes lit up when he smiled, how his gaze shifted to her, then flitted away again. She'd been obsessed with Dylan Becker, but she hadn't liked him at first, just the way she'd doubted Carter's authenticity. Dylan had been the football star, a senior, so full of himself that he believed he could get any girl he wanted. With those first glances thrown her way, she was sure he thought she'd fall adoringly at his feet. But after being allowed into his select group, invited by girls who didn't think she was a threat, she began to see Dylan in a different light. The day he'd saved a pimply kid whose name she couldn't remember, her opinion changed as quickly as it had with Carter. When Dylan found the boy circled by a gang of bullies, he'd stepped in, telling them all to get the hell away, and he'd walked the kid to his locker to get his books. No one had bothered the boy after that.

And Sienna had fallen in love with Dylan Becker.

It hadn't ended well. Her mom had gotten her dad to agree she was too young to date a senior, and they wouldn't allow her to go to the prom. Dylan had taken someone else, and that was that. The other girl became his girlfriend.

She tightened her grip around Carter's waist as they made a turn, and he patted her hand as if he thought she was afraid. But she was thinking how similar the incident had been to what her father had done with Mr. Smithfield, deciding something wasn't right for her and acting on that decision. Back then, he'd blamed her mother. *Your mother says...* He'd used that phrase so often. But now she questioned whether her mother had been the one to say she couldn't go. Or had Dad used her as a scapegoat, making her the bad guy so Sienna wouldn't blame him?

She wondered what he would say about Carter Ellis. She could already hear it, the same thoughts she'd had, realizing now that they came from her father's mouth. Carter didn't work as hard as he should; he shouldn't take a three-week vacation in Santorini; his father was setting a bad example by ending his work day in time for dinner. They were slackers. They were posers.

She saw now that her father's modus operandi was sabotage, and she knew in her belly, maybe even in her heart, none of that was true. Carter deserved his vacation. And being with family should come first.

She wanted to enjoy the flirtation for what it was, a holiday romance. She'd be going home in a week and a half, and it would all end. But what fun it was for now.

Carter guided the moped down the road to Amoudi Bay. They were lucky to find a couple of parking spaces that accommodated all the scooters.

They'd all worn swimsuits under their shorts and brought towels in case they wanted to jump into the sea along the way. Now they stripped down.

Self-conscious in her bikini, Sienna wrapped her towel around her. She'd taken off her shoes and bought a pair of water sandals at a nearby stall, and now they trooped past fishing boats in the harbor and restaurants packed with sunburned tourists. The cliffs rose above them, stabilized by red brick walls that had crumbled in places. Heading along a pathway beyond the harbor, they rounded a corner, the cafés and shops disappearing behind them. The path turned to a dirt trail at the base of the cliffs, their feet kicking up red dust motes. The trail ended at a small outcropping covered with towels, shirts, and shoes tossed down haphazardly.

Carter jutted his chin. "You can't see it back there from the harbor, but that big rock is where we'll jump off."

The rock loomed out of the water, and the only way to get to it was to swim. Heads bobbed on the surface beneath a small plateau, and the swimmers shouted and waved, laughing as a teenage girl took a running jump off the cliff and cannonballed into the water. Terror rose in Sienna's throat, choking her, until the girl's head popped above the surface, and she high-fived another swimmer.

Honestly, it didn't look all that bad. It wasn't as if they'd be jumping from the cliffs of Oia. That would be insane. This was doable, maybe twenty feet. It was the rocks below that worried her more. What if she didn't jump out far enough to miss them?

She kept her water shoes on, and the others were halfway across when Carter took her hand, helping her down. "This'll be great. I promise," he said, as if he saw the fear in her eyes and felt the tenseness of her muscles. But if Alyssa, Irene, and Tamryn could do it, she sure as heck would.

Climbing down, she immersed herself in the blue water. The swim was refreshing after the warmth of the sun. Carter stayed abreast of her even though he could have sprinted ahead. Reaching the rock, they hauled themselves up after the others, and she sluiced water out of her eyes. Carter held out his hand as they crossed the concrete landing to a set of wide stone steps she hadn't seen from the shore.

At the top of the short flight, she marveled at the smallest church she'd ever seen nestled into the rock. It had a door, so people must be able to get inside. Did they have to crouch? Rounding the church, they came upon the plateau from which the teenage girl had jumped.

A short line of people waited their turn, with Carter's group gathered at the end. An old lady stood on the precipice, catcalls rising from the sea below. Or maybe they were just cries of encouragement to Grandma. It struck Sienna that though she'd called the woman old, she was only her mother's age. Was fifty-something really that old? The woman turned, walking back several paces, then took off at a run, jumping far out. The sound of her splash accompanied cheers rising up from sea level.

Carter held her hand. "Looks like a blast, don't you

think?" He gazed at her as if he was her cheering section. She wasn't afraid, at least not much. She could do this. So what if she wasn't a risk taker. This couldn't be that much of a risk. Could it?

There were kids and teenagers and older couples holding hands. When it was their turn, Reed went first. He'd been on the university diving team, and he effortlessly arced through the air. Irene made a running jump and squealed as she went over the edge, then popped up in the water. Everyone below cheered as if they knew her. Bill went next, then Alyssa, followed by Jamal, who burst out of the water laughing and fist-bumping the others. Finally, only Tamryn, Sienna, and Carter remained.

Tamryn turned to Carter. "Sweetie, I can't do it," she cried, hands over her mouth.

A man in line behind them called out, "Just grab her up and throw her off! She'll love it."

But Tamryn looked as if she might burst into tears. "Carter, I can't."

Something in her voice made Sienna look harder at the glint in her eyes. Was she playing Carter?

He called back to the man. "You come and throw her. I'm afraid."

Amid their jeers and laughter, Tamryn's expression morphed into angry lines. She flipped the guy off, then ran to the edge and jumped.

Carter didn't seem to care. "She's a drama queen," he said good-naturedly. "But she's damn good at marketing, and she amuses me."

Sienna found Tamryn irritating, but here was another thing she liked about Carter. Other people's nonsense didn't get to him. He never seemed to have a bad mood. He was kind to her mother, always including her. It brought back that day with Dylan and the bullies. Carter would save a kid from a bully without blinking an eye. Then he'd make that kid his friend.

As if he recognized her nervousness, Carter held out his hand. "Let's jump together."

She clasped her fingers around his. She couldn't let Tamryn beat her. But as they stood on the edge, she saw the rocks and the clear blue sea below. It wasn't as tall as a high dive, but you had to jump out, not straight down, or you'd hit those rocks just under the surface.

Carter squeezed her hand. "Let's take a running jump." His eyes glittered like an excited ten-year-old.

She felt his warmth, his comfort, his strength seeping into her. They backed up a few of steps, and he whispered, "Ready?"

And they ran. She screamed as they went airborne, but it was exhilaration rather than fear. It was the joy of her hand in Carter's.

They hit the water, sinking deep into the blue sea, far from the rocks, Carter's strong hand around hers, pulling her back up. They popped above the water amid a round of cheers from below and cries from above.

All except Tamryn, who watched Sienna with a glare.

Sienna scooped the hair out of her eyes and the water off her face, and shouted a laugh. "That was awesome. Let's do it again."

And as she jumped with Carter time after time, she grew fearless.

THEY LAY DELICIOUSLY ENTWINED FOR LONG MINUTES after their lovemaking. When Xandros moved to relieve his weight off her, Angela clung to him. It had been so long since she'd luxuriated in the weight of a man, breathed in that musky male aroma, reveled in the feel of slightly rougher skin against hers. She was loath to let the sensations go.

He peppered her face with kisses, his mustache a delightful tickle, then her neck, her earlobes, her collarbones, hardening inside her the closer he drew to her breasts.

He rose above her, his arm muscles taut. "I'd rather make love to you in my comfortable bed." His eyes were a dark blaze. "There's so much more I can do to you when I have you stretched out beneath me."

She leaned up to give him a long, delicious kiss. "And there's so much I can do to you."

They spent long, lazy hours in his bed. Exploring each other, renewing all the things they'd known about each other's bodies so long ago.

Until her phone rang.

Xandros had given her a comical look, half sad, half wink-ing-emoji, when she'd brought her phone downstairs with them.

"I really need to look." She hadn't checked in with Sienna all day.

The text invited her to meet them for dinner. But Xandros ran his hand down her flank beneath the covers, and she texted back that she was fine, to go ahead without her. She didn't mention that she was in her lover's arms and couldn't leave him.

"Let's take a dip." Xandros pulled her from the bed, and they padded naked to the pool where the water was deliciously cool on her overheated skin.

She gave his body a long, lingering sweep of a look. "What if your son comes back?"

Xandros laughed. "We can hear anyone coming from miles away." He kissed her sweetly, lazily. As if they had all the time in the world.

But Angela knew the clock was ticking.

He held her loosely in the circle of his arms, floating in the water, her legs wrapped around him, his body luscious between her legs.

"Let's go down to Oia and watch the sunset." He nuzzled her ear.

She tipped her head back to laugh. "You have a much better view from up here."

He shook his head, water spilling from the ends of his hair. "It's so much better with all the tourists."

She snorted. "I thought you hated all the tourists."

His swift kiss cut off her objections. "Tourists are my bread and butter, even if they're a nuisance to us locals." He rubbed noses with her. "But I feel the need to hug you close in a big crowd and listen to their exclamations while I bury my face in your hair and drink in your scent as we watch the sunset."

It was so romantic her heart leaped.

They showered, giving themselves a bit of playtime. Until Xandros had her breathless up against the wall, pushing her over the edge with exquisite ferocity.

Once they'd dressed and gone outside, he announced, "We'll take the quad bike. Much easier to park."

True to his word, he found a narrow spot between two cars and backed the bike in.

Like the crows in Alfred Hitchcock's *The Birds*, the crowds were already roosting, filling up walkways, sitting on stairs, lining railings, leaning over balconies, and enjoying restaurants.

"There's not a single spot," she complained, but Xandros grabbed her hand, wending his way through the crowd, forcing breaks in the waves of people with his big body. He found a perfect spot and turned his back to the wall, pulling her in front, his chest warm and muscular against her.

Nature's light show began as the sun fell toward the horizon, its rays streaming across the sky, yellows and oranges, streaks of purple. The facades of the houses lit up with a yellow glow, as if spotlighted by the sun. The windmills turned lazily, picking up speed as the wind blew while the sun set. As it hit the horizon, the colors intensified, and the oohs and aahs of its audience rose to a frenzy.

She'd often come to Oia with Xandros to watch the sunset. The crowds had been just as thick, the cries of delight just as fervent, and the brilliant colors threw her back to all those evenings with his powerful arms around her. With his sea-salt scent drifting over her, she understood he'd wanted to come here now for all the memories they'd left behind. Memories of magnificent sunsets, of their lovemaking, their laughter, their love for each other.

She imagined that the Santorini sunset, with its brilliant colors from yellow to orange to pink to purple to red, must be like what the northern lights were to the people in the north.

They stayed until the very last ray faded, until the fingers of light darkened into the twilight sky, until stardust sparkled on them and the man in the moon smiled.

The crowds dispersed, clogging the pathways out of Oia as if they were leaving a stadium after a Super Bowl win.

Xandros took her hand so they didn't lose each other in the throng. "I know a trick to getting out of here."

She followed him like a woman besotted or obsessed. Or both.

He entered the back gate of a packed restaurant, leaning down to her. "I know the owner. He won't mind if we slip through."

An older man, with perhaps ten years on Xandros, waved at them, and Xandros made hand signals to indicate their intentions. Yet the man came down the tiered patio, slapping Xandros on the back, then man-hugging him.

It was then that she saw them, Sienna and her new friends, Carter seated beside her.

Tamryn's gaze pierced Angela, as if she could see all her secrets. The girl pointed, skewering her like the Grim Reaper's bony finger. Carter turned then. And finally, Sienna did, her mouth an *O* of surprise, before she waved.

Angela took a step toward her, then a step back to Xandros, hissing to him, "I have to go. Talk to you tomorrow. Will you be at the café?"

As hard as she tried to get rid of him, Xandros had already picked up on the stares directed at them. "Is that your daughter?"

"Yes. I don't want her to know I had dinner with somebody else since she asked me to go with them." She threw the words at him as if yet another lie didn't matter. Pleading welled up in her eyes. "Tomorrow?"

He nodded. She thought for a moment he might try to kiss her, and she flinched away.

She left him behind without looking at his face, feeling as awful as she had the day she'd boarded that ferry thirty-one years ago, as if she was leaving pieces of herself behind. She hadn't known about Sienna then, but she knew now. And she was running from him all over again.

"Who was that?" Sienna asked.

Angela's throat was parched as she waved a hand nonchalantly behind her. "Just a man I met when I came here before. He saw me and cleared a place to watch the sunset. There were just so many people blocking my view. Amazing to see him, isn't it?" Feeling all eyes boring through her, she flushed with guilt.

"So," Tamryn said, winking exaggeratedly. "You blew off dinner with us for a sexy silver fox you used to know?"

In that moment, Angela hated the girl. It wasn't fair, it

wasn't right, but she hated her for saying aloud what everyone else was thinking.

Carter laughed, breaking the tension. "What an awesome coincidence."

He looked at Sienna, and she smiled, though Angela thought suspicion glinted in her eyes. Then her daughter asked the most innocuous question. Or maybe it wasn't. "How did you get here?"

"The bus." The lie tripped off her tongue. "It was packed with tourists."

"You should have texted me."

"I'd have come to get you," Carter added.

Angela felt yet another lie forming on her lips. "I forgot my phone back at the villa. Is that stupid or what?"

The hole she was digging got deeper and deeper.

"And then you just happened to see a friend," Tamryn added, her voice as sweet and bad for you as processed sugar. "Did you have a drink with him? Maybe dinner?"

It was ridiculous, but the excuses kept coming. How would she keep them all straight? "Actually, I was going to ask him to give me a ride back. I didn't want to get caught in the crowds at the bus stop." She glanced over her shoulder. Still talking to his friend, Xandros's gaze was as hard as diamonds.

As if he'd seen the truth.

But he couldn't have. There were four girls at the table. He couldn't know for sure which was her daughter.

Except that Sienna was a clone of his Juliana.

"We're just waiting on dessert," Carter said. "Then you can come back with us. Ride on the back of Reed's moped."

Reed's eyebrows rose a fraction before his smile widened. "Sure. No problem."

The waiter arrived with dessert and an extra chair for Angela. Taking the seat, she braved a glance at the second-tier patio.

Xandros was gone.

They drank black coffee and shared several Greek desserts. Maybe it was the delicious baklava, or the Greek donuts, maybe the custard tart drizzled with orange syrup or the almond shortbread. Angela's blood pressure finally lowered. She could breathe again. Sienna wasn't suspicious, talking excitedly about their day, the moped ride around the island, Akrotiri Lighthouse, the black sand beach, jumping off the rock into Amoudi Bay.

"And tomorrow we're visiting the ruins at Akrotiri. Do you want to come?" Sienna was excited, buoyant, her eyes bright with enthusiasm, as if her work worries had melted away. Always focused and driven, this was a totally new Sienna.

It had to be Carter Ellis's influence. Maybe it was even the beginnings of a romance.

"What time are you planning to set out?" She absolutely had to see Xandros at the café.

Tamryn, Bill, and Alyssa groaned.

"Please don't make it the crack of dawn," Jamal begged.

Carter shrugged, smiled. "Who knows with this gang? Probably not until noon. I've got to see about renting the mopeds again. Do you want your own or to ride on the back?"

"I'll ride my own."

Sienna's eyes sparked, her gaze on Carter. "Can I share again?"

"Absolutely." There was a sweetness in his smile.

Maybe they were both a little smitten. Or a lot.

At least when they returned home, there wasn't a continent, an ocean, and an engagement separating them.

Not like her and Xandros. Even if he forgave her for ditching him tonight, there was still so much to keep them apart.

18

Before saying good night by the hot tub last night, Angela had told Sienna she'd go for her morning walk and be back in plenty of time for the trip to the ancient Minoan village.

She jogged along the path to Fira, feeling frantic, until her heel slipped on a stone and she almost turned her ankle. Yet she kept to a fast clip. By the time she rushed through the café gate, she was out of breath and half afraid Xandros wouldn't be there.

But he was gorgeous in the early morning sunlight. He'd already ordered her usual coffee and *bougatsa*. The coffee refreshed her, but the sugary pastry made her stomach lurch.

And so did his first words. "Sienna is mine, isn't she, Angelika?" He said her daughter's name as if he knew her, though Angela thought she'd only mentioned it a couple of times.

The cream in her coffee curdled in her stomach.

Xandros pulled out his wallet, opened it to a fan of pictures, and pointed to one of his youngest daughter. "They could be twins."

Angela's heart jumped to her throat, choking her. Different from the one in his home, this was professionally posed, a graduation picture. It could have been Sienna's graduation photo.

There was no hiding from it, no lying, no half-truths. She shouldn't even want to lie. She nodded. "I planned to tell her on this trip. I wanted to show her the beauty of Santorini and hope she'd see how easy it is to fall in love here."

Xandros raised an eyebrow, saying softly, almost deadly, "Easy?"

Her skin flushed. She couldn't meet his eyes, gazing around the terrace café instead. Like usual at this time of the morning, it wasn't full, just two couples, each sharing a pastry, a family, three kids with their parents, getting ready for a day of sightseeing, an old man reading a book, the photographer. Eleni filled his cup as she rushed by.

Angela turned back to Xandros, his thick, wavy salt-and-pepper hair, the grooves of his face that hadn't been there when they were young but which added to his depth of character. "It was so easy to fall in love with you. Because of who you are, because of who I am, because we were meant to be together even back then."

He didn't agree or disagree. "Why didn't you tell me about her?"

She couldn't meet the drill of his gaze, closing her eyes just to start the explanation. "It was the early nineties. We barely had email. The internet was still a mystery. There was no social media. And I didn't have your phone number." They were lame excuses.

He didn't let her get away with it, his face stern, his features immovable. "You could have written me a letter. You could have flown back to Santorini and told me face to face." All of it was true.

It was time to tell the whole story.

She concentrated her gaze on her coffee, hating herself for not being able to meet his eyes. "I told you about my mother. She could be so domineering, especially back then. I know I was twenty-two and I'd been to college and I was a grown-up, but it just seemed like when I got around my mother, I was a teenager again and unable to assert myself."

The explanation sounded so weak, so pathetic, even fake, but she couldn't deny him her gaze or her truth for long. It was up to him whether he felt sympathy or anger or disbelief. "I allowed my mother to undermine everything I felt for you. I take full responsibility for that. If I'd been older, more sure of myself, I never would've let that happen." Then she confessed the worst. "I let my mother make me believe you were just a beach bum who went from woman to woman, finding someone on every tour. I allowed her to make me doubt you would even show up the next year. And that if you did, you certainly wouldn't want the baby."

In his pain, the color of his eyes faded from cerulean blue to a pale imitation. "You had so little faith in me?" Hurt turned his voice harsh.

She couldn't let him think it was about him. "It was myself I had so little faith in." She put her hand to her chest. "I didn't think you could fall in love with me so easily, so quickly. I didn't think that a mere three weeks would make you mine." She reached out, letting her hand drop to the table inches from his. "Isn't that why we said we'd meet after a year, so that we'd know our true feelings by then?"

She'd had so many insecurities. He was beautiful. Women looked at him with desire glittering in their eyes. And she was just... pretty on a good day, with a decent body. She could hide the flaws with shorts and a T-shirt, but not the slight bulges when she wore her bathing suit. He had kissed her stomach, not caring that it wasn't flat. But maybe he'd done that with all women. Or maybe he'd liked that he could get her to try new things, and she'd willingly done just about anything he wanted. But those were things a man tired of when they eventually wanted someone new.

As if he'd been watching each separate emotion flicker across her face and shine from her eyes, he closed the short distance between their fingers. Taking her hand in his, he held her with his touch and his gaze. "I understand. You were afraid. You were alone. You didn't know what to do. I married the woman my parents wanted me to because I had doubts and fears as well. You and I were young. It was such a fleeting time. Could we actually make it after having known each other for only three weeks? When you didn't show up, I knew my fears were right, that I was just a vacation romance for you."

"I'm so sorry," she whispered, blinking back tears.

He gripped her fingers for a moment. "You have no need to apologize. Neither of us does. It was simply what happened. Perhaps we should have said we would write to each other. Or call. But we cannot go back or live with regret or anger. We have to move on."

She wondered exactly what moving on meant.

Xandros told her. "Yesterday on the beach, I said it wasn't our time back then. But it is our time now. I will not let doubt ruin us. I will not let what others want or think get in our way. I will not let you go again."

Her heart beat faster with each word. "I don't have any doubts about you or me. But my daughter. She doesn't know and..." She didn't finish the thought.

He sat straight. "I should be there when you tell our daughter."

Our daughter. A thrill rippled across her skin as he spoke. But she shook her head. "That's a bad idea. She's going to freak out as it is. I need to handle this. I won't put you through that. And it's not fair to her either. She doesn't know you. She still thinks Donald is her father."

After a brief silence and the slight tilt of his head as he looked at her, he asked, "Why do you need to tell her at all? Maybe it's better that we let sleeping dogs lie."

God, how she wished she could do that. Just put it all away, let her relationship with Sienna grow from this vacation on. But she couldn't. "Thank you for not pressuring me or putting a claim on her. But when you lie down with dogs, you get up with fleas."

Nodding, he obviously knew the old saying.

"That's what I did. I got into bed with Donald Walker. He'll eventually tell her, and he'll chose the time when he believes it will do the most damage. I feel that deep in my bones." Her body quaked. "The worst thing that can happen is for Donald to tell her. Sienna needs to hear it from me. She deserves that. And I owe her that."

"How did your husband even know? She looks like you. Even if I see a resemblance to my own daughter, no one else would know."

"She takes after my Mediterranean genes." She breathed deeply, the story still painful even after all these years. "Sienna was eight years old when she fell out of a tree. She was such a tomboy," she said with fondness and the love she felt in every fiber of her being. "We rushed her to the hospital, but she'd lost a lot of blood from a branch that tore her leg." She licked her lips, took a sip of coffee to wet her throat. "Donald's blood wasn't a match." She held his gaze. "What type are you?"

There was a dark pleading in his eyes, as if he needed this. "AB." He waited a beat. "Am I a match?"

Breathless, speechless, all she could do was nod. Then she told him about Donald. "He punished me for years after that, but I couldn't leave because of the children. He would have taken them both away from me."

"But why not divorce him once they were out of the house?"

"Donald always held the truth over my head. He didn't need to say it out loud, it was just always there, that he could tell, even after the kids had gone to college and started their own lives. I knew Sienna would hate me. So I stayed." She shrugged helplessly, the corners of her mouth drooping in a frown. "I thought after the divorce and his remarriage, the emotional blackmail might end. But I know it'll never stop. I can't live with that for the rest of my life. I need to get out from under Donald's thumb, and the only way is for Sienna to know the truth."

He curled his fingers around hers. So racked by guilt and regret, she'd almost forgotten his touch. "You're right," he said. "You need to be the one to tell her. My presence will only make it worse. When do you plan to do it?"

She breathed in, realizing she'd been holding her breath until she felt lightheaded. "This is what I'd like to do. The gang wants to go to the Minoan ruins at Akrotiri today. I'd like to invite you. I want you to get to know her. I already told her last night that you and I met when I was here before. I want to start off telling the truth, even if it isn't the whole truth. Let that percolate for a couple of days. Then I'll tell her."

"You want me to tour with you for two or three days?"

She learned nothing from his inflection. "Can you take the time away from work?" Then she added, "Would you want to?"

He laughed, a deep sound that made her want to feel him inside her. "I have a good staff, good family, and Niko and Juliana. And they like it when I'm not asking them questions every minute. They don't really need me."

How different he was from Donald, who had to control everything. "I'm so glad they support you that way."

He smiled wide, his teeth gleaming, his eyes bright with possibilities for the future. "Since I have a travel company, I can arrange the trip using a company van, if you'd like."

Honestly, she didn't want to share him yet. She would have been happy spending the day with him, helping him cook, floating beside him in the pool and stealing kisses until he took her to his bed.

But she had to put Sienna first.

"What do you think your children will say?" she asked softly, tentatively.

He breathed deeply, his nostrils flaring. "I don't know. But we are Greek. We take things in stride, as you Americans say. I think they'll be fine once they get used to the idea."

She could only pray it would happen that way. She had enough to worry about with Sienna's reaction.

HE DROVE HER BACK TO HER VILLA ON THE QUAD BIKE, AND as he watched her bound down the stairs to tell their daughter and her friends about the change in plans, he wanted to run after her, as if once she was out of sight, he might never see her again.

He could castigate her for not telling him about Sienna. He could even hate her. For a moment in that restaurant last night—after they'd made love in his house, after he'd held her against him as they watched the sunset, after they'd shared so much, yet nothing at all—he'd seen her daughter, *his* daughter, and he had hated Angelika. He'd wanted to shake her and make her tell him why she'd kept his daughter from him.

And yet, understanding hadn't taken long to come to him. They'd both been kids. He was three years older than her, twenty-five, but he hadn't been the man he'd thought he was. He should have written her, should have flown to her. Instead, he'd become engaged to another woman without ever going to Angelika. And if she'd told him she was having a baby?

He didn't know what the young man he'd been would have done.

So who bore more blame?

He had a daughter he'd never known. The realization filled him with as much sadness as it did joy. He wondered if she'd ever want to know him.

But he was no longer a young man. He no longer had the same fears. And no matter what happened with their daughter, no matter how she took the news, he was never letting Angelika leave him again.

"That's an awesome idea," Carter agreed when her mom said she'd like to invite a friend.

Sienna's stomach sank, yet she said, "Great." She'd been looking forward to another day wrapped around Carter on the moped, not a day spent with her mother's new flame.

But that was mean. Mom deserved some happiness.

The others cheered.

Except Tamryn, who muttered under her breath, "Who is this guy anyway?"

Mom had returned from her walk with the news that she'd found a way they could all get to the Minoan ruins without having to rent mopeds.

"Remember I said I knew the man I was with last night at sunset?" She didn't wait for an answer, but rushed on. "Well, he was our tour guide on my previous trip."

Irena waggled her eyebrows like a lecherous old man. "Ooh, your tour guide."

She felt Carter staring at her mom.

"And now he owns that company, Exotic Adventure Travels."

Carter whistled. "They're the tour group we used for the catamaran. That's also who I've rented the mopeds from. I'd say he's far from *just* a tour guide."

Her mother blushed, as if she was proud that she'd known the man when he was on his way up. Now he was probably as rich as Croesus. Or was it Midas? Sienna couldn't remember.

A bus. Old ruins. Sienna was planning. She'd find a way to be close to Carter. No problem.

Tamryn was the only one harrumphing like an old woman.

Xandros Daskalakis arrived at eleven-thirty, driving an air-conditioned bus. He was tall, maybe six-three, and handsome for an older man, a silver fox like Tamryn said. Sienna had to admit it was nice to have a ride out of the heat and dust. Even Tamryn seemed mollified.

Mom sat in the seat behind Xandros, pointing out the front window, and listening to his tour monologue.

Sienna snagged the back row next to Carter, her thigh pressed to the warmth of his. It was crazy the way her heart pitter-pattered like an old spinster from a vintage movie.

He leaned close to say, "Your mom looks excited. Happy."

She didn't want to think about her mother's happiness, however deserved. She wanted to concentrate on last night, sitting in the hot tub with the gang after Mom went to bed. Carter had been glued to her side. He insisted Tamryn was just a friend, that they were all friends. And none of them seemed to partner with anyone, at least not in a sexual sense, though the girls hung on the guys, whispered with them, followed them inside to refresh the drinks. But they were a gang, not couples.

Still, Sienna couldn't help but wonder about Tamryn. She looked at Carter with what Sienna could only call a hungry gaze, as if she wanted to eat him up. And she often caught Tamryn looking at her with narrowed eyes.

But on the bus, Carter sat down next to Sienna, not the other way round. "Since your mom's been divorced for a year, it's nice to see her have a little fun."

She wondered why he was feeling her out about her mother. Maybe he wanted to see if she was one of those kids who begrudged their parents a new relationship after a breakup. Sienna didn't. "My dad's getting remarried. And Mom deserves whatever happiness she can find."

It was odd how suddenly that had become the truth for Sienna. She'd resented her mother for so long that bitterness became ingrained.

But somehow, on this trip—or even earlier, when her dad had sabotaged her life—Sienna was finding empathy for her mother, who'd always been the bad guy. But now Sienna saw that Dad had often set Mom up, playing the children off against her.

She admitted as much to Carter. "I don't think she had it easy with Dad. It was probably never a great marriage. So if she can have a little fun on a holiday, more power to her."

Carter laced his fingers through hers, caressed her thumb, and she knew that's how he'd hoped she'd feel.

They bumped along the road—Santorini didn't have highways—and took the curves, swaying with the bus. Sometimes Xandros pulled off when a fast-moving car wanted by, waving them on, smiling. Even if she'd rather listen to Carter, Xandros was interesting, telling them about the history of the island, pointing out the sights through the windows.

Then they rattled into the car park. It was probably later in the day than most people came out here. Tourists didn't sleep in, they started early to beat the heat. The lot was almost full, with reserved spots marked for Exotic Adventure Travels. One of those was open, and Xandros expertly wheeled in.

Climbing out, Xandros helped the ladies down like a practiced tour guide. The day was hot, the sun beating down and the wind whipping dirt across the lot. She was glad they hadn't come in July or August, the hottest, windiest, and most crowded months on Santorini.

He smiled as he helped her out of the bus. "I've got our tickets." He fanned them out.

When Carter opened his mouth to protest, Xandros said, "I get them at a fraction of the cost."

They approached the low-slung building as Xandros explained, "We had to enclose the ruins to preserve them from the winds and the hot Santorini sun. Buried for 3600 years and discovered in the 1800s, they weren't excavated properly until the 1960s. And yet, after only a few decades, they were crumbling with the heat and the feet of so many tourists. Now, with the walkways above the site, you can enjoy, but we still preserve the archeological find for future generations."

Tamryn leaned in and snorted at Carter. "He really is a tour guide," she said with disdain.

Carter shushed her in a singsong voice. "Don't be a bitch."

Tamryn grumbled, but said nothing about Carter calling her a bitch. Maybe she was used to it. Probably because she got bitchy a lot.

The building was temperature-controlled, and rows of skylights bathed the ruins in natural light. Raised walkways and platforms allowed a good view without wear on the ancient stones. Like any good tour guide, Xandros related tidbits about the site, the ancient Minoans, and the eruption that destroyed them and created Santorini. He described how the 1956 earthquake once again played havoc with the ruins.

He wasn't annoying or intrusive, giving them the bare facts, then letting them wander as they liked to read the informational placards, only answering questions or explaining when he was asked.

Sometimes she caught him looking at her, and he'd smile. She wondered what her mother had told him about her.

Tamryn soon became bored. "It's just a bunch of rubble," she groused. At least Xandros was at the next platform with Sienna's mom and couldn't hear the dis to his beloved island.

"Uh, that's what the word *ruins* means." Reed punctuated with an eye roll, and Tamryn elbowed him, though a friendly smile lit up her face.

"It's interesting," Irene said. "This place is sort of mystical, don't you think?"

Carter read aloud from an interpretive sign describing some of the artifacts uncovered, amazing frescoes, evidence of underfloor heating and hot and cold running water, and even an ancient toilet.

"How fascinating," Tamryn drawled. "That's what I came to Santorini for, to learn about ancient toilets."

Unoffended, Carter let the others wander ahead, and Sienna stayed with him.

He pointed once again to the interpretive sign. "They found nothing indicating remains like they discovered in Pompeii. And only one gold object. So these guys must have been able to get out before the eruption."

"That's pretty cool."

Sienna gazed out over the ruins. It was good to know people hadn't died here. Yes, it was rubble, but it was intriguing to see the way the village had been a community, walkways, houses with doors and windows. Some walls were just a few stones, others taller than she was, but she could make out the outlines of the village, and it allowed her to imagine all the lives lived thousands of years ago.

There were signs of current excavations, ladders, wooden scaffolding, and tunnels as if they were digging deeper. It would have been incredible to walk down the stairs and wander through the ruins themselves, but she understood the irreparable damage so many tourists would cause.

She glanced at her mom standing beside Xandros on the next platform, reading another of the interpretive signs. They never touched, never even walked that close together, and yet there was something in the way her mom looked at him. Sienna shivered before she could even think the word *desire*. There was definitely something there in the way Xandros looked at her too, as if he was controlling the number of times he glanced her way so no one else would notice.

But Sienna noticed. And she wondered exactly what was happening between the two of them.

19

Making the rounds faster than the rest of them, Reed, Jamal, and Tamryn were talking and laughing amongst themselves on the opposite side. Sienna had the odd sensation they were laughing at her. Or maybe she was imagining things, and her suspicion stemmed only from Tamryn's antipathy.

Carter caught up with Xandros and peppered him with questions. "What other artifacts did they find?"

"In recent digs, they've uncovered bits of clothing, even burned fruit, bronze objects, beads from necklaces, as well as a lot of black and white pottery shards they believe were part of a Minoan burial site. And of course, they discovered wine casks." He spread his arms. "So we know the people of Santorini have been making and enjoying wine for thousands of years."

Carter listened, fascinated. He seemed more mature, even though he was only a year younger than Sienna. He was the grown up versus his friends' college-age ways.

"Due to the eruption, the frescoes are among the most well-preserved examples from the period," Xandros told them. "A thick layer of pumice and ash kept them virtually intact. We can visit the museum in Fira where you can see many of the artifacts that have been found."

They spent another half hour wandering through the exhibits, reading all the signs. Alyssa, Irene, and Bill remained with them, attentive to Xandros's comments.

He looked at Sienna often, smiling with their eyes met. She wondered if he was trying to ingratiate himself with her, hoping she'd put in a good word with Mom.

Once the tour was over, her mother took that same seat behind Xandros, as if she couldn't bear to be too far away from him. Sienna could have sat with her and learned more tidbits about the island, but she headed to the last seat, crossing fingers Carter would sit with her.

She had to laugh at herself, because who was acting college-age now, or even high school? A grown up would simply have taken the seat beside him. But she was playing silly games, waiting to see if Carter sought her out.

And he did.

Once the bus was rolling, he leaned close to say, "He's actually pretty cool." He jutted his chin at Xandros at the front of the bus. "They make a good couple."

"They certainly seem to have eyes for each other." She prodded him in the ribs.

He nodded, still looking ahead. "Does it bother you?"

They'd discussed her parents' marriage, and she'd admitted her mother deserved something better. And yet she said, "I'm not sure. I mean, we were supposed to take this vacation together."

Carter looked at her, and she felt forced to return his gaze. "Yet you're spending most of your time with us."

She nodded, turning to her mother again. "Maybe it's okay. I think we're both having a good time."

Carter nudged her. "You *think*?"

She bumped his shoulder, glad they were at the back of the bus so Tamryn couldn't send her dirty looks. "I *know* I'm having a fabulous time."

They trundled along a winding, dusty road when Xandros called out, "How about a late lunch?" He didn't use the microphone, as if he didn't want them to feel like they were on a tour. "I know a great place near Thera. And afterwards we can mosey around the ancient ruins there. Our tickets for Akrotiri will get us in there as well."

Mosey? It wasn't a Greek word. It wasn't even a modern word. He was dating himself. Or maybe it said something about the time he'd known her mother way back when. And how close they'd been.

Everyone called out agreement, punched the air, the guys getting in a rounding huzzah.

Thirty minutes later found them all seated around a large table, a trellis above them threaded with blooming bougainvillea that shaded them from the afternoon sun. Xandros obviously knew the proprietor as they slapped each other's back in big man hugs, laughing boisterously.

He ordered a feast of Greek delicacies, starting with deep-fried calamari and Greek salad, followed by traditional foods from dolmades, the stuffed grape leaves, to souvlaki, skewers of lamb and beef, to moussaka, the spicy eggplant lasagna. Tzatziki with toasted pitas accompanied the meal. To drink, he ordered retsina wine, because it was very Greek, he said, and Greek beer.

"What about ouzo?" Bill asked.

Xandros guffawed. "You do not want ouzo during the day unless you're very used to drinking it."

He made sure to seat her mother on his left, with Sienna on his right and Carter next to her. Between breaks in the courses served, he asked her questions as if he was really interested. "Your mother tells me you're a financial advisor."

She wondered when the two of them had talked about it. "I've actually got an interview at a new firm when I get back, and if I get the job, I'd like to think that my clients will come with me. They're more geriatric," she explained, hoping he didn't think that was a dig at his age. "Many of my clients aren't tech savvy, especially the widows, and I like helping them." She grinned. "I've also come across those who are far more knowledgeable than I am, and they teach me a few computer tricks."

Carter put his hand on her leg, sending a shiver through her. Xandros asked him questions as well, and the lunch was lively with talk and shared histories. By the end, she liked the older man. If her mother wanted a flirtation on this vacation, Sienna was fine with that. It gave her time for her own flirtation.

A bill for the meal never arrived, Xandros once again taking care of it. When Carter protested, he said, "The proprietor is an old friend of mine. I send many tour groups here. He is charging us only what it cost him, and it is my pleasure to treat all of you."

Everyone thanked him, even Tamryn, who gave him a hug.

They walked the streets, stopping to look at the touristy offerings. Sienna bought a royal blue and yellow scarf that would remind her of the holiday. Carter purchased a scarf for his mom, and the girls loaded up on tchotchkes, especially since Xandros got them good deals in the shops. Even the guys succumbed to Santorini key chains.

In the same shop she'd bought the scarf, Sienna looped her arm through her mother's. "That's pretty," she said of the blue blouse Mom was eyeing. "You should get it."

"You think so?"

She hadn't given her mom the time of day since she was eight years old. She'd punished Mom for the way Dad had acted. It was only in the last few weeks that she'd realized her father might be the villain of the story. Maybe it was long past time to be kind.

"The Santorini blue complements your coloring," Sienna said. "Xandros will like it on you." Her words were tacit permission to have that flirtation with the handsome Greek.

She was unprepared for Mom's broad smile and the mistiness in her eyes, as if Sienna had just given her the greatest gift. "I'm so glad you think so. Thank you."

Sienna felt as if she'd finally done something nice for her mother, something long deserved.

THE DAY HAD BEEN BEYOND ANGELA'S WILDEST DREAMS. Xandros treated them all to Akrotiri, then that fabulous meal, a tour of the ancient ruins at Thera, and finally the museum housing many Akrotiri artifacts.

When he finally dropped the group off outside the villa, she stepped back onto the bus to say goodbye after the others had exited.

"Would you like a winery tour tomorrow?" he asked.

"That would be wonderful. I'll check with everyone." He said nothing else, and she wondered if he was waiting for an invitation. "I'd invite you in, but I'm worried about what they'll think. At least until I'm ready to talk to Sienna." She touched his arm. "Is that okay?"

He nodded, his beautiful smile doing things to her insides. "It's okay, as long as you meet me for coffee before the tour. I want some alone time." He'd been around enough Americans to know the sayings.

"Absolutely."

Glancing at the stairs leading down to their villas, she made sure the others had disappeared. Then she cupped his cheek, leaning in for a kiss, savoring his taste, his scent, the feel of his skin beneath her palm. His tongue flitted into her mouth, his mustache soft against her, reminding her of the hours they'd spent pleasuring each other yesterday.

"Tomorrow," was the last thing he said before she climbed off the bus and he motored away.

She and Sienna had dinner with Carter and his group, and Angela brought food up from their fridge, not wanting it to go to waste. She ate lightly, a salad, after the big lunch.

Tamryn batted her eyelashes. "Xandros is totally dishy, Angela. You work fast," she said with what Angela thought might be a sneer.

"It was just the surprise of seeing him after we'd met when I was here before." That didn't truly explain why he was taking them on tours and treating them to delicious meals. "Xandros wondered if we'd like to go wine tasting tomorrow. He can reserve another bus."

"Way cool." Irene and Alyssa were ecstatic.

"You're amazing," Carter said. "Finding us the perfect tour guide."

From her seat beside Carter, Sienna looked at her with an unreadable expression. Then she smiled. "I'd love it, Mom."

Angela savored the infrequent use of *Mom*, just as she'd savored Sienna's opinion on the blouse she'd bought, especially that Xandros would like it. It had smacked of approval.

"It's nice that you've found someone your age to hang out with," Sienna said, and Angela felt the jibe before her daughter rushed on. "He knows all the places to go to. You couldn't have found a nicer guy."

"I'm tired of sitting on buses," Tamryn said huffily. "We've hardly had any beach time this week. I want some sunbathing."

Carter snorted. "Hitting the beaches was all we did the first two weeks we were here."

Bill boomed out. "You're giving up wine tasting? Are you nuts?"

Jamal and Reed shot their fists in the air with a rousing huzzah. "Count us in."

They shamed Tamryn into going on the jaunt. Angela almost told her to forget it. She was pretty sure the girl's antagonism was jealousy of Carter's attention to Sienna.

The group decided on another late start at eleven o'clock, and when someone suggested a turn in the hot tub, Angela finally excused herself.

"I'm not as young as you," she said with a smile when Carter protested.

"I'll be quiet when I come in," Sienna said, making it clear she was staying.

Angela laughed. "No one can be quiet after margaritas." Carter was already making them.

Though she was tired, she wanted to call Xandros and let him know the time for tomorrow. She wanted to hear his voice, calling him after climbing into her bed.

"They're not an early bunch," she told him.

His deep, thrilling voice sent shivers through her. "Eleven is good. It will give me time to make a few calls after our coffee." Then he added in a soft, delicious tone, "Come early."

"Thank you for today. They loved it." She'd loved it all, walking beside him, eating next to him, remembering how they used to feed each other morsels of food when they were young.

"It was my *pleasure* to show you." He emphasized the word, meaning so much more than the tour. "I wish you were here now."

"I wish I was too."

He murmured so sensually that she felt as if he'd run his

fingertips across her skin, "I could come down and pick you up. No one would ever know."

God, how she wanted it. But... "Sienna usually peeks in when she returns. I can't risk the bed being empty."

"Alas, my bed is so empty."

There was more talk, not actual phone sex, just desires to spend more time together. The call left her feeling delightfully sexual in a way she hadn't for years.

WHEN SIENNA SAW HER MOTHER WAS AWAKE, SHE PERCHED on the edge of the bed. "I like Xandros," she said, her gaze a little blurred, her brain slightly fuzzy.

"I like Carter too." Her mother touched her hand.

They weren't touchy-feely, but this was nice. "It's just a vacation thing." She tucked her hair behind her ear, nervous even though she didn't know why she should be.

"But he's in San Jose. If you wanted..." Mom didn't finish, but the suggestion was there.

"I'm too busy with work." But what would it be like? She felt a giddy thrill in her stomach, even if it was impossible. She had to be satisfied with what she had now. "Do you like Xandros?"

Her mom blinked, looked up at the ceiling, as if the answer was written there. "I like him very much."

"Did you like him when you knew him before?"

Her mother blushed, the lamplight highlighting her pinkened skin. "I did back then too."

"But he lives out here and you're back home. Could it turn into something more?"

Her mother's smile lit up her face. "I chiseled your father out of a very nice settlement. If I want to come back, I can even fly first class again."

Sienna giggled, her hand over her mouth. "It's like a long-distance booty call, you naughty woman."

Mom laughed with her. "We'll have to see." But her smile was sweet, almost secretive, as if they'd already had a booty call and that's why they'd watched the sunrise together. Maybe Mom was having a holiday fling.

It didn't bother Sienna the way she'd thought it might. Her relationship with her mother was changing.

She'd never had a mother she could talk to. She'd only had her aunt.

Maybe it was time to give Mom a chance.

X andros was great, Sienna decided. He arrived the next day around eleven for wine tasting, and Mom turned all pink-cheeked, like a woman entranced. She wore the blue blouse and basked in Xandros's compliments.

"I really don't mind if she has a fling while we're here," Sienna told Carter as they sat together on the bus.

Xandros's smile was wide, his gaze flashing often in her mother's direction in the rearview mirror. He never truly stopped looking at her mom. Except when he smiled at Sienna as if he was asking permission for something.

"Are you just trying to convince yourself?" Carter wanted to know.

"I mean it. We had a nice talk about it last night. They might even see each other again after the trip is over."

"Good." He stroked her thigh. She liked the way he touched her intimately, as if they were an item, though they hadn't even kissed yet. What were they waiting for?

The wines they tasted were amazing, and so were the vineyards, the vines coiled on the ground like woven baskets, a growing method that protected the vines from the wind and heat.

They tried mostly whites, because the majority of grapes grown here were white, but there were reds. And retsina, of course, which was fermented with pine resin that left behind its unique aroma. She found it overpowering, preferring the sweet dessert wine, *Vinsanto*.

Xandros chose wineries off the main cruise route so there were fewer people. The tastings were no less delicious. Well known to the proprietors, they gave him the red-carpet treatment with a variety of appetizers and flights of wine.

Sienna was tipsy by the time it was over, but she'd had fun. On the return trip, with her head on Carter's shoulder, the sway of the bus and the warmth of his body lulled her.

Xandros kept up the tour guide gig the following day, taking them on a catamaran to Nea Kameni, a small island created by the volcano itself, its last eruption back in 1950.

Birds roosted on the rocks as they landed at a small wooden dock. Tamryn whined that she hadn't brought appropriate footwear for hiking, and Xandros climbed back onto the catamaran, reappearing with a pair of shoes that fit.

Tamryn's favorite pastimes seemed to be complaining or creating drama.

Lava rocks rimmed the cemented path along with scrub and grasses dried brown in the sun. Wind whipped through trees that looked like little more than tall, thick weeds. The path changed to steps as the group climbed, then finally to gravel.

It was a good hike, though not strenuous. Her mother enjoyed it as well, taking the hills faster than the rest of them, right alongside Xandros.

Finally, they gazed down into the crater that had formed as the magma cooled, Carter reading all the interpretive signs while Tamryn and the guys sat in the shade of a picnic structure.

She'd thought that was the top, but Xandros waved them on. "There is more," he called, leading them along the rim. Several benches had been erected beneath umbrellas for those who needed to escape the sun.

Santorini and the blue water came into view. She stopped to take pictures while her mom trudged on with Xandros, Carter not far behind. The higher they went, the windier it got, until it was almost a struggle to walk, but the panorama was stunning.

Trails crisscrossed the crater, smoke and sulfur fumes rising out of the ground.

"The vents are called fumaroles." Xandros had them squat to touch the ground. "Feel the heat coming from below."

The volcanic earth was warm to the touch. The island was like walking on the surface of the moon.

She murmured to Carter, "I've definitely decided that instead of working out in the gym, I'm going for a hike every day during my lunch hour."

He laughed, not at her, but with her. "What about your high heels and skirts?"

She shrugged. "I change to work out in the gym. I'll do the same for a hike. There's a trail by the Presidio." It was where she'd seen Mr. Smithfield that day. "I don't get there often enough." She pumped a fist in the air. "But now it's a priority. And I also plan to do some hills."

Carter pulled her in and kissed the top of her head. "You go, girl."

She liked how easy they were together. Wasn't that the better way, friends first?

They headed back to the catamaran for a light lunch and the cruise to the hot springs.

When they arrived, tourists already packed the small bay.

"A hazard of Santorini," Xandros commiserated. "Tourists everywhere." Though tourists were his company's mainstay.

The water bore a reddish tinge due to the hot springs emanating from the volcano. They all stripped down to swimsuits and dove in.

Sienna came up ready to squeal. "It's a lot cooler than I thought. Where's the hot in hot springs?"

Xandros bobbed in the water beside her mother. "We must get closer to shore." He swam with a powerful stroke.

Once they hit the warm flow, it was wonderful, despite the crowd. They splashed and played and floated for at least an hour before Xandros herded them back to the boat.

Over dinner that night, he tagged along, seating himself next to her mother. "What can I arrange for you all tomorrow?"

Tamryn was the first to whine her opinion. "I want a beach day. I'm tired of ruins and volcanoes and hiking."

Sienna realized Carter had kicked Tamryn under the table when she squeaked, but she didn't apologize for her rudeness. "What Tamryn means," Carter interpreted, "is that we appreciate all the tours you've given us, but tomorrow is our last full day on Santorini and swimming and relaxing in the sun would be super."

Tomorrow was their last day? All right, Sienna had known that from the beginning, but she'd put it out of her mind, letting herself imagine this vacation with Carter could go on and on.

The sparkle in Xandros's eye showed he wasn't offended at the rejection. "We all need a beach day, especially since you're so close to the end of your holiday. If you go to the black sand beach at Períssa or Perivolos, you'll find shops and cafés, beach bars and restaurants. I can arrange for mopeds to get you down there."

"That's nice of you, Xandros," Carter said.

"Aren't you coming with us?" Sienna asked, looking at her mother. Was it terrible that she didn't want Xandros or her mother along? She wanted Carter to herself on this last day.

Xandros declined with an elegant shrug. "Paperwork and phone calls to catch up on."

On the heels of that, her mother said, "I think I'll walk to Skaros Rock."

With a lift of one eyebrow and a smirk, Tamryn asked, "Didn't you see everything when you were here before?"

Mom smiled as if she didn't hear the snide edge. "That was thirty years ago. I'd like to see it all again." She and Xandros exchanged a look, and Sienna was sure that no pictures of Skaros Rock would be taken tomorrow.

As if he followed her train of thought, Carter squeezed her hand. "It's sweet," he murmured in her ear.

And it meant she could spend the day with Carter.

AT THE CAFÉ THE NEXT MORNING, ANGELA THREW HERSELF at Xandros. "Thank you for having the mopeds delivered last night. Now they can go whenever they want."

He held her tight. "And we can do as we please."

She felt giddy enough to giggle. "Do you want to see Skaros Rock?"

His mustache twitched. "Absolutely not." Nuzzling her ear, he whispered, "I have bigger plans for you today."

"I'm looking forward to something huge," she said with a laugh.

His answering chuckle vibrated through her. "Are you talking about sex, naughty woman?"

They sat down, and Angela leaned over the table to say, "Are you up to it?"

He grinned. "Definitely. Drink your coffee, then you—" He leaned in for a kiss. "—are all mine."

It was the most delectable day she'd known in thirty years. The first day she'd returned to Xandros had been amazing, but they filled today with long, lazy bouts of lovemaking, extraordinary food, lounging by the pool, playing in the water, then doing it all over again.

In a bedroom, he found a swimsuit that fit her, even if it was skimpier than she was used to. The back plunged and see-through lace ran down the center, reaching almost to her belly button. She'd slathered sunblock all over, and he climbed on top of her on the lounger, the sun beating down on them, their skin sliding deliciously together.

"Are you afraid of helicopters?" he asked.

She let out a laugh that didn't make a sound. "You want to take me for a helicopter ride?"

He shook his head, slowly, then bent to kiss her, his taste luscious with the rum drink he'd made them both. "I meant helicopters flying overhead." He marked her with a love bite. "I want to make you cry out right in this spot."

Her skin heated far beyond the temperature of the sun. He could seduce her so easily. "What exactly do you have in mind?"

"This." He kissed his way down her throat, slipped her swimsuit straps down her arms. He licked and lightly pinched her breasts, bringing her nipples to hard peaks. The pull of desire reached straight to her center as he kissed all the way to her belly, dragging the suit with him. She held up her leg, and he tugged it off, letting it hang from one knee. Then he spread her legs with his strong, warm palms and feasted on her.

If a helicopter flew over, she never heard it as she threw her head back and clasped him hard between her thighs. His tongue was like liquid gold, heating her up to a fever pitch with the slow roll of his fingers inside her. She cried out, shook and shimmied and shivered until her voice rose to a wail, her climax shooting through her body.

She was naked in the open air, and she didn't care. When he crawled back up her body, she rolled with him, shaking the bathing suit off and sitting astride him. He played with her breasts, and she went to the tie of his swim trunks. He was rigid as she palmed him, then she shoved the trunks down his legs.

"How old did you say you were?" she asked with a twinkle in her eye.

"Fifty-six."

She took him in her mouth, all the way down and slowly back up. "You must have popped Viagra when I wasn't looking."

His belly laugh made his stomach muscles tremble. "Around you, I don't need any help."

He'd certainly demonstrated that over and over.

She took him again, just the tip, until he groaned and all his laughter fell away. He tangled his fingers in her hair, and she reached below to squeeze him the way he liked.

She made love to him with her mouth and her tongue and sometimes the slight graze of her teeth or a squeeze of her hand. When he was close, she backed off, bringing him down, prolonging the seductive tease.

Until finally he held her head in his hands, showing her the rhythm he craved. He squeezed his legs tight around her as his body shook. Then he filled her mouth, a low groan falling from his lips.

She didn't let him go until he latched onto her arms and pulled her up. "Enough. Can't take anymore. Too damn good."

She crawled up his body, lying flat on him, breast to chest. He kissed her then, sharing his taste on her tongue and lips.

"I may be crazy," he said softly, sweetly. "But I love you. I never stopped loving you. And I won't let this end, no matter how we have to manage it."

"I love you so much, Xandros. I don't care if we can only see each other a couple of times a year. I'll take whatever I can get."

He trapped her face in his hands. "Twice a year will never be enough. Maybe you will be here six months, and I come to you six months. It doesn't matter. We will make it work."

Reality washed over her, bringing goose bumps to her skin despite the heat. "I still need to tell Sienna about you before we plan anything."

"When?" he whispered.

She took a deep breath, held it, drew on all her courage. "Tonight."

The thought made her queasy, but it had to be done. She couldn't wait until they got home. After the stunt Donald had pulled, sabotaging Sienna's interview, when he learned that she still planned on Smithfield and Vine rather than taking a job with him, he would rain down retribution on them both.

Xandros pulled her close for a tight hug.

Her heart and her soul shouted that he was right. They would never be parted again.

PERÍSSA BEACH, WITH ITS COARSE BLACK SAND, WAS everything Xandros had said. Cafés and tavernas and restaurants abounded. They rented loungers and ordered drinks from a beach bar. The sun was hot and the water deliciously cool.

Carter had taken the lounger next to hers and helped her slather on sunblock. She willingly smoothed it all over him, loving the feel of his skin beneath her fingertips. When the sun became too much, they took a walk, and she snapped photos of their footprints in the black sand, the rows of colorful sunbathers, a lone towel on the beach with someone's hat sitting atop it, a blue-domed church gleaming in the distance.

They headed back to their loungers, and as she lay next to Carter, he curled his hand around hers. "It was the biggest stroke of luck that you and your mom were staying in the villa below ours."

She smiled, her eyes crinkling against the blaze of the sun. "You're just happy we got a tour guide all to ourselves."

His laugh was soft, seductive. She loved the way Carter laughed. He wasn't loud and rowdy, but toned down in everything he did. And she liked that. She liked that they could sit in the background with no one bothering them while the others shouted and laughed in the sea, body surfing, throwing each other into the waves. Not that Carter didn't like to share in the fun as well, but he was understated, more like her.

Still chuckling, he teased her. "You just like me for my hot tub."

He would be gone tomorrow. She didn't know if she could stand it all alone with just her mom. Not that she wouldn't have a good time, but she craved the jolt she felt with Carter. Leaning over the armrests between them, she kissed his cheek. "I adore your hot tub."

But when she would have flopped back on her lounger, he cupped her nape, holding her there. "I'm going to kiss you, Sienna Walker. Is that all right with you?"

"Do men even ask anymore?"

"I do."

She answered softly, "Yes, you may kiss me."

His kiss was soft and sweet and closed-mouthed. Until he licked the seam of her lips, and she opened to him, touching her tongue to his, testing him, tasting him. It was slow and honeyed, just the way a first kiss should be, lingering, a silent conversation, getting to know each other.

When he backed off to look at her, he sighed. "Way better than I imagined."

Would he call her when they were back home? She wanted to ask. She was thirty years old, a year older than him, and she should be able to ask. But somehow, she couldn't.

He grabbed her hand. "Let's dive in." Hauling her up, he ran with her into the sea.

They played like his friends, splashing each other and rolling with the waves as Sienna's body grew accustomed to the water. Someone said the sea would be warmer in July, August, and September, and while she certainly wouldn't call it cold now, she enjoyed its freshness.

They all climbed out together when Tamryn said she was starving. The guys took everyone's orders and jogged up to a restaurant along the front.

Tamryn threw herself down on Carter's lounger, and when Sienna opened her mouth to protest, Tamryn waved her off with a smirk. "I'll move when they come back." Then she flopped back, closing her eyes to soak up the sun. Without even looking at Sienna, she asked, "So, like, how old are you?"

Sienna turned her head and stared. Tamryn's eyelids didn't flicker. "Thirty," she said. What an odd question. Did Tamryn think she was too old for Carter?

"So, like, when's your birthday?"

"Why do you care?"

Tamryn cracked one eyelid. "I'm curious about everything."

Sienna still didn't see what Carter saw in Tamryn, even as a friend. But then maybe that's why Tamryn acted the way she did, because Carter was *just* a friend. She wanted more, and she didn't like that Sienna was spending so much time with him.

"March," she said.

Tamryn whispered something under her breath, then lay in silence for several minutes. Sienna thought she'd fallen asleep.

Until Tamryn speared her with a look. "So, like, when was your mother over here?"

Tamryn knew very well. Sienna's mom had said it more than once, and she didn't have to feign her frustration. "Thirty years ago."

The woman stared, unnerving Sienna. She was about to get up and find Carter when Tamryn said, "So, like, isn't it weird that you're thirty, and your mom was here thirty years ago?"

Sienna wanted to shout at her to stop prefacing everything with those words, *so, like*. And yet Tamryn was making her think. Was it exactly thirty years ago? Her mom was fifty-three, and she'd gone to Greece right after college graduation. She would have been twenty-two. Which made it thirty-one years.

Tamryn's unblinking gaze made her itchy. Her parents got married right after Mom returned from Santorini, July or thereabouts. They'd never celebrated anniversaries, so she wasn't sure of the exact date. Her parents were unsentimental about that stuff. Then she'd been born in March. Her mother had always said she was premature. But Sienna read somewhere that first-time babies were much more likely to go past the due date.

She didn't like the turn of her thoughts. She didn't like the way Tamryn eyed her. She didn't like the way her stomach churned.

Her mind feeling blurred, she counted the months on her fingers. Numbers were her thing, but she couldn't seem to make them work.

If she hadn't come early, the way her mother always said, if she was a week or two late...

She forced her mind to go quiet. She couldn't allow that thought, absolutely could not.

Until she couldn't block it any longer. If she wasn't premature, she would have been conceived in June.

When her mother was in Santorini and her father was back in the U.S.

The gyro made her want to throw up.

Sienna wanted to throw up all her hate and anger on Tamryn, as if she was to blame.

But if her fears were correct, her mother was to blame.

Beside her, Carter asked softly, "Are you okay?"

She jumped up then. She couldn't sit there, couldn't look at the food or the drinks or Tamryn or Carter's friends. Not even at Carter himself. As she marched down the beach, she thought she heard Tamryn laughing.

Carter caught up, his hand on her arm. "Sienna." Her name was his only plea.

Her voice was hushed. "My father never liked me. He always preferred my brother."

He murmured agreement. "It hurt you that he never let you go on any trips, always making them just for father and son."

"I thought he didn't like me because I was a girl, and he only wanted a boy who would take over the business. That's why I refused to work at his company." She turned, unable to see him clearly through the tears scarring her eyes. "But what if he resented *me*? And that's why he shut me and my mom out. Why everything fell apart. Because he *knew*." She put her fingers to her temples, trying to recall every detail, thinking until her head hurt.

"What are you saying, Sienna?"

She wanted to shout at him so badly that she forced her voice to barely a whisper. She didn't want Tamryn to hear her scream. "I don't think I'm my father's daughter." She pointed into the hills of Santorini, to her mother somewhere out there. To that man. "*He's* my father."

She expected Carter to wrap her in his arms, so she could pour out all the things Tamryn made her think. And Carter could tell her it wasn't true.

But he did none of those things. "Would it be so bad? You told me your dad made you feel second best. Maybe this could be good."

She backed away from him, her face rigid, as if her muscles had frozen. She wanted to run, but her feet wouldn't move. Carter closed the space between them, put his hands on her arms, said her name again, just her name.

She closed her eyes, tapped her head. "My mother was here on Santorini in June. I was born at the beginning of March. She always said I was premature. But what if I was right on time?" She opened her eyes, stared at Carter's handsome face, the mouth she'd kissed only an hour ago. "What if my dad always hated me because I wasn't his daughter?"

Carter didn't let her go, as if he was afraid she might run. "Sleep on this. Don't rush to judgment."

She thought of the look in her mother's eyes when she gazed at Xandros. About the looks he gave her mom when he didn't think anyone was watching. What if it had been far more than a flirtation on a tour all those years ago?

"I have to get out of here," she whispered.

"I'll take you back to your villa."

She shook her head, her hair flying. "I can't go back there, not after she's been with him. I can't bear to look at her."

Carter laced his fingers through hers. "You can stay with me. There's a sofa in my room. I can sleep on that. I want to be there for you."

She couldn't even thank him for his gracious offer. "I can't stay there either, in case she comes looking for me."

"Then we'll get a hotel room with two beds. I won't tell the others where we're going." He squeezed her hand. "But you have to talk to her at some point. What if it's not true?"

She looked at him, gazed into his beautiful, trustworthy eyes. "You weren't surprised when I said it. You've been thinking something too, just like Tamryn."

He muttered under his breath, a swear word that included Tamryn's name. "I don't know anything,"

"But you're suspicious."

He closed his eyes as if he couldn't handle her pain. "There was just something familiar about his face that first night." He rushed on to add, "But that sense of familiarity disappeared the more I got to know him."

"You don't have to tell me lies to save my feelings. You see him in me, don't you?"

She'd always thought her olive skin and dark curly hair came from her family. But what she'd thought was an Italian nose could be Greek. She touched it now as if she could somehow learn the truth from her face.

"Let's sleep on it," he said again. "And see your mother tomorrow."

"I never want to see her again," she said with all the venom that had grown since she was eight years old. Since her father began to hate her because of what her mother had done. "She's made her bed and now she can lie in it with *him*."

THE DAY WITH XANDROS HAD BEEN THE MOST AMAZING OF her life. They pledged themselves to each other all over again, and this time, it wouldn't end. Both divorced, they were free. They could be together now.

As soon as she told Sienna the truth.

He kissed her goodbye at the top of the villa steps. Angela didn't want to leave him, but she had to talk to Sienna. It was long past time.

He rested his forehead against hers. "No matter how hard it is, remember I love you. I have always loved you, and I will go on loving you for the rest of my life."

Tears pricked her eyes. "I love you too. I'll make it all okay." But what if she couldn't?

Before she changed her mind, she dashed down the stairs. She owed Sienna the truth.

Opening the French doors, she called out, "Hello?"

The villa was silent. She headed out the gate of her unit and opened the one to Carter's, taking the steps tentatively, her nerves getting the better of her.

They were all on the patio, drinking beer or spritzers or wine. She tried to sound bright. "How was your day?"

Sienna and Carter weren't with them.

"It was great," Tamryn said with a smile so beatific it scared Angela. The girl never smiled without a hidden meaning.

"I was looking for Sienna."

Irene waved a hand. "She went off somewhere with Carter. They didn't say when they'd be back. Did you try her phone?"

There'd been no answer. "Could you call Carter, just so I know where Sienna is?"

Tamryn clucked like an old woman. "Okay, *Mom*," she said with an annoying drawl.

Then she called Carter. At least Angela thought she did.

"Wow!" she exclaimed, eyes wide with feigned surprise. "He doesn't answer. Isn't that weird?" Her phony tone grated on Angela's nerves.

Tamryn said to the rest of them, "Did they say where they were going?"

After a lot of headshaking, Angela asked the question she was afraid of. "Did anything strange happen at the beach?"

"Not much," Tamryn said with a nonchalant shrug. "We were talking about our ages, our birthdays. Stuff like that. Come to think of it, she got all weird and ran off."

That sunset in Oia, Tamryn had pointed at her with the Grim Reaper's bony finger. Angela knew deep in her gut that Tamryn had figured it out even then. She'd been probing when she asked about birthdays.

Almost with glee, Tamryn added, "We both thought it was strange that you were here just the summer before." She finished her spritzer, smiled. "I'm getting another. Do you want one?"

She could hate this girl. Yes, she'd hated Donald, but she'd never felt quite this level of rage. Her eyes burned with it, and her body trembled.

Yet it wasn't about Tamryn. It was about what *she'd* done from the moment she left Xandros thirty-one years ago. She should have told her mother to take a flying leap. She should have walked into Donald's office and called off the wedding. She should have gotten right back on a plane and flown to Xandros. She should have trusted him. She should have believed in him.

She should have told him she was pregnant with his child.

❀

SHE CALLED HIM, TALKING IN A FRENZY HE COULD BARELY understand. It could mean only one thing. The talk with Sienna had gone badly.

"I'll be right there." He couldn't bear the weight of her tears. "Stay on the line with me so you don't feel alone." He would do anything for her. He would take the car so he could use the Bluetooth, even though parking would be harder to find. But that didn't matter. Only she did.

But she denied him. "No. I'll be okay. I'll wait for you."

She'd said those words so many years ago. She hadn't waited.

There were so many things they both should have done. None of that mattered now. They couldn't change it.

Sienna was his daughter. He and Angelika had made her together. It still amazed him, thrilled him, terrified him. He'd known of her existence only a few days, yet now, just like Angelika, she was part of him. He could never let her go.

And he would move heaven and earth to fix this.

On the quad bike, he found a space he could slide into right above her villa, and he dashed down the steps, through her open gate, laughter from Carter Ellis's patio raining down. Maybe Sienna was out there with them.

But Angelika needed him.

The French doors were wide open, and she was curled into a ball on the sofa, her face buried in her hands. He could do nothing more than stroke her arm as she cried, his heart breaking into tiny pieces.

"Tell me what happened, Angelika. I will help you."

She raised her head, her cheeks tear-stained, her makeup smudged, mascara slipping down the trail of tears. "I didn't tell her," she whispered.

He dipped his head, knowing his confusion was written all over his face.

"She figured it out sometime this afternoon. Tamryn said

they were talking about birthdays and my trip here thirty years ago."

He didn't say he'd never liked Tamryn. Something always displeased her, and she bored easily. Now she'd caused trouble the first time she'd gotten Sienna away from her mother.

He'd recognized trouble from the moment he laid eyes on her. He just hadn't known what kind of trouble. She'd done it on purpose, of course. The oldest reason in history, jealousy. She wanted Carter Ellis for herself.

But that didn't help Sienna or his Angelika. He wrapped her in his arms. "Is she upstairs with them?"

She shook her head. "She and Carter went off. I've called, but neither of them answers."

He had Carter's number. The young man had given it to him in order to make all the arrangements. But now it rang and rang while Angelika's ragged breaths ravaged his heart.

He waited five minutes, then called again, planning to leave an urgent message.

This time, the young man answered. "I appreciate the call, Xandros. But her mother needs to give Sienna time. We've taken a hotel to have some space away from the others. I'll call you when she's ready."

"Is she okay?" His heart hammered in his ears.

"Of course she's not okay." Neither of them needed to say what was wrong.

"I mean physically."

"I'll make sure nothing happens to her. But you don't have to worry about her doing anything to herself. Sienna isn't like that."

It pained him to acknowledge that he knew barely anything about her.

"Thank you. We'll wait for your call." Xandros hung up, wrapping himself around Angelika, whispering sweet nothings into her hair before he told her the situation. "She is okay, I promise. She and Carter are at a hotel. He'll keep her safe. She needs time."

Angelika turned her tear-streaked face to him. "She's going to hate me forever."

"No. She will get over it." But he wasn't so sure. He kissed the top of her head as if that could make her believe. "Have you eaten?"

She shook her head, her hair falling over her face. "I'm not hungry."

"You must eat to keep up your strength during this time."

After kissing her softly on the lips and murmuring comfort words, he left her on the sofa. The refrigerator revealed a bag of salad. Under other circumstances, he would have laughed. With all the fresh produce on Santorini, they'd bought bagged salad. He discovered fresh tomatoes and a tub of marinated olives, setting them out for salad. He found dried pasta, and with the milk, fresh cream, and scraps of cheese, he made a creamy sauce. With everything cooked and the salad prepared, he carried it all to the kitchen table.

Angelika was still curled on the sofa, and he knelt beside her, stroked her hair. "Eat." It was a soft order.

She said yet again, "I'm not hungry."

"You're exhausted. You need sustenance." He helped her to her feet, walking her to the kitchen table as if she were an old woman. Emotion and fear exhausted her, and she slumped at the table, eating as he'd ordered.

"This is good," she said, as if obligated.

They didn't talk about Sienna. They didn't talk about themselves or the emotions that had drained her completely. But they sat close, thighs touching, body warmth comforting each other.

Finally, she pushed away the half-finished plate. "I'm tired." And though the sun hadn't set, he helped her up the narrow stairs. He tugged off her shoes, toed off his own, tucked her beneath the covers, and climbed in fully clothed.

It was dark when he woke again. She'd woken long enough to undress, and he stripped down now, crawling back in beside her, sleepless. Holding her, he kissed her hair, her cheeks, her shoulder. He stroked her arms, comforting her as she slept. Until finally she turned, seeking the comfort of his lips.

He hadn't intended it, but as her need to forget grew, so did the ferocity of her kiss. Her fingers roamed his body, reaching for him, squeezing him to life and unbearable need. He rolled her to her back and slid deep inside her, holding her as she wrapped her legs around him.

Until she clutched his buttocks, urging him to move, and he stroked deep inside her. It wasn't the frenzied sex of that first afternoon or the seductive dance on the lounge chair. It was exquisitely slow lovemaking, a melding of mind and body, an attempt to soothe each other's soul. They sought oblivion, a place where there was no fear, no loss, no pain.

Her tears fell silently, sliding down her temples. He came with a grimace, she climaxed with a spasm around him, and they held each other as if neither would ever let go.

And yet their future together was in terrible jeopardy.

22

C arter had booked a room with two singles, but they lay atop the bed closest to the window. He held her tight as Sienna shivered with all the emotions she couldn't put a voice to.

This wasn't how she wanted their first night to be. The kiss on the beach had been so sweet, so full of longing and promise, and she'd dreamed of making love with him.

Now there was just this, his arms around her, his soothing kisses on her hair and forehead, the gentle stroke of his fingers along her arms, and her lacerated heart.

"She lied to me all my life." She could no longer keep in the pain.

"I know how it hurts." He didn't tell her to stop feeling, for which she was grateful.

Everything poured out. "That's why he's always hated me, why he favored Matt. He said it was my mother who kept me behind, but he was the one who didn't want me."

"Maybe he turned your mother into the bad guy so you'd blame her."

"It worked. I was always angry with her for holding me back."

"It must've been hell."

"I yearned for him to love me." She fisted her hand on Carter's chest. "I hated her for not letting him love me. And it was all her fault in a way I never imagined."

"Do you think he knew from the beginning and married her anyway?"

She lay quiet, thinking. "I don't know. When we were little, he would send Mom and me and Matthew away on vacation and only joined us on the weekends because he was working."

"But you had a good time?"

She had to think again. "We had a great time. If we went to Disneyland or SeaWorld or stayed at the beach, we always did the fun stuff during the week because he didn't want to deal with the crowds on the weekend."

"What about when you were a teenager? Did you go places? Europe maybe?"

She shook her head. "There weren't any trips like we took when we were young. He said I couldn't do this or that. I couldn't date till I was sixteen. I couldn't get my driver's license until I was eighteen. I couldn't go on school trips with my friends. But he always said my mother had made the edict."

"And you hated her for it."

She nodded, her cheek brushing the soft hair of his chest. He'd stripped down to board shorts. She wore a tank and panties, their legs entwined, comforting, healing, enticing.

"When did all the vacations stop?" he asked so softly she almost didn't hear.

In a near dreamlike state, she said. "When I was eight and fell out of the tree."

"Didn't you say they had to give you blood?"

She twined herself around him, and he wrapped her in his arms. In that gentle fantasy state, it felt almost like hypnosis. "Yes. They gave me blood."

He was silent so long that she woke up fully to the feel of him against her. To all the things he wasn't saying.

Until finally he told her. "Maybe it was the blood."

"What do you mean?"

She had to strain to hear him over revelers on the street. "Maybe they asked him to give blood, but he didn't match."

She shook her head, almost wildly, her hair tumbling over his chest, and he stroked it away from her face. "If I wasn't his blood type, they would've known all along, wouldn't they? Isn't the blood type on the birth certificate?" She couldn't remember what hers said.

"My blood type isn't on my birth certificate. I don't even know it. Do you know yours?"

She had to think a minute. "I should. But I don't." Then she murmured, "That's crazy."

"And yet it makes sense. You don't remember vacations with your father after that. And you remember being at odds with your mother since you were young."

She said softly, almost in wonder, "She ruined my life."

Carter wrapped her tight. "Maybe your father ruined your life."

"He's not my father," she said. "I don't have a father."

Donald Walker had never loved her. He'd only ever made her feel unwanted and unloved.

"He should have divorced your mother and let you both go."

"She should've divorced him." She wasn't about to give her mother the benefit of the doubt.

He cupped her cheek, tipped her chin to make her look at him. "Maybe she was between a rock and a hard place. She might have been afraid your father would take you both away from her. Maybe he even threatened to."

"Don't defend her," she hissed.

Staring into his eyes, she put her hand behind his head, pulling him close and kissing him defiantly. It wasn't the sweet, longing kiss of the afternoon. It was savage, their lips smashing, their teeth knocking. Then he opened his mouth, and she devoured him.

She didn't want to talk about her mother. She didn't want to think about her father. She didn't want to know if Xandros Daskalakis had a fling with her mother and got her pregnant. She wanted to blot out the last thirty years, the job she hated, the new firm where she faced rejection yet again.

Backing off, she muttered against his lips, "I won't fail."

Then she put her mouth on his and took command, diving into him, climbing on top of him, straddling him. She knew he wanted it. She could feel him between her legs, hard and hot. Bending down, she sucked his nipple, biting lightly until he gasped in need rather than pain. She slipped a hand inside his board shorts. Only to stop.

He was so beautiful, so full, so thick, and her mouth watered. She'd never enjoyed putting her mouth on a guy. That had always been for them; they begged, and you were supposed to give in. But now she felt the pleasure of it, hearing him groan, knowing how good she could make him feel. Wrapping her fist around him, she took him in her mouth, first the tip, then his whole crown, and finally she gave him everything. He groaned, then a growl rose from his belly, and he arched into her, quaking beneath her. She used her body to hold him on the bed. She took him the way a man took a woman, the one on top and in control and loving it.

She wasn't graceful as she slipped out of her bikini panties without letting him escape her mouth.

And when he said, his hands in her hair, "Wait, wait, I want to come inside you," she reared up, sat astride him, and buried him deep inside her,

"We don't have a condom," he hissed on an intake of breath.

It was too late. She didn't care. "I'm on the pill, and I haven't had sex since my last checkup. So I'm clean. What about you?"

"Me too," he said in a strangled voice as she tightened her muscles around him

"Then we're good," she whispered.

She took him then. Until there was nothing left but sensation. Nothing but oblivion.

And finally, there was bliss.

SHE WASN'T ASLEEP AS CARTER HELD HER, HIS FINGERS gently caressing her arm.

"Feel better?"

She shook her head. "Not really."

"It was still awesome." He kissed the top of her head. "But it wasn't how I wanted our first time to be."

"How did you want it to be?"

He rolled her slightly until they were face to face, and he cupped her cheeks in his palms. "Like this."

His kiss was gentle, sweet, and she opened to him. He delved deep, going slow. Then, still cupping her face in his hands, he kissed her ear, her cheek, the corner of her mouth, her chin, her throat. He dropped to her breasts, plumping her in his hand as he sucked the bead into his mouth. And everything inside her tightened.

The sex had been satisfying, but this was more. He slid down her body, gently pushing her to her back, spreading her legs. He kissed the scar on her thigh, rubbed his nose along it. And the mark that had always made her self-conscious suddenly became beautiful.

He put his mouth on her center, fitting his fingers inside her and stroking her gently. He learned what she liked, played his tongue over her slowly, until she was delirious.

It was so much better, so much sweeter. She thought of that old song, *Killing Me Softly*. That's what he did to her, killed her with pleasure and sweetness and caring.

The sensations were too much, a tsunami building inside her. When it crashed over her, she cried out, squeezing him tight between her legs, but even before it was over, he slid inside, all the way, hitting that perfect spot and forcing the sensations to go on and on.

Until she needed more.

Wrapping her legs around his waist, she clapped her hands on his butt and pulled him deep, forcing him to pound her deliriously hard. Until this time, the tsunami dragged them down together.

XANDROS WENT OUT EARLY FOR EGGS, BREAD, POTATOES, and tomatoes to make breakfast.

Angela was groggy with emotion even though it was past ten in the morning. They'd slept late. She called Sienna; her daughter didn't answer. She hadn't expected her to. But Carter was leaving today, which meant Sienna would have to come back to the villa at some point.

The phone rang. She grabbed it, praying it was her daughter, but it was an unknown number. She took the call anyway.

"Angela?" He said as if he wasn't sure. "It's Carter."

"Is Sienna okay?" Her heart was pounding so hard she thought it would beat right out of her chest.

"She's okay, Angela. But—"

She cut him off. "Can I talk to her? Please."

She could hear his breath as he thought about it. Finally, he said, "I wanted her to talk to you, or at least text you. But she's not ready."

The heart that seemed to beat so hard ceased altogether. She'd lost her daughter forever. The knowledge paralyzed her.

"We've changed her ticket, and she's flying home with us today. I wanted to let you know. I'm talking to her, comforting her, trying to get her to see that she at least needs to hear your side of the story."

The subtext of his words was that Sienna didn't want to hear anything her mother said. Angela was sick deep in her bones, as if a fast-growing cancer had overpowered her cells.

"When you're home, please get her to talk to me." She begged Carter to give her hope.

"She needs time, Angela."

There was no time. As soon as she got home, Sienna would go to Donald, and he'd tell her everything in the worst way possible.

"Don't let her talk to her father." She stopped herself. That was the problem. Donald wasn't her father. "Don't let her talk to Donald until I can talk to her. Please."

"I wish I could make you promises, but I can only say I'm taking care of her. I won't let her go through this alone. I'll do whatever I can to make things easier."

"Thank you for looking out for her. I know you're doing your best in the situation, but please let her know I'm so sorry. I didn't want her to find out like this."

"I'll tell her. Just give her time, Angela." Then he was gone.

She flew out of the villa and up the stairs to Carter's terrace. The cleaners were already vacuuming and mopping the floors. She was too late. They were on their way.

A brainstorm struck, and she raced to her room for her phone. She had to change her flight, catch up with them. But when she checked, there was no way she could get on a flight out of Santorini that would make the San Francisco connection in Athens.

Xandros, grocery bag in hand, caught her coming down the stairs. "What's wrong?"

She tried not to cry, but tears stole her vision. "Sienna changed her flight. She's going home with Carter, and they've already left." She held up her phone. "The flight from Santorini is already boarding, so there's no way I can get on the afternoon flight out of Athens."

Xandros dumped the bag on the table and pushed her into a chair. "Just change your Athens flight to today. I can get you there."

"How can you possibly do that? There are no flights, and the ferry will take hours."

He cupped her cheek. "I own a tour company, remember? I have helicopters and planes at my disposal."

"Oh God, Xandros." She threw her arms around his neck, hugging him tight, and whispered, "Thank you."

"I will cook breakfast while I make arrangements. Change your flight and pack your bag." He put in his earbuds, went to the kitchen, and she heard his voice amid the sound of banging pots and pans.

It was impossible to quantify how lucky she was that she'd found Xandros again, even more that he still wanted her.

Xandros arranged a helicopter to fly them both. They arrived in Athens in time for her to check in and hand over her bags.

They stood on the concourse outside the security gate. "Thank you." She cupped his face and pulled him down for a last kiss.

"I could come with you."

She'd gotten the last first-class seat. "I'll be back. I promise."

He put his finger to her lips. "No promises. We promised last time, and it didn't work."

She closed her eyes, breathed out a sigh. "Then it's not a promise. It's a knowing deep in my soul. We will be together."

He rubbed his nose down her cheek, kissed the corner of her mouth. "What if Sienna doesn't react the way you want?"

Her breath hitched. "She'll react however she reacts. She might never speak to me again. She might never want to see you. Or maybe everything will turn out perfectly. But no matter what, my feelings for you won't change. This time, nothing will get in our way."

He held her close, tightened his arms around her. She breathed in his scent and his desire as he kissed her, long, luscious, and loving. She was aware of people sidling by them to enter the security line, but she didn't care.

Finally, he let her go. "I love you. If you don't come back, I will fly over to get you."

"I love you. And I will be back." Then she smiled at him. "Although it might be nice to have you hunt me down."

"A deal."

They parted slowly, their hands entwined, their fingers lingering in each other's before they finally parted.

She repeatedly looked back as the line progressed. He watched her until she lost sight of him in the crowd.

But he was there.

And they would be together again.

23

"First class is spoiling me," Sienna said as Carter slid into the seat beside her.

"We're young. I bet we can handle economy again."

"Nothing less than premium economy." Until they delivered champagne, and she was positive she could never downgrade again.

The strange thing was that since she'd changed her flight to go home with Carter, she'd been able to stop thinking about her mother. The pain in her chest had eased. Carter even made her laugh as they studied the on-board menu.

That was another gift Carter gave her. He made her laugh so much more than she ever had, even when her life was falling apart.

Reed, Irene, Jamal, and Alyssa chose the economy section. While Carter had footed the bill for the villa, they'd all paid for their own flights.

Tamryn and Bill, however, had splurged. Perhaps they were like Carter, throwing everything into one yearly trip. Or they had enough miles to cover the upgrade.

The economy people were boarding and the rest of their group shouted cheers and jeers, shooting glares at them as they passed the first-class doorway.

Just when the commotion died down and she thought all the passengers had taken their seats, the flight attendant greeted a late arrival into first class. Sienna turned, all the oxygen sucked out of her lungs.

Her mother stood there, her gaze traveling the cabin, not seeing Sienna right away.

How the hell did she get here? Sienna hadn't let Carter call until they were already at the Santorini airport.

Everything zip-tied inside her, all her organs jerked out of place. She wasn't ready to face her mother. She thought she'd have another week. And oh God, what if her mother had brought that man with her? The situation would be untenable.

As the flight attendant showed her mom to her seat, Sienna grabbed Carter's arm. "My mother's here," she hissed. "Don't let her see me."

It was too late. Mother had already spotted her.

Sienna dug her nails into Carter's arm. "Don't switch seats with her."

He caressed her hand. "I won't do anything you don't want me to." Stroking a finger along her jaw, he leaned in for a sweet kiss she wanted to lose herself in.

That was the thing about Carter. She could lose herself with him. Was she ready for that? She had so much happening in her life. She didn't know if she could handle a relationship, not that Carter had talked about anything serious. Yet they'd only known each other a week, and he was treating her like a girlfriend, not just a girl he'd hooked up with on holiday.

Not that it mattered. Right now, he was her lifeline, her protection, her comfort.

And she clung to him.

The flight was getting close to take off as the attendant brought her mother a glass of champagne.

"I know we have to talk," Sienna said softly to Carter as if her mom could hear even rows away. "I just don't know what I'm going to say. I don't even know what I feel."

"Practice on me. Get your feelings out, whatever they are."

She rolled her lips between her teeth and bit down, feeling the tears ready to spring to her eyes. The pain of the bite pushed them away. "I'm angry. I feel duped and lied to." She looked at him, blinked, feeling something new, something that she'd never fully allowed into her head, and certainly never talked about, not even with Aunt Teresa. "I feel like I was my parents' pawn. They were both using me to get at each other."

Carter laced their fingers over the console between them. "I can see how you'd feel that in hindsight. But is it really true? A *pawn*?" He stressed the word, making a point.

"I was a pawn. I don't have to think about that. But I'm not sure if I was *her* pawn. Maybe it was just him."

She let the thought percolate as the flight attendant brought them each a bowl of warmed nuts. She crunched, the sound filling her head. Then the engines powered up, and the plane pulled away from the terminal.

Carter voiced her musings for her, something he'd already conjectured last night, but now it was more direct. "From what you said, it sounds like your father held you and your brother over her head, threatening to take you both away from her."

She shook her head. "He wouldn't have threatened to take me away. It would have been Matthew. He was the important one, the one my father groomed to take over the business."

"But you said he wanted you in the business as well."

She rolled it over in her mind before saying, "He didn't want me to go to his competitor. And he wanted to make sure I didn't turn to my mother for anything." She gripped his hand tightly. "My aunt Teresa even said something like that."

She kept the thought as the flight attendant refilled their champagne and the pilot came on to say they were next in line.

"It was when I asked Aunt Teresa why Mom didn't divorce Dad right after both Matthew and I went off to university. She said my father would never willingly give up his control."

"But he divorced your mother."

She looked at him, forgetting whether she'd told him that part of the story. "Only because he wanted Bron."

"Your soon-to-be stepmom?"

She nodded vehemently at the sudden realization. "He pushed that divorce through like lightning." She paused, thinking. "And she's pregnant. Even before the wedding."

"Wow. You'll have a half sister or brother young enough to be your own kid."

She rolled her eyes in an oh-my-God gesture.

"But don't you see? Now he's lost control of your mother."

She thought it through with her words. "Not if he's still holding me over her head. He can threaten her by saying he'll tell me and my brother. And it's worse if I'm actually working for him." She squeezed Carter's arm, feeling the flex of his muscles beneath her fingertips. "If he thinks he has complete control over me because I work for him, he can make her believe he'll hold me back, keep me down, make sure I never make it into partnership." Her voice hushed at the horrible thought. "That's why he wants me to work for him so badly. He's never tried so hard before. And he squashed that inter-view I had with Smithfield and Vine."

"If that's true, he's pretty diabolical."

"I just don't know." Then she lost her breath as the plane roared into the air. Her ears plugged, and the force of her thoughts pushed her back in her seat.

Could her father be that diabolical? Could he have been punishing her, and especially her mother, since she was eight years old?

She wanted so badly to talk to Aunt Teresa. To figure out the truth. To decide if she could forgive her mother for the lie that had lasted a lifetime.

She clutched Carter's hand for comfort and in fear of what the future held. "Right now, I don't want to have anything to do with either of them. Never again." Then the tears were unstoppable.

Even strapped in, Carter wrapped her in his arms, holding her while her tears and her anger and her fear flowed like a river.

Carter was safety. Carter was comfort.

Carter just might be everything.

ANGELA WANTED TO RUSH TO SIENNA AS SOON AS THE captain turned off the seatbelt sign. Her daughter, however, had seen her and made no move, though the discussion would have to come at some point.

The champagne tasted like cough syrup, the nuts were like bark, and the gourmet steak was as chalky as liver. Her saliva had dried up, her head ached, and she wished she'd let Xandros come with her.

But she'd created this mess over thirty years ago, and what had been a dilemma back then was now a tidal wave of gigantic proportions.

Maybe she should talk to Teresa first, figure out a plan.

She dismissed the thought immediately. Sienna was probably drawing her own battle plans. There was no way Angela could wait.

She demolished her dessert, even though she hadn't tasted a bite, and the little glass of Bailey's Irish Cream made her knees feel weak. But she went to the bathroom, scrubbing her hands in the sink as if she were Pilate trying to wash away the biggest mistake he'd ever made.

When the flight attendant knocked on the door, there was no time left. She opened, saying, "I'm sorry. I'm okay. I didn't mean to take so long."

Then she made her way down the aisle to Sienna.

EVEN THOUGH HER MOTHER WAS RIGHT THERE, LOOKING down at her, Sienna could still tell her to go away. Better yet, Carter could do it. Or she could close her eyes and pretend she was asleep.

But that was just delaying the inevitable. Procrastinating had never made things easier. It only complicated everything.

She let her mother open the discussion. "There's a small bar area up front. We could have a drink." Then she added, after a beat of hesitation, "And talk."

Carter squeezed Sienna's hand, saying softly, "I support whatever you'd like to do."

Suddenly Sienna didn't want to wait. This needed to be done, then she'd never have to speak to her mom again. Stepping past Carter into the aisle, she was inches taller than her mother. And only an inch shorter than Donald Walker. Their relative heights had never been an issue before, but now it reminded her how tall *that* man was. How she probably took after *him*.

"I'll talk," she said, trying to sound unaffected.

"Thank you." Her mother turned and led her to the bar

where a couple of guys had taken seats. Her mom sat in one of the remaining two.

The bartender brought two glasses of champagne, and Sienna wondered why he thought they had something to celebrate.

Her mother fortified herself with a sip. "I can't explain away what I did all those years ago, all the lies I've told. But this trip was about telling you the truth. Even as late as it is."

Sienna gulped the champagne. Not because she wanted it, but because she needed it. "So you planned to let me see him and figure it out. And then you wouldn't have to say it aloud?"

Her mother stiffened. "The last thing I expected was to see Xandros again." She took a breath, as if the truth she planned to tell had stolen it. "I don't expect you to understand or forgive me. But you deserve to know what happened. I should've told you years ago. And I should never have married your father."

Sienna cut her off. "But he's not my father."

Her mother swallowed, pressed her lips together, breathed in deeply. And started again.

"No, he's not. I made so many mistakes. And the biggest one was letting you live your whole life with a lie." She waited then, as if she needed permission to go on.

Sienna finally nodded. "All right, give me your spiel." The word was nasty, so was her tone, and she felt nasty. Yet she fell into her mother's tale.

"I met Donald at college. He was a senior, I was a sophomore. He was rich and everything I was supposed to marry. His father ran the premier investment house in the city. They were San Francisco elite, and that's what Nonni thought I needed."

Sienna choked out a laugh. "This wasn't a hundred years ago when women had to marry a rich man because their parents wanted them to be taken care of. It was the nineties, and you had a college degree."

"I know." Her mother nodded, closing her eyes briefly. "I was never like you. I wasn't a strong person. My mother thought teaching was an acceptable career until I got married. And I just did it." She rubbed her temples, then slid her fingers across her lids as if her eyes ached. "But you're strong, and I'm so proud of you. I never wanted to tell you what to do with your life. You needed to figure it out on your own. I didn't want you to be weak like me."

Her mother was wrong. Sienna wasn't strong. She worried all the time, fearful of the future, afraid of failure. She didn't have relationships, not because of her career the way she told everyone—and even herself—but because she was afraid of rejection. But she'd made sure no one ever knew any of that.

"Go on, she said.

"Donald and I were engaged, but I wanted one last thing of my own before I got married. A trip, something amazing. Something without Nonni hanging over me. She wanted Teresa to go, but your aunt had met your uncle, and she didn't want to leave. And I wanted to do this on my own. I wanted to prove something to myself."

Sienna could understand that. It was another reason she didn't want to work for her... for Donald Walker.

"I met Xandros on the tour. He was..." She shrugged, as if she couldn't find words to describe what she'd felt.

Sienna wondered if it was the same way she felt about Carter. That he was solid and brought her comfort, that he made her feel strong despite all her doubts.

"I just fell, hard, and there was nothing else but him. I planned to go back to him. When I got home, I was going to tell Donald I couldn't marry him, that I wouldn't fall in line with my mother's plans. I felt strong for the first time in my life."

As her mother relived the decision she'd made, Sienna saw her strength in a way she never had. "Why didn't you go back? In fact, why did you leave him at all? You could have sent your family an email, a text, called them, anything."

Her mother laughed without humor. "Because it's the kind of thing you tell people face to face. We didn't have Skype or FaceTime or Zoom. And I didn't want to start my new life being the weak person I'd always been."

What was so bad about a phone call? Sienna didn't get it. But she let her mother go on.

"Xandros and I agreed we'd meet each other at a special café on Santorini one year from the day I left. It was a kind of test for ourselves, to make sure what we felt was real. I already knew I'd never feel that way about Donald and that I couldn't marry him." She reached down to take Sienna's hand, squeezing her fingers as if they were family instead of strangers.

"But the fear settled in as soon as I got back. My mother was so busy making wedding plans. I should never have gone home first. I should've gone straight to Donald and called off the wedding. And then—" She shrugged. "—I figured out I was pregnant. It must've happened so fast on Santorini."

Sienna couldn't help herself, as cruel as it was, as unfeeling, as horrible. "So you shacked up with your tour guide the first night?"

Her mother closed her eyes, breathed in and out as she absorbed the blow. Then she looked at Sienna with such sadness and pain that it cracked the wall Sienna had built.

"It might seem like that," her mother said. "Not exactly the first night, but there was an immediate connection. I just knew. And he knew. And when it happened, it was the most beautiful night of my life." She held Sienna's gaze. "I'm never leaving him again."

Yet she was on a flight back home, and that man was still

on Santorini. Yet Sienna knew what her mother meant, and the words stole her breath. "He feels the same?"

Her mother nodded. "I never felt that way about Donald. I never stopped feeling that way about Xandros. But when I found out I was pregnant with you, all my terrible fears came back. I listened to my mother tell me he was a beach bum, and there was absolutely no way he was going to want a baby, and the best thing to do was let Donald think you were his."

Sienna recoiled. "And now you're blaming Nonni?"

Her mother shook her head. "I'm not blaming her. She thought she was doing the best thing. I blame myself for being so weak."

"But you both cooked up this lie for my father." Really, what else was she going to call Donald Walker? He'd been her father for thirty years. She couldn't shake that off so easily, even if she was angry with him.

"That's exactly what I did," her mother admitted solemnly. "I duped him. And I've been paying for that lie ever since. Now I've made you pay as well. And I am so, so sorry."

"Why didn't you just get an abortion?"

The gasp out of her mother's mouth drew stares from all directions. The horror in her eyes was unmistakable. "I wanted you with all my heart."

Did that actually make a difference? Sienna didn't know what to think, what to say. How did you live with a thirty-year-old lie? How could she ever forgive that lie? "You've stolen my father. He and I have our issues, absolutely, but now I have no one."

Her mother had the gall to say, "You have me. You have Aunt Teresa and Matthew, your cousins, your uncle, Nonni and Poppa. You have so much. All you're losing is Donald."

She said it as if Donald Walker meant nothing.

"He figured it out when I had that fall, didn't he?"

"Yes."

"They needed blood, and he didn't match."

Her mother nodded.

"That's what Carter thought. Because everything changed after that."

"That's when I ruined your life. He punished me, but he also punished you. And he's still threatening to tell you and Matthew. I wanted you to come with me on this trip so I could tell you first, before he told you in some horrible way."

"But you never banked on Xandros showing up again."

She shook her head. "I never dreamed of that."

"But you must have seen every single day how much I look like him."

"I did. And I saw how Donald always made you feel unwanted. I will live with the pain of that forever. And yet it made you the strong woman you are, a woman who knows her own mind and what she wants to do."

"Strong?" Sienna laughed. "Every day I'm second best."

Her mother rubbed her palm around Sienna's fisted hand. "You're the strongest woman I know. You've done so much. Look at all the elderly people who depend on you to make their golden years the best they can be."

"But I've never been strong enough to let a man into my life. I've been afraid of relationships."

Her mother wagged her head sadly. "I'm to blame for that. But I look at you and Carter, and I know you have the strength to let him in if you really want to."

Did she have the strength? Sienna wasn't sure. She'd push him away eventually, the way she'd always done. Afraid he'd leave her, she'd leave him first.

"He won't let you push him away."

Suddenly, as if someone had slapped her face without warning, she couldn't take anymore. She couldn't let her mother spin this fairytale of who she thought Sienna was. "You don't know me at all." That was partly her fault, but her mother's lie had started it all. "I've listened to your story, your explanation, but it doesn't change anything. I am who I am, and you are who you are, and Donald Walker isn't my father. It doesn't change my life. But at least I know. And you're free. He can't hold anything over you anymore. Except Matthew. Do you want me to tell him for you?"

It was a stab, she knew, and she wanted to hurt her mother, as terrible as that was. She wanted her mother to feel the same pain she did.

Yet all Mother did was shake her head. "It's my duty to tell him."

"Good. Let me know as soon as you have. When he needs a shoulder to cry on, I'll be there for him." It was another cruel jab, and she actually hated herself for it. But she didn't take it back. "Now, I'm going back to Carter. I need to think this through. Please don't bother me for the rest of the flight." She almost added, *and never bother me again*.

But even in this mood, she couldn't be that brutal.

Maybe it was because her mother had said she'd wanted Sienna with all her heart.

✤ 24 ✤

It seemed so natural to lay in Carter's arms after making love. He'd taken her home with him after the plane landed. His apartment was minimalist, although his TV, stereo, and computers were all state of the art. His bedroom was manly, with a big wood headboard and a walk-in closet that was less than half full. Carter wasn't a clotheshorse.

"I'm glad you listened to her." He didn't need to say he was referring to her mother. "Now that you've had time to think about it, how do you feel?"

Sienna had half the flight and the rest of the evening to think about it. But she'd made love with Carter instead. "I don't know how I feel. I may never know." She tipped her head on his shoulder. "I need to talk to my father."

Carter raised an eyebrow, and she knew what he meant.

"I'm not suddenly going to call him Donald," she said. "He's always been my father." Despite the crap he'd pulled over the last few months. She'd told Carter everything, from how much she cared about Bron and the baby to how her dad tried to cut her out of the wedding to his sabotage of the Smithfield and Vine job the first time around. She knew in her gut that those actions supported what her mother had said, that her father was controlling and threatening, that he'd emotionally blackmailed her.

But Sienna wanted his side of the story. "I need to know how he's felt all these years."

Carter kissed the top of her head. "I'm not going into the office till Wednesday. I'll come with you for support."

Her heart lurched. Carter was so good, but she had so much baggage. "I don't deserve someone like you," she whispered.

He hugged her tight. "You deserve the best of everything."

She drank in the feeling of those words. Refusing to let her go home alone after the tumultuous trip, he'd prepared a delicious dinner of chicken cacciatore. Afterward, he'd made love to her until she felt weak and sated. He was so good to her.

She didn't know how she could have thought he was a lazy loser. Carter was amazing. He was smart, funny, and caring. He was the best thing that had ever happened to her. But no matter what he said, she wasn't sure she deserved this kind of happiness.

Not that *deserve* mattered. She needed him.

She stroked his chin with gentle fingers. "Can you wait outside while I talk to him? I have to do this alone. But I'm going to need you when I'm done."

He held her tight. "I'll be wherever you need me to be. For as long as you want me."

She was afraid she would need him forever.

Though her confession to Sienna had gutted her, Angela could wallow in the pain until she'd told Matthew.

The day after her return from Santorini, she made a lunch date with her son. Though she hadn't been able to tell Sienna before she figured out the truth, she wanted Matthew to hear it from her.

They'd never been close. He never called her on a whim, never invited her to lunch, had never even shown her his condo in the city. But he didn't turn down today's invitation.

She'd chosen a posh restaurant in the city frequented by executives entertaining investors, with white tablecloths, quiet conversation, and floor-to-ceiling windows providing an amazing view of the bay. Matthew approached the table wearing an expensive pinstripe suit. He was only twenty-eight, but he looked every bit the confident businessman. Her heart melted for him, and because he, like Sienna, would probably never want to see her again.

She couldn't let that stop her.

He bent to give her cheek a perfunctory kiss, like he always did.

"You look wonderful, darling." She tried to sound as if she hadn't a care in the world.

"Santorini seems to have suited you." He reached out, but didn't touch her, taking the seat opposite. "You got a lot of nice sun." He didn't mention that she was back early. He probably wasn't aware when she and Sienna would return.

The waiter took their orders, and once he was gone, she didn't see any reason for idle chitchat. "I have to tell you something. I should have told you a long time ago."

Matthew smiled easily. "You're going to tell me that Sienna is only my half sister, not my full sister, right?"

If a person's jaw could actually drop, hers did. A rush of blood went straight to her head, making her dizzy. "Did Sienna already talk to you?"

He laughed softly. "She didn't have to. I've known for years. Does this mean you've finally told her?"

Angela could only nod. She'd had a speech prepared, but now it took her long moments to reply. "She guessed while we were on Santorini. But how do you know?"

"Dad told me when I was like..." He raised his gaze to the ceiling. "Thirteen."

Her head pounded as if someone had taken a jackhammer to it. "He told you when you were thirteen?" She couldn't keep the horror out of her voice.

Somehow, despite everything, Matthew's eyes softened. "He wanted me to know that I was his son and Sienna was your daughter and that I would always be the special one. I suppose he believed that would endear him to me. He probably thought I'd rush to tell Sienna so I could have one up on her. I never did. It was my secret. And I already knew —" He shrugged indifferently. "—that Sienna was your favorite."

Her heart ached. "I don't have a favorite. I love you both with all my heart."

"But you knew Sienna needed you more because Dad was such an ass to her."

She was shocked. She hadn't thought Matthew, just a child, would have characterized Donald's behavior that way.

As if he could read the look on her face, he said, "She was always more delicate. When Dad told me, I sort of understood why you had to coddle her. I suppose I felt some resentment, but..." He shrugged as if it no longer mattered, though she knew it must.

"You shouldn't have had to deal it. You were only thirteen. I wish you'd come to me." She couldn't stop herself from reaching across to curl her fingers around his. And he let her. "I'm so sorry. I had no idea you knew or how you felt. I always thought I treated you exactly the same."

His voice was soothing. "It's not that I thought you didn't love me. Just that Sienna took precedence." His eyes crinkled with a smile. "When Dad told me, it all finally made perfect sense."

"But we've always been distant with each other, haven't we?" She had to say it aloud.

"I guess. I couldn't tell you what I knew. And I wouldn't tell Sienna. It's hard to be close when you have a big secret, especially with Dad hovering, waiting for the explosion. And he was grooming me for the business right from the beginning. It made me feel special. He always wanted to do everything with me and not Sienna, taking me on school trips, teaching me how to play golf. I just figured I belonged to him and Sienna belonged to you. So yeah, I never felt close to you." He shook his head regretfully. "A couple of months ago, Sienna said something about me holding a grudge. But I don't. And I don't hate you. We're just not close." He shrugged. "But that's okay. I don't mind."

She started to cry. She hadn't meant to. No matter what Matthew's reaction was, she'd told herself she would remain stoic. She'd stand by him and be whatever he needed her to be. But knowing he'd had the truth all along, that he'd been such a grown-up about it even at thirteen, made her face that she was as guilty for the distance between them as Donald was. "I really thought I was doing my best for you."

"You did what you had to do. And I'm fine." He didn't even seem hurt by it. He didn't seem to have much feeling about it at all.

But while he said the words that absolved her, she still had so much to make up for.

"I didn't take care of you," she said. "I was so concerned about Sienna's feelings that I never realized how much I wasn't giving you." She wiped her eyes.

"Please don't cry, Mom. I never intended to make you feel bad. I should have let you tell me and pretend I didn't know."

A sob welled up. She only held it back by grabbing a tissue

and blowing her nose. "My God, you don't have to apologize for anything. Your father and I are the ones to blame. We let our mistakes affect both of you in terrible ways."

"You can stop feeling bad, Mom. I'm totally fine." He nodded his head as if none of it was a big deal. "And Sienna will be fine too." When he smiled, he looked like Teresa. She'd always thought he was the image of Donald, but his smile was pure Teresa. Maybe that meant it was also purely her.

"I'll be honest," he went on. "I love Sienna, even if she's only my half sister, but the truth is I don't want to fight her to be head of the company. With his marriage and the new baby coming, I can see Dad stepping away. And I want more responsibility. I want to be a full partner." His words were harsh, almost callous, and yet there was nothing heartless in her son's eyes. It was simple practicality.

"And you're saying don't rock the boat."

He wagged his finger at her. "I'm saying he's controlling and autocratic and manipulative. But if you accept that about him, you can figure out how to work around it. He trusts me. He lets me do pretty much whatever I want. And I really like what I'm doing." He must have seen something on her face because he added softly, "But I'm not like him. I don't treat people like crap. I don't manipulate them or try to control them. I have a knack for getting people to see things my way. Fear doesn't work. Dad never learned that, but I have."

Her heart felt close to bursting. "You are so amazing. Exactly the man I always knew you'd grow up to be. And I love you so much. I'm sorry if you ever thought Sienna was my favorite. I want us to be a family. Can we do that?"

He smiled, but he didn't touch her. "We've always been a family, even if we don't act like it. I'm not a demonstrative person. Ask my girlfriend."

She wanted to weep again for everything they'd missed. "I didn't even know you had a girlfriend."

"She's pretty important to me. Would you like to meet her sometime?"

"You're going to make me cry again," she whispered.

"For the record, I'm sorry too. I never made an effort, since you obviously thought I'd cut you out of my life. Even Sienna thought I was holding a grudge. I never meant to be that way. I'm just busy and I don't pay attention to all that stuff."

She should have talked to him years ago. She'd decided he hated her—or maybe Donald had made her believe that—and she'd never confronted the situation. By letting fear dictate her actions for so long, she'd missed years of getting to know her son.

She wasn't unrealistic, however. This reconciliation was too easy. She had more work to do, and they might never have the closeness she craved. But this was a start.

She pushed out of her chair, rushed around the table, and held Matthew in her arms.

He was one of the best gifts she'd ever had.

IT WAS A SUNNY DAY IN SAN FRANCISCO, BUT CARTER rubbed his hands up and down Sienna's arms as if it was cold and foggy.

"I'll wait for you in the café over there." He pointed across Market Street. "Call me if you need me. And I'll be there in a second."

Then he held her face in his big, comforting hands and kissed her until she knew she'd have to stop in the restroom to fix her lipstick. She smiled and wiped the smudges off his mouth. "Thank you," she whispered.

Though she'd called earlier to make an appointment, her father made her wait ten minutes, because that's just what her father did. She texted Carter to let him know.

Then Heather, her father's admin, showed her in.

Naturally, Dad didn't get up from his desk. He only did that for important clients. "Sienna, it's so good to see you." He flicked his gaze over her frame. "You look terribly tanned. That Santorini sun is too hot for human habitation."

She didn't want to fight, but she didn't want a lot of chitchat either. She didn't engage, saying, "It was a good trip. While I was away, Mom told me." The name slipped out. Not Mother, not Angela, but Mom. What she'd said wasn't the full truth, but it wasn't a lie either. Mom had told her the whole story, even if Tamryn was the one who'd opened Sienna's eyes.

"Told you what?" he asked, his mouth agape as if he was mystified. Yet his eyes gleamed with an image of the confrontation, and it made him giddy. Now he wanted her to fill in all the dirty details.

"She told me you're not my natural father." As she said the words, she found them almost soothing. She didn't want to think about why right now.

He smiled, still with that satisfied gleam. "I'm glad she finally decided to tell you. I've wanted her to for years. You deserved to know, but your mother fought me every step of the way. She was afraid you'd hate her." He raised one eyebrow. "But I truly hope you don't." The eyebrow was his tell. He wanted her to despise her mother.

"It was a shock," she admitted, then probed him on his latest lie. "But I got the impression you enjoyed holding it over her head."

He laughed. It didn't sound natural, as if laughter was a tool rather than an emotion. "Of course she would say that." His tone was soothing, almost melodic. "She always liked to paint me as the bad guy."

She wondered if he actually was.

"But I didn't know the truth when I married her," he had to add, his voice deepening with affront.

"Would you have married her anyway? If you'd known, I mean." What Sienna really wanted to ask was whether he'd loved her despite the lack of DNA connecting them, but she was afraid she already knew.

"It would've been disingenuous if I knew and married her anyway, don't you think?" He smiled as if she were a foreigner who didn't grasp the nuances of a second language.

He didn't say that she was important to him, that it didn't make any difference, that she was still his daughter. But this was the man whom she'd thought of as her father all her life, and he'd never been one to reassure her. He'd saved that for Matthew, his real firstborn, his son.

"Well," he said, still smiling, "that settles the wedding then."

It wasn't a question, but she had to ask, "What do you mean?"

That smile. She'd never seen how cutting it was. His laughter had an agenda, his smiles had hidden meanings. And he was moving in for the kill.

"It's obvious you need to back out of the wedding. After all, you're not actually related."

She sat before him, utterly stunned. His words were like a knife she hadn't seen coming until it slid right between her ribs. Then he turned it, slicing all the way to her heart. "You're not the baby's half sister. You're not even a stepsister." He raised a brow as if suddenly seeing the truth. "You're not really family at all."

She couldn't take another second. Standing, she said, "Thanks for letting me see you."

She had seen everything about him that she needed to.

CARTER WAS ALREADY LEAVING THE COFFEE SHOP AS SHE exited her father's headquarters. After waiting for a break in traffic, he jaywalked to her.

"Are you okay?"

She was too stunned for words. Or maybe there were just too many words fighting inside her head.

Carter hooked his arm through hers and headed her down the street to a burger bar. "Are you hungry?"

She shook her head, but he settled her into a seat anyway. It was an old-fashioned fifties diner where the waitress slapped menus down on the table, then brought glasses of water, splashing and grumbling as she wiped the mess with a dirty cloth.

As the woman stalked away, Sienna found her voice. "I might throw up if I eat."

Carter pushed into the same side of the booth and wrapped his arm around her. "You'll be okay," he whispered into her hair.

"I don't think so," she muttered in barely perceptible words. Then she looked at him. "He's a monster." She could feel her eyes wide in her face, and Carter let her go on. "He told me he didn't want me in the wedding because I'm not family."

"That's maniacal." He pushed the glass of water closer in case she needed it. "Maybe you're better off being out of it."

But she was thinking ahead. "I wish there was a way I could stop the wedding. Bron is too sweet and nice for him. He'll crush her."

"She's going to have a baby. Would she really back out now?"

She was silent, ignoring the menu.

When the waitress arrived to find they hadn't decided,

her lips pinched with irritation, and Carter said, "We'll be ready in a minute."

Sienna blurted out, "I'll have a cheeseburger and fries, no onions," just to get rid of the woman. Carter ordered the same. He could have eaten hers, she thought, but whatever.

"What can I do?" she asked as the woman left to toss the order at the cook. "Should I send Bron a text? Maybe an email? Or I could be old school and send a letter?"

Carter's arm was still around her, still comforting. "Don't you want to talk to her?"

She trembled and, in a little girl's voice, said, "I'm afraid to talk to her."

He cupped her chin, forced her to look at him. "You're not afraid of anything. The truth is probably more that you don't want to be the one to tell her what a scumbag her future husband is. Or maybe you think he can be different with her. Or maybe it's even that you know a person can't be told something, that they have to learn for themselves." He kissed her softly on the lips. "Just like you needed to learn about your father. Your mother could've told you long ago what he was like. But would you have believed her?"

He was so right. "Even on the plane, when my mother told me her story, I didn't think he could be as bad as she said, trying to turn Matthew and me against her, emotionally blackmailing her. I thought she was exaggerating." Her heart was in her eyes as she looked at Carter. "I didn't truly understand until he callously told me I'm not family."

He hugged her then, so tightly she thought he'd never let go. "You do have family. Your mom, your brother, your aunt and uncle and cousins, your grandparents. That man isn't your only family."

She drew in a breath, trying to fill herself up again. "He's always held me at arm's length, always preferred Matthew.

And I've always tried to get him to love me. Now I know it's all because I'm not his daughter."

"That fact isn't your fault, and yet he punished not only your mother, but you as well. From the time you were eight years old. You didn't deserve that. He could say anything he wanted to your mother, but *you* didn't deserve it." He tipped her chin, held her gaze. "And that makes him a monster."

She saw the truth with powerful clarity. "I always blamed my mother. At times, I barely tolerated her, at others I actively hated her. But I realized that wasn't good for me, and I thought this trip would be a way to see if we could have some sort of relationship."

He asked her the important question. "Do you still hate her?"

It took a minute, maybe two or three, but she finally shook her head. "She made a mistake. I wish she hadn't lied to me. I wish she hadn't married Donald Walker. But I understand in a way I never did before. She was scared. She didn't want to face him or her mother. And she certainly didn't want to tell everyone she was pregnant with another man's child. I think my ex-father—or my father who never was or whatever the hell he is—I think he would've rained holy hell down on her. She would've been a pariah. And even though it was the early nineties and not the fifties, it would've been really hard on her."

"Does that mean you forgive her?" His voice was gentle, and yet so loud inside her.

She said, with no preamble or platitudes, "Yes." She grew stronger, more certain, less afraid. "Yes, I can forgive her."

Carter wrapped her in his arms, holding her tight. "I love you, Sienna Walker. You're the strongest woman I've ever met."

She admitted to the emotion she'd never felt for any other man. "I love you, too."

❦ 25 ❦

Even though it was eleven at night for Xandros, Angela called him after her lunch with Matthew. "I got home last evening," she explained. "But I didn't want to wake you."

"I don't care if you wake me. I am glad you're home. Are you safe?"

His voice was a soothing balm. "I'm safe." She told him about the daunting conversation with Sienna on the plane, but now at least her daughter knew the truth. "I don't know what the future holds for any of us, but Matthew surprised me completely today. He's known for years. And he doesn't hate me. I'd been envisioning this horrible confrontation, but..." She searched for the right word. "It was just so easy. Too easy. But it was a good start."

"I am so glad. I had to rearrange a few things, but I have booked a ticket."

"Have you said anything to your kids yet? About me? And Sienna?"

"I said only that I've met a woman, and I am flying out to

see her. I will deal with them when I get back. But for me, right now, it is all about you and Sienna."

She wondered if they were putting off the inevitable blow-up. Or was he right, that his family would deal with it so much more easily than hers? But he was coming to her now, and that was the most important thing.

"I will be there late tomorrow afternoon, and we can handle this together. If you don't want me to meet Matthew, I understand. If you don't want me to see Sienna right away, I understand that too. But I will be there for you."

Tears pricked her eyes, and she blinked them away before they obscured the traffic. "I was going to beg you to come. I never want to be without you again. And I'll work this out. Even Sienna." She wasn't as sure as she sounded.

"I love you."

His words reached deep inside her, easing her fears about Sienna and boosting the joy she felt over her lunch with Matthew.

"I love you too. But I'll let you go you. I want you rested for your flight tomorrow. Send me all your info, and I'll pick you up at the airport."

"I want to make love to you all night long."

When he was gone, she called Teresa and told her the entire story, from finding Xandros again, to the week of love-making that renewed their feelings, to the ghastly scene with Sienna, and finally the reunion with Matthew.

"I'm so happy for you," Teresa said. "Especially about Matthew. He's a good boy." Angela could almost hear her sister gulp then. "Sienna called me, and she wants to come over for dinner tomorrow." She stopped, as if she was stalling or trying to figure out the right words. "She wants you to be there because she has something to tell us."

Angela sucked in a breath. "Good or bad?"

"Honestly, I don't know. But your daughter isn't a vindictive person. She wouldn't invite you to dinner at my house if she was going to ream you a new one, especially not in front of other people. Will you come?"

Angela hoped her sister was right. "Xandros arrives tomorrow afternoon. I'm picking him up at the airport." She paused. "I want to bring him with me."

"It's fine with me. Sienna's bringing Carter Ellis. She told me all about him. He sounds wonderful. But tell her about Xandros. Let me know what she says."

They hung up without Angela even describing the holiday. There would be time enough for a trip diary later on.

She bucked up and called Sienna, but her daughter didn't answer. Rather than freak out and come up with all the worst reasons why Sienna didn't pick up, she used her Bluetooth to speak a text.

Sienna texted just as Angela pulled into her driveway, and the tinny voice read aloud, "It's good that Xandros is here. We have to talk and get this out. Carter's coming with me."

There were no emojis and no tone of voice to gauge her daughter's words. Angela didn't know what to think, but neither would she work herself into a frenzy. She wanted to believe what Teresa said, that if it was a bad thing, Sienna wouldn't hold a dinner meeting.

The thought gave her strength.

ANGELA SAW HIM ON THE ARRIVALS MONITOR, TALL, strong, handsome.

When he exited the customs area, she ran to him. Dropping his carry-on with a thud, he gathered in his arms, holding her before setting her back on her feet and kissing her until she was breathless.

"I've missed you," he whispered. His eyes seemed bright

with tears.

She stroked his chin, his skin smooth and his mustache trimmed, as if he'd shaved before the plane landed. People flowed around them, shouting with joy, hugging relatives heartily.

But for her, there was only Xandros. "I love you. I always have, I always will."

"And I love you." He picked up his bag, then wrapped her beneath his arm. "Take me home. I need to make love to you. Now."

She laughed. "I like the way you say home."

"Anywhere you are is my home."

She stopped him in the middle of the arrivals hall to kiss him soundly.

Walking swiftly to the parking garage, her arm around his waist, his around her shoulders, she knew they'd never let go of each other again. But first there was Sienna.

"My sister Teresa invited us for dinner. And as much as I want you to make love to me now, we need this dinner."

He looked down at her. "Is it an intervention?"

She laughed at his Americanism. "I don't know what it is. But Sienna called it, and she's bringing Carter. I texted her to say you'd be coming too, and she said that was fine."

"Fine?" he murmured, his brow knit.

"That's the best we're going to get. But, as my sister said, if Sienna was going to ream me a new one—" She looked up to see if Xandros got the euphemism. And he did. "—she wouldn't do it in front of everyone. So I've got high hopes."

He hugged her against him. "Then I have high hopes too."

As she kicked her foot under the SUV to open the hatch, Xandros said, "No matter what happens with our daughter, we will always have each other. No matter what she says, no matter what anyone says, your family or mine, no one will tear us apart again."

He threw his bag in the back, punched the button to close the lid, and gathered her into his arms. "You never have to be afraid again. You have me."

"And you have me."

They sealed the vow with the tenderest of kisses.

THEY STOOD ON HER SISTER'S FRONT PORCH, ANGELIKA'S hand in his, his heart in her palm.

Then she rang the bell.

He was so in love that he'd do anything for her. And yet a fist had closed around his heart that he couldn't tell her about. He wanted his daughter to love him, but if she couldn't, he wouldn't be able to bear the rift that would grow between him and Angelika.

Reality hadn't hit him this hard on his home earth of Santorini. They'd been keeping it a secret from Sienna, and everything had been about not letting her know until the time was right. He hadn't even begun to feel what it was like to have another daughter, a child he'd made so long ago with Angelika, a girl he hadn't known existed.

And now, he would finally face his daughter when she knew exactly who he was. It felt so much more momentous than the evening in Oia when he'd seen her for the first time and instinctively knew the truth.

His family was entirely different. He didn't believe his kids would have any big issues. They had their own lives, their own dreams, their own families.

But Sienna's world had blown apart, her identity stripped from her. He wanted to make this as easy as possible, though he didn't know how. And he didn't want Angelika to feel his trepidation. For her, he wanted to be strong, with no doubts.

Then there wasn't a chance to back out or rethink as the big front door opened wide.

Teresa, the sister, was a duplicate of his beautiful Angelika, but her smile was broader, her eyes holding a less darkness, as if her life had been far happier.

He wanted that look for Angelika. Perhaps someday she would have it.

Teresa opened her arms wide. At first, he thought it was for her sister, but then she enveloped him, the unexpected action stealing his breath.

When she said, "I'm so glad to finally meet you," he felt a tremor inside for this warm welcome. He wished he'd known Teresa all these years. He felt in his belly that she would be good family.

Then she led them both into the living room, introducing her husband, William, a stocky, balding man with a smile as big as his wife's.

Carter Ellis stood tall beside Sienna, but Xandros had eyes only for his daughter. He hadn't let himself brood on her. In fact, he'd distanced himself, unwilling to contemplate the pain of her rejection. Now he would face it head on.

She was so beautiful, so like Juliana, like Thea too. And he opened his heart fully to her, his skin tingling and his palms clammy as Angelika puts her hand in his.

Just when he was about to speak, Sienna said flatly, "I know you're my father."

Angelika nodded. "Yes, he is."

Xandros forced himself to say, "I know it is a shock."

Sienna sat with a plop on the sofa. "The shock is that the man I thought was my father told me there's no reason I should be in the bridal party at his wedding since I'm not any relation to the baby Bron is carrying."

Angelika rushed to her side, sitting beside her. "Oh my God, Sienna, I'm so sorry." Though she was so close to her daughter, she restrained herself from putting her arm around Sienna, though Xandros knew how desperately she wanted to.

He would gladly beat the man to a pulp. And this was the man Angelika had been married to for thirty years? How did she survive?

He said solemnly, meaning every word, "You will always be a welcome part of my family."

She looked at him, her eyes shiny with tears. "Are you sure they're going to want me?"

"Absolutely." Then he added, "I will always want you in my family." He looked at his Angelika. "I love with your mother. I have been in love with her for over thirty years." Then he turned back to the daughter he hadn't known he had but whom he would love no less. "Will you allow me to be part of your family?"

He waited for her answer with bated breath, his heart ready to break or burst with joy.

Angela waited to hear her daughter's answer, either absolution or condemnation, even as her heart broke for what Donald had said, once again making Sienna worthless in his eyes.

But there was Carter Ellis, sitting beside Sienna, holding her hand, letting her lean on him. Sienna had never had anyone to lean on.

And finally, her daughter said, "I don't know even know you."

"I'd like to know you," Xandros answered with the gentleness of a father gazing at his newborn. "We can try."

Sienna sniffed, and Carter squeezed her hand, giving her support. He was a good man. Sienna wiped beneath her eye. "I'd like to try."

Angela was close to tears, of joy, of fear, of relief, of nerves. Because while Sienna might want to know Xandros, she still might not forgive her mother.

It was up to Angela to ask. She plucked up her courage, wishing that she had Xandros's hand wrapped around hers the way Carter had curled his around Sienna's. "I have a lot to apologize for. I should have told the truth years ago. I should never have let your—" She stopped herself. "—I shouldn't have let Donald ostracize us. I should have left him. There are so many things I should have done but didn't. Can you ever forgive me?"

Sienna breathed in, held it, looked at Carter, then exhaled in a rush and echoed her words to Xandros. "I'd like to try." Tears filled her eyes. "It might take a while to get used to all of this. It feels like my whole life has upended. I don't even have Bron and the baby anymore."

"But you have a whole family in us." She touched Sienna's hand. "Aunt Teresa, Uncle William, your brother, me. Xandros." She had to add him. He was part of their lives now. "And maybe Bron doesn't feel the way Donald does. She cares about you." Then she couldn't help herself, and whether it was right or wrong, she added, "I love you. You're my baby girl. I'll do whatever I can to make things up to you."

But Sienna turned away, looked at Carter.

And Angela felt nothing but loss.

SIENNA DIDN'T WANT TO CRY IN FRONT OF THEM. SHE didn't want to feel that vulnerable. Not now. But she looked at Carter's handsome face, at the sincerity in his gaze, at the love shining from his eyes. It felt as if she'd been bitter and lonely all her life, keeping everyone at arm's length. She hadn't wanted to risk rejection, to risk her heart.

But she wanted to try again, with a new job, with Carter, with her brother, with Bron. She'd even been willing to give her father a chance, though he wasn't her real father.

But then he'd trashed her.

Maybe things would be different with Xandros. Maybe she could never call him Dad or feel the things a girl should about her father. But did she even know what that was like? Maybe she could give Xandros a chance. She could give herself a chance.

Could she do no less for her mother?

She met Carter's gaze, looked deep into his eyes, into his soul. She knew what he would do, what he would want her to do, what he would feel was the best thing for her.

"Mom, did you say I couldn't go to the prom with Dylan Becker?"

Her mother's eyes widened as if she'd thought Sienna had lost her mind. Maybe she had. But she still needed to know.

"Was that when you were sixteen?"

Sienna nodded. "He was a senior."

Her mother drew in a deep breath, let it out. "I don't think so. Actually, now that I really think about it, I was excited to take you out to buy your first prom dress."

Sienna sighed. "That would have been really fun." Reaching for her mother's hand, she held it in both of hers and said what was in her heart. "I was always angry with you. I blamed you. But today, when he said I wasn't even a relative —" She couldn't say his name, certainly couldn't call him Dad. "I saw all the small cruelties he dealt. Death by a thousand scratches. What were you supposed to do?" She shrugged, putting herself in her mother's place, feeling the helplessness. "Could you have said when I was eight or ten or thirteen, 'Hey, guess what, he's not really your dad, so don't worry about what he says?'"

Her mother flinched. Sienna couldn't help that. "But once

you married him, I don't think you had any other choice but to keep that secret."

"I should never have married him in the first place."

Her mother looked at Xandros, and it wrecked Sienna to see the love in his eyes. He adored her mother. And Mom loved him. Everyone had suffered for that decision. But would Sienna herself have done anything differently in her mother's situation? She knew Nonni. Her grandmother meant well and had such a big heart, but she could be so opinionated and stubborn, telling you what she thought you should do, angry if you didn't take her advice.

Then her mother added, "But if I hadn't married him, you and I wouldn't have Matthew."

"No, we wouldn't have Matthew," Sienna echoed. Finally, she squeezed her mother's hand. "Let's start over without all the petty cruelties your ex-husband perpetrated." She gave him the name he deserved, an ex. Then she looked at Xandros. "Let's all start over." She felt Carter's warmth, his support, his love.

Her mother cried, and Xandros was there only a moment later, his big hand on her back, soothing her tears. Tears of joy.

She wondered what it was going to be like to have a Greek father, to be half Greek, to have half siblings she'd never known.

And what it would be like to have an amazing man like Carter by her side, talking her through it all?

Aunt Teresa clapped her hands, beaming with a huge smile. "Let's all eat, drink, and be merry."

It sounded like an excellent plan, especially when she stood and Carter wrapped his arm around her shoulder, holding her close.

There was no place she'd rather be.

EPILOGUE

The doorbell rang. Xandros. Angela dashed to the door like a girl waiting for her prom date. It seemed like forever since she'd seen him. Two weeks was a lifetime, even if they'd been apart for thirty years before that.

Opening the front door, she threw herself in his arms, dotting his face with kisses until he took her lips with a long, sweet kiss that left her drunk with desire.

Pulling back, he framed her face in his big hands. "I missed you."

"I missed you more." They both smiled at her one-upmanship.

She took his hand, pulled him inside. "I could have picked you up at the airport."

"I didn't want to disturb your party preparations. And I needed a car. I cannot have you driving me all the time."

"I love driving you around." But she knew what he meant. A person needed freedom.

He wrapped an arm around her shoulder. "I wanted to arrive yesterday to help you."

She laughed. "It's just family. And I catered the whole thing."

His mouth dropped in mock shock. "But I would have cooked for all of you."

She patted his chest, went on her tiptoes to kiss his cheek. "Next time."

He pulled her in for another full-body hug. God, he felt so good against her.

Her bed had been so empty the past two weeks, even though she'd talked to Xandros every day. "Did you get everything done?"

A month ago, only a few days after what she liked to call her reconciliation with Sienna and Matthew, she and Xandros flew to Paris. There they met his eldest daughter, Thea, a lovely woman. Her husband was a quiet, handsome Frenchman, and Xandros's grandchildren were adorable. Thea took the news with a joy Angela couldn't have dreamed of. She'd hugged Angela, whispering, "I am so glad to see my father this happy." Then she'd pelted them with questions. When would they get married? Where would they live? When would she meet her half sister Sienna? Maybe it was the way Europeans dealt with things, calmly, no hysterics. Maybe it was the thirty years, before her parents had even married.

They'd headed to Athens next, meeting Christos and his family, then onto Crete where Juliana's cruise ship had docked for excursions, and finally back to Santorini to speak with Niko and Xandros's mother.

Everywhere Angela was greeted with open arms, even Mama Daskalakis.

She'd stayed a few days on Santorini, then left Xandros to his arrangements. He planned to spend the summer with Angela and he needed to pass off his duties. Of course, he would only be a phone call or video chat away and would still do his fair share of work.

And, she smiled to herself, doing his fair share of pleasuring her too.

"Everyone's out by the pool. Are you ready to meet my mother?"

He shuddered dramatically. "I am shaking in my boots. Your mother terrifies me."

She laced her fingers with his. "She terrifies me too. But together, we can vanquish her."

She smiled, and Xandros leaned in for a kiss. "For luck," he whispered.

They could hear the noise even before they opened the French doors. "I thought it was only your family?" Xandros put a hand over his ear as if the noise was deafening.

Angela laughed, shaking her head. "It is. And you've met most of them already."

It was odd, a funny odd, the way the patio fell silent as they stepped out, as if they were a couple ready to make their wedding vows in front of all their guests.

She'd dressed the garden for celebration. Hydrangeas, rhododendrons, camellias, and azaleas surrounded the pool deck, though a little past their spring blooms. She'd interspersed the beds with petunias, impatiens, pansies, and minion bells, filling the backyard with glorious color.

Looking at Xandros, she thought how beautiful he was, how strong, how kind. He saluted Sienna, who'd been catching up on the latest gossip with her cousins, her hand curled in Carter's.

Carter had become a fixture. Angela had never seen her daughter happy. She'd seen her determined, focused, angry, complacent, even pleased, but never lighthearted or joyful, not like she was with Carter Ellis.

Santorini had changed both their lives. Angela had found her lost love. Sienna had found a new love.

Matthew, too, was happy, dating Fay, a beautiful woman

seven years older than him. It had come to Angela that Matthew was an old soul, so of course he would be with an older woman. Her son had a beautiful, even temper, taking everything with equanimity, never flustered, never reckless. Which was probably why he could handle his father. Fay, a pediatrician, suited him perfectly. They matched in looks as well, both with hair a russet brown that Fay highlighted with amber. Shorter than Matthew's five nine, Fay could still wear heels. Though Angela wasn't sure young people these days even cared about that.

And there was Mama. She sat with Poppa and William and Teresa at the table under the patio umbrella. She was on her second margarita. While the others rose as Angela and Xandros took the three steps to the pool patio, Mama remained seated, like a grand dame or even a queen.

At eighty, her mother was remarkable. She'd blessed her daughters with her full figure. Angela had once heard a society matron refer to her mother as a battle-ax. And Mama was definitely sturdy. For years she had dyed the gray out of her hair, but after moving to Scottsdale, she'd allowed her hairdresser to let the gray take over. She still wore her long hair in a neat chignon at the back of her head, and she had aged well, like Sophia Loren, her mother's idol.

But she was not the battle-ax that society matron had called her. She was strong, she was opinionated, she was stubborn, and she was formidable. Yet she loved fiercely. Love had been in the mix when she'd pushed Angela to marry Donald. In her world, a child needed a father. Even if he wasn't a biological father. How could she know Donald wasn't father material?

As they approached, Mama looked down her nose, if it was possible to look down your nose when you were five foot one and seated. When Xandros stood in front of her, she held out her hand like a queen who expected him to kiss her ring.

In regal tones, she said, "I suppose you're no longer a beach bum."

Xandros laughed boisterously, full of happiness and love. "With the red, white, and black sand beaches of my Santorini and the blue Aegean Sea, one cannot help but be a beach bum."

For a moment Mama appeared stunned, her brow furrowed, her lips pinched, as if she'd expected Xandros to bow and scrape before her. But then, as if a light had turned on or the sun had come out from behind the clouds, her mother smiled. Mama had a beautiful smile. "Sit, young man."

That, of course, made Angela's lips twitch. Xandros was not a young man. But he was a man in his prime, and he was hers. And she would love him for the rest of her life.

She no longer had to subsist on memories of Santorini.

XANDROS CHARMED HER GRANDMOTHER. HE SEEMED capable of charming anyone. He was so different from the man Sienna had believed to be her father. Quick to smile, quick to laugh, his dark eyes seemed to dance, especially when he looked at her mother.

But she couldn't call him Dad yet. Maybe she never would. Maybe he would always be Xandros. But she didn't hate him. She was no longer angry with her mother. And she tried not to think about Donald.

She squeezed Carter's hand. "Nonni likes him."

"How can you tell?" Charlotta wanted to know. Her cousin was a ballerina through and through, delicately boned, finely featured, slim with a dancer's grace.

Sienna held up both hands. "Because she's like a giggly teenage girl impressed with the captain of the football team."

"Oh my God," Bianca gushed, her hand over her mouth. "She's actually fluttering her eyelashes."

Sophia laughed with them, and whispered, as if Nonni had the best hearing, which maybe she did, "She's just so cute." She started to raise her hand to point, but stopped herself. "Look at Poppa. He's fading into the background so Nonni can have her day."

Their grandfather wasn't usually a wallflower, but he sat back in his chair, his arms crossed over his beefy chest, and smiled. He was a stocky man, three years older than Nonni. You'd never guess they were both in their eighties. Maybe it was the Italian genes. She hoped she was just like them.

Carter tipped his chin toward her mother. "I've never seen your mom look more radiant."

They all nodded, agreeing. Her mother had started to glow weeks ago, perhaps even that night at Aunt Teresa's house, when Sienna finally admitted that Donald, who was *not* her father, had shown his true cruel colors. Sienna had finally realized what her mother had gone through over the years.

"She looks beautiful. And happy," she murmured. They all fell silent, watching her mom, watching Xandros charm Nonni, watching Poppa's delight.

So much had happened in just a month. She'd had her interview at Smithfield and Vine, who'd offered her the job on the spot. She jumped at it, turning in her two-week notice at that "soulless corporation." They promptly issued her walking papers, not even accepting her offer of two weeks. That had been fine with her.

She'd left her cell phone number on the voicemail, and, oddly enough, it hadn't been cut off, which was strange since they'd rushed her out the door as if she might steal state secrets. Her favorite clients were now calling her, scheduling appointments. Everything was working out.

And there was Carter. She pressed against him. His body felt so good, his strength so towering, his compassion melting her heart. And his lovemaking made her knees weak.

They'd talked about moving in together, but hadn't made a decision since her office was in San Francisco and his was in the South Bay. They'd discussed getting something halfway between. Nothing was decided, everything was on the table, and the possibilities were limitless.

Was it love that made her so happy? Was it the new job? Or was it everything rolled together, finally reconciling with her mother, finding an amazing man, the perfect job, and tossing to the curb all the insecurities her father had helped to build.

Her phone vibrated in her back pocket.

Who could it be? Everyone was here, Matthew, her cousins, her aunt, uncle, Mom, Xandros, Carter. A sick lump rose in her stomach; the only other person it could be was Donald.

He'd called her twice since she'd gotten the job at Smith-field and Vine. She hadn't answered his voicemails.

But with Carter by her side, she squashed the nausea.

Only it wasn't Donald. It was Bron.

Sienna crossed to the far side of the pool so she could hear.

"Bron?" Surprise made her voice rise. She'd had one brief phone call with Bron since her meeting with Donald. "What's up?"

"I need to talk to you."

"I'm at my mom's. We've got that family get-together today."

"I know. I saw it on your Facebook page. I'm outside. Will you come get me?"

Outside? It sounded crazy. "I'll be right there."

That brief phone call right after she got back from

Santorini had not gone in Sienna's favor. In fact, it was disheartening. Bron said she didn't like it, but she understood Donald's feelings about not having Sienna in the wedding. And when Sienna had asked her to lunch to talk about it, Bron said it would be better to meet after the wedding. She'd ended the conversation with, "There's a lot going on. I just need to take care of all this stuff on my end. But I will see you. We're friends, I promise."

Sienna never got the chance to tell Bron what Donald had said and done. Would it have mattered? Like Carter and her mom said, Bron was having a baby, and it was difficult to leave.

But she still felt the guilt of letting her friend walk blindly into the marriage.

She whispered to Carter, "It's Bron. She's outside. I'm going to bring her in."

Then she looked at her mother. "Could you tell my mom? I don't want her caught off guard. But I think Bron really needs me. She sounded weirdly desperate."

Bron was already on the front porch when Sienna opened the door.

She was enormous, and while the last time Sienna had seen her, she'd been glowing, her hair was now bedraggled, her face pale, her eyelids drooping with fatigue. Sienna pulled her inside. "Oh my God. Are you okay?"

"I need to talk."

"We can sit in Mom's living room. Everybody's outside. We won't be disturbed."

Bron shook her head. "Your mom is exactly the person I need to talk to, as well as you." She tugged Sienna in for a hug, her belly keeping it from being full body. Then she pulled back, wiping her eyes as Sienna led her to the sunporch's French doors.

The whispers buzzed like bees, then everyone went quiet as they took in Bron, her belly so huge that she waddled.

Sienna's mom rushed forward, taking Bron's arm as she descended the deck steps. Nonni vacated her royal throne for Bron, who eased herself down, hands on the armrests. Xandros dragged another chair closer and indicated for Sienna to sit. Carter brought a chair for Mom.

"Could I have a glass of water?" Bron asked, her voice cracking.

Poppa poured from a pitcher on the table and leaned over to hand it to her.

Bron gulped, then gulped again, and finally set the glass down. After a deep breath, she started to talk.

"The baby's due in less than two weeks." She put her hand to her incredible belly, rubbing the child inside. She would be a good, caring mother. "And right when I'm packing a bag to go to the hospital in case the baby comes early and I'm fretting about every little thing and hoping I got everything done for the wedding, because I can't remember a thing—" She tapped her temple. "—Donald springs a prenup on me." She shook her head. "He never said a thing about a prenup, not when we first got engaged, not when we were planning to get married in May, not when I got pregnant, never." Her eyes narrowed, and her lips flattened.

Mom said softly, "I'm so sorry. This must be so hard right now."

Bron tapped her temple again. "I think he did it now because I have foggy baby brain. I'm not thinking straight. I'm worked up all the time. And he thought I'd sign without reading it." Her voice was hoarse, her eyes red, as if she'd been crying all the way here.

Sienna touched her hand. "We'll do whatever we can to help. Just tell us."

After a deep breath, Bron told her rapt audience everything. "He said it was just a formality." She rolled her lips between her teeth and bit down, as if fearing she'd cry again. "And I told him to leave it on the bureau and I'd have my lawyer look at it. And Donald said it was ridiculous to give it to my lawyer, that it was just a simple document to protect us both and I'd be taken care of. And I said I always have my lawyer look over any big contracts. And he said I'd never had a big contract to sign before. I was getting mad by then."

Not having taken a single breath, she sucked in air. "I said fine, just leave it and I'll read it when I'm done packing. And he said it was just a bunch of legalese that I probably wouldn't understand anyway. And I said I'd been his secretary, and I understood all the legalese in the contracts. Honestly, I thought he'd apologize then, but instead he got stubborn."

She gulped more water. "So I grabbed it and we played tug-of-war, me pulling this way and him pulling that way and I thought it would rip in half." She filled her lungs with a deep breath, rubbed the baby. "I knew something was up. He didn't want a lawyer to read it. He didn't even want me to read it. He just wanted me to sign. Then I doubled over and gasped, clutching my stomach. It shocked him so badly that he let go, and suddenly I had the prenup. And when he looked like he'd try to go for it again, I said, 'Are you really going to fight a pregnant lady?' And he just threw his hands in the air and walked out."

"So you read it," Sienna said. She was dying to know what was in it.

"I planned to take it to my lawyer, but I started reading." She smiled, transforming completely into glowing motherhood. "I sat in the beautiful rocking chair you sent me, Angela."

Sienna looked at her mom, who returned her gaze with a shrug. She'd never held anything against Bron or the baby. Sienna should have known that. Mom only ever wanted the best for Bron. Everything else was just lies Donald Walker had spread.

Bron tipped her head, hair falling out of her hastily pinned twist. "As I was reading, I actually felt bad, because he was right, it was a generous settlement that would keep me for the rest of my life even if I left him. Even if I cheated on him. And I was thinking, gosh, he doesn't get anything out of me because I have nothing. I was almost ready to run to him and apologize for being bitchy."

It was that word *almost*. Sienna knew deep in her bones that something bad was coming. Bron was good at heightening the drama.

She lowered her voice. "Then I found one little line that said in the event of a divorce, no matter who was at fault, I would give up all parental rights to any children I had with him."

Mom gasped. Even Nonni burst out with, "Good Lord." And Aunt Teresa growled, "That man is evil."

Sienna looked at her mother. "Did you have a prenup?"

Mom answered in barely a whisper, "No. But it didn't matter."

Looking at each other, Sienna pictured what her mother's life had been like. If she'd left him, he would have made sure she never saw her children again.

And he was trying to do the same thing to Bron.

It was Xandros who asked, "What are your plans now?"

"I took the prenup to my lawyer, had him strike out that line and write in that in the event of a divorce, no matter whose fault it was, I got all parental rights and Donald got none."

Carter clapped. Sophia, Charlotta, and Bianca pumped their fists in the air.

Bron smiled. Actually, it was more of a smirk. "I took the prenup back to Donald, and I told him I'd made one itty-bitty change that wouldn't make much difference to him." Her smile got bigger, reaching her eyes. "When he read it, he tore up the whole thing and said we didn't need a prenup."

Everyone waited with bated breath for the rest of the story.

"I told him we didn't need a prenup because we weren't getting married. Then I rolled my suitcase out to my car." She made a little moue. "Or course I had three suitcases and had to go back, and on the last one, something terrible came over me. And I told him I wasn't putting him on the birth certificate because I wasn't sure he was the father."

"Oh my God," Sienna blurted.

Bron smiled evilly. "Did I ever tell you I was one of the mean girls in high school?"

Mom was the first to hug her. "I'm so glad you're not marrying him."

Then Sienna held Bron. And suddenly it was a hugfest all around.

Finally, she found herself in Carter's arms, and she whispered in his ear, "I am so relieved."

He hugged her tightly.

"I love you," she whispered.

"And I love you. Maybe we should get rid of Walker as your last name, so you aren't associated with that man anymore."

She gasped. "Are you asking me to marry you or something?"

He smiled. "Or something."

They'd only known each other a couple of months, and this could be a holiday romance that wouldn't last.

But this was Carter. And he was so much more to her than any holiday romance ever could be.

Holding him against her, she whispered for him alone, "I would absolutely love to 'or something' with you."

She'd run away from so many relationships in the past. With Carter, her running days were finally over.

"You don't need Donald," Angela said. "You have us. We're your family."

That was his Angelika, so kind, so caring.

The girl brushed a tear from the corner of her eye. "Thank you, Angela. I'm so glad you're all here for me." She narrowed her eyes, something steely in her gaze. "But I'll make sure Donald does his duty by this child." Then she laughed. "Of course, after what I said, he'll probably make me take a paternity test." Glancing at Sienna, she said, "He told me you'd backed out of the wedding because you'd found out he wasn't your real father and that you didn't want to have anything to do with a baby who was absolutely no relation to you."

Sienna blanched at her words, and Xandros had the strongest urge to hug her to him. But they weren't there yet. They had so much more to learn about each other. It was Carter Ellis who pulled her close. Carter, a good man.

"I was pretty sure that wasn't true," the pretty pregnant Bron went on. "But sometimes we put blinders on because we have to. The baby was coming, and I thought I could make everything okay after the wedding, that we could be friends again." She sniffed as if thinking about what she'd lost. "But Donald ripped the blinders away."

"I'm glad you're not marrying him," Sienna said quietly.

The girl smiled, rubbing her enormous belly. "I'm glad you're still my family."

Xandros looked at his Angelika then, and she held out her hand to him. He took it with his whole heart, thanking God she'd rid herself of that horrific man.

"When is it safe for a baby to travel on a plane?" he asked.

Her eyes widened with surprise. "I've heard as early as three months. As long as the baby is full term and doesn't have any medical issues."

Three months after the baby was born. He could wait that long. After all, he'd waited over thirty years.

Holding up his hand, he signaled for attention. "I have an announcement."

Angela looked up at him. "Do I know anything about this announcement?"

He smiled, shook his head. "No. I should have told you before, but it just came to me in a flash of brilliance." He raised his voice for the entire family. "I would like you all to come to Santorini to meet my family." He looked down at Bron, the extremely pregnant girl. "Once the baby is old enough to travel." Then he gathered everyone in with his gaze. "And since there will not be a September wedding, we will replace it with a Santorini wedding."

His Angelika smiled at him. "Are you proposing to me?"

"Who else would I propose to?" He cupped her face in his hands and dropped a gentle kiss on her lips. "I've waited for you for over half my life. Will you marry me?"

A hand on his cheek, she traced her thumb over his lips. "Yes, I'll marry you."

There were whoops and hollers and hugs and kisses on the cheeks all around.

The happiness that had been missing from his life for more than thirty years welled up from deep inside him.

He pulled Angelika close, whispering for her alone, "I will never lose you again."

Once Again, a later-in-life series that will whisk you away to fabulous foreign locales where love always gets a second chance.

Look for **Siesta in Spain** coming your way soon!

ENGLISH TEACHER NITA JEFFRIES IS STUCK. SHE CAN'T move on from a brief fling with a grieving widower and decides to forget him by making the trip of a lifetime to Spain. Who can be sad in Barcelona, between the amazing markets, the whimsical Gaudi architecture, and the fabulous beaches? When she finds the perfect rental, she packs her bags, intent on savoring every moment of her vacation... and finally getting over the beautiful man who could never fall in love with her.

Widowed more than a year ago, Thomas Hunt is still grieving his wife. For 25 years, she was the only one for him, and yet, only months after her death, he had a brief encounter with another woman. Suffocating in guilt, he ended it badly—but he can't forget the woman who made him feel such passion.

Then, on a business trip in Barcelona, he sees Nita Jeffries again. And this time, he can't walk away. They embark on a whirlwind exploration of southern Spain, and they spend the nights exploring each other.

Can a two-week holiday heal Thomas's broken heart? Or is this love affair destined to end when their Spanish siesta is over?

Take a trip through scenic Spain in this second chance holiday romance.

Readers met Thomas in *Wishing in Rome*. Now it's time to enjoy his story...

The *Once Again* series, where love is in the stars.

Dreaming of Provence
Wishing in Rome
Dancing in Ireland
Under the Northern Lights
Stargazing on the Orient Express
Memories of Santorini

And coming soon... **Siesta in Spain**

ABOUT THE AUTHOR

NY Times and USA Today bestselling author Jennifer Skully is a lover of contemporary romance, bringing you poignant tales peopled with hilarious characters that will make you laugh and make you cry. Look for Jennifer's series written with Bella Andre, starting with *Breathless in Love*, The Maverick Billionaires Book 1. Writing as Jasmine Haynes, Jennifer authors classy, sensual romance tales about real issues such as growing older, facing divorce, starting over. Her books have passion and heart and humor and happy endings, even if they aren't always traditional. She also writes gritty, paranormal mysteries in the Max Starr series. Having penned stories since the moment she learned to write, Jennifer now lives in the Redwoods of Northern California with her husband and their adorable nuisance of a cat who totally runs the household.

Learn more about Jennifer/Jasmine and join her newsletter for free books, exclusive contests and excerpts, plus updates on sales and new releases at **http://bit.ly/SkullyNews**

ALSO BY JENNIFER SKULLY/JASMINE HAYNES